C
FOR
HELP

BOOKS BY WENDY DRANFIELD

Shadow Falls

CRY FOR HELP

WENDY DRANFIELD

Bookouture

Published by Bookouture in 2021

An imprint of Storyfire Ltd.
Carmelite House
50 Victoria Embankment
London EC4Y 0DZ

www.bookouture.com

ISBN: 978-1-80019-134-1
eBook ISBN: 978-1-80019-133-4

This one is for Don. Thanks for your support.
(Maybe now you'll actually read one of my books!)

PROLOGUE

September 2012— Lost Creek, Colorado

Detective Madison Harper is startled by an aggressive thump at her front door. Not wanting to leave her son's bedside while he's feeling unwell, she waits.

Two more thumps follow. Instinct makes her glance at the Batman clock on Owen's nightstand as dread creeps up from the pit of her stomach. Even if she wasn't a cop, she'd know that a knock at the door after ten o'clock could only mean bad news.

"Who is it, Mom?"

She looks down at her son and pushes a sweaty curl of blond hair from his forehead. His cheeks are still pink with heat, but the thermometer shows his fever is leveling off. Hopefully it will subside as quickly as it arrived.

"I don't know, honey. Stay here, I'll be right back."

He sits up, her anxiety reflected on his face as she slips from the bed and pads downstairs with bare feet. Her front room is illuminated by red and blue flashing lights. She swallows, wondering who could have been hurt. Is it Stephanie, her ex-girlfriend? Or someone from work, injured while on duty?

She pulls the blinds back from the front door just to be sure she's opening it to someone she knows. She recognizes the tall man staring back at her: Detective Don Douglas from the Lost Creek Police Department. *Her* police department. He signals for her to open the door, but she hesitates as her gut tells her something is seriously wrong. She doesn't know Detective Douglas well as he's new to the department, but he arrived in Lost Creek with a bad reputation.

She can see a few uniformed officers standing behind him, but it's dark out and the cruisers' flashing lights mixed with the heavy rainfall make everything blurry. She can't identify them. She unlocks her door and opens it enough to let in a gust of cold wind. The rain hits her bare feet. "What's wrong?"

Douglas doesn't wait a beat before shoving his shoulder against the door, pushing past her and pulling her arms behind her back, cuffing her within seconds.

"Detective Madison Harper, I'm arresting you for the murder of Officer Ryan Levy." He spins her around to face him.

Madison's mouth goes dry. She stares up at him in silence, waiting for the punchline. Ryan can't be dead; they were on duty together earlier today. At the end of their shift he treated her to coffee and cake to celebrate her birthday.

Detective Douglas doesn't even blink.

"This is a joke, right?" she asks.

"I'm going to assume you don't need me to read you your rights," he says, pushing her toward the doorway. "They won't help you now anyway. We both know murdering a cop is the worst thing you can do. You're screwed."

He tries to force her out of the door without even letting her slip on some shoes, or a jacket. She leans back against him but he doesn't move.

"Are you resisting arrest, Detective?" he hisses into her ear.

His warm breath on her neck makes her cringe. She turns to look at him, wanting to scream in his face, but she spots her ten-year-old son standing at the top of the stairs in his pajamas.

"What's happening, Mom?" asks Owen.

Douglas notices him for the first time. "Hang tight, kid. Someone from child services is on their way."

Madison stares at him in disbelief. "You can't do this."

He shoves her out of the front door and into the rain as she yells behind her, "Owen! Call Stephanie. Tell her to bring you to the station."

With another forceful push, she is crammed into the back of a police cruiser. She looks back at her house through the car's wet rear window and manages to see Owen trying to get out the door—reaching for her—before someone closes him in.

She has a terrible feeling she won't ever see him again.

CHAPTER ONE

July 5, 2019— Lost Creek, Colorado

Ricky Gregor sings to himself as he meanders through the sleeping amusement park on his early-morning rounds. He's got a rock song in his head picked up from the car radio on the way over, and alone on the grounds he belts it out as loud as he likes.

There's no sign of the sun rising yet, as it's only just gone 5.30, but Ricky thinks it's going to be another scorcher today and that's just fine with him.

Ever since he scored this job as maintenance manager at Fantasy World amusement park, life has been good to him. Working in the great outdoors—the park sits alongside Lake Providence and at the bottom of Grave Mountain—has its perks, especially in summer. He likes to watch the girls wander around the park in their skimpy shorts and bikini tops. Yes, this job beats prison any day.

If his employer had known about his long rap sheet, he would never have given him the job, and rightly so, but Ricky's not stupid: he faked his references and moved down here from up north, so there's no risk of anyone ever finding out. With that knowledge and the thought of a pleasant day ahead, he whistles the song's chorus as he switches on the power to the food concession stands. They need warming up ready for the packed house that's expected again later.

He stops whistling when he thinks he hears something. His skin prickles like he's being watched. He shouldn't be: he's solely responsible for opening this place in the mornings. He squints into the darkness for any movement. There's no one here. And the only sounds are the thrum of the generators and the rusty rides creaking in the morning breeze.

He laughs to himself and pulls out the pressure washer. There's usually plenty of vomit to clean up from the night before, but today will be worse than usual, what with last night's Independence Day celebrations. Normally it's brightly colored kid vomit from too much cotton candy, but he just knows this morning will include hot dogs and fried chicken from the teens who couldn't hold their alcohol. He doesn't touch the stuff himself. Knows too many people who've ended up addicted. He'd rather spend what little cash he has on weed.

As dawn gently breaks, he sprays water all around the carousel and works his way up toward the Ferris wheel, his favorite ride. As he approaches, he notices that all the cars are gently swaying. All except one. He drops the pressure washer's nozzle and walks closer for a better look, certain he can see the outline of someone in the bottom car; maybe a teenager. But they don't move.

"Little shit," he mutters. "Hey! You're not allowed in here until we open."

He squints as he gets closer, trying to see through the dark. Something about the way the kid's body is positioned sends a chill down his spine. They're seated but slumped. He can make out shoulders, but from where he's standing it looks like the body has no head.

"What the hell?"

At the wheel's ticket booth he flips the switch that powers up the ride's many lights.

"Holy crap!"

The body of a teenage girl is illuminated in a halo of colored neon lights. He instantly recognizes her from the long red hair that spills over her cheeks. Her forearms are slit down to her wrists and her eyes are fixed on the pool of blood beneath her dangling feet.

Ricky backs away. If ever his freedom was at risk, it's now.

CHAPTER TWO

Route 191, Utah

Madison Harper shivers as she stands in the middle of a vast empty scrubland next to the eerily silent highway. It's a little before six o'clock and the sun has yet to fully rise, leaving her standing alone in the twilight. With cold hands, she feels for the cigarettes and lighter in her sweater pocket. The flame from her lighter startles a rabbit nearby. He freezes, stares in her direction, then hops into the darkness when it's clear she's not a threat. The smoke from the cigarette warms Madison up from the inside as she slowly spins around to see if she can make anything out through the dawn, but there's nothing to see: just miles of sun-scorched vegetation and a few passing trucks and cars making their way either south to Arizona or north to Wyoming, or perhaps as far as Montana.

Thanks to the clear night they've had, she can still see a few stars. The far-off twinkling makes her feel small, as if her problems might be trivial. But down here on earth they're serious. And they need fixing, fast.

She taps the ash off the end of her cigarette and exhales smoke into the cool morning air. Yesterday was Independence Day, and as she and her companion drove through a succession of small towns in Utah, they passed firework displays and plenty of drunks waving patriotic flags or shooting off rounds from their assault rifles. Madison can't remember the last time she celebrated Independence Day. Or any public holiday for that matter. As she tries to think back, it dawns on her that the last celebration she had was on her thirtieth birthday; the day she was arrested for murder. And that was just coffee and cake with Officer Ryan Levy, followed by unwrapping some presents her son had made her. It's a bittersweet memory, since her friend is now dead and her son is lost to her.

When she's finished her cigarette, she pulls out her cell phone. There are no calls or messages waiting for her. The last call she took was from Mike Bowers, two days ago. He was her sergeant at Lost Creek PD in southern Colorado when she worked there. While she was doing time for a murder she didn't commit, he was promoted to detective; to the role left empty as a result of her arrest and subsequent conviction. And it was his recent call that prompted her to make this road trip to Lost Creek from northern California as fast as possible.

Mike gave her the news that Stephanie Garcia, her ex-girlfriend, had been killed. As if that wasn't bad enough, Madison's pretty sure it happened because someone was looking for *her*.

But that's not the only reason she's returning to Lost Creek after seven years away. As well as spending six years in prison for manslaughter, she lost the job she loved, her ten-year-old son, and her freedom.

Today she's heading home to find out who framed her, and why. And she's not in the mood to play nice.

CHAPTER THREE

Nate Monroe opens his eyes and is greeted with blackness. He feels confined. His mind betrays him, unable to tell him where he is, but his body reacts quicker; it's trembling with fear. The all-consuming feeling of panic convinces him he's back on death row.

He tries to move his arms but they're weighed down. His legs won't move either. His heart races in alarm, fear rising in his chest. How is he back here after serving seventeen years of someone else's sentence? He must be strapped to the lethal injection bed, but he doesn't understand how this is happening when he was finally exonerated. Or was that a dream? The thought makes him want to scream. Instead he says a silent prayer to a God who has evaded him ever since he chose love over the Church.

"No." He gasps, trying to fill his lungs, but they feel constricted. "Not again. I can't." Lifting his head off the bed, he tries to focus on anything but the blackness, but there's nothing to be seen. Has he gone blind, or have they pulled a hood over his head?

He feels a cold hand on his arm.

"Nate?"

He turns to the female voice, but there's no one there.

"Nate? It's me, Madison." A cell phone lights up and she points it downwards to avoid blinding him. "Are you okay?"

He looks across at her. Madison Harper: his employee, and maybe his friend.

"Holy crap." He leans back against the car's headrest as goose-bumps consume his entire body.

CHAPTER FOUR

Colorado state line

Back on the road but feeling the need for coffee and courage, Madison suggests they pull in at a truck stop diner for breakfast.

The waitress pours their coffees then disappears to get their food order. As Nate goes to freshen up in the restroom, Madison notices a young brunette waitress giving him the eye. He's bound to attract attention; he's a good-looking guy. He's also the only guy in here not wearing a flannel shirt and dirty denims. Some women can spot outsiders a mile off, especially ones with money.

Nate's not completely oblivious to the attention because he smiles at her as he passes. The waitress spots the rosary around his neck and whispers to her friend, "Forgive me, Father, I'd like to sin." They explode into laughter and Madison can't help but grin. She doesn't think Nate heard them.

Hugging her hot coffee mug with both hands, she looks out of the partially steamed-up window at the highway beyond. It's still early, so there's not much traffic yet, but the diner is almost half full already with truckers. Most of them are sitting at the counter watching the TV and ogling the waitresses. Brody is outside scouring the parking lot for trouble.

As she and Nate get closer to her home town of Lost Creek, she's feeling increasingly uneasy about the final leg of the journey. She thinks about what's waiting on her arrival. Not only will she have to face her old police colleagues for the first time since her trial, but she also has to arrange Stephanie's funeral. While they were a

"We're in Utah. We pulled off the highway last night to get some sleep. Nate, listen to me: you're not back on death row." She squeezes his right hand. "Are you awake now?"

Nate swallows the lump in his throat and nods. He silently thanks God, then looks down at his chest. Brody, the former police cadaver dog they seem to have adopted, is curled up on his lap and chest for warmth. Nate doesn't understand how such a large dog—a German shepherd and husky mix—can fit on top of him in the driver's seat of his Jeep Grand Cherokee, but he's managed it.

The dog yawns, looks up at him and licks his face in greeting. His tail gently beats against Nate's thigh.

"Shit, Brody." He looks across at Madison. "I thought I was strapped down for my lethal injection." This isn't the first time he's woken with that feeling. After all, at the time of his release, his execution date was just three months away.

"It's the dark," says Madison. "There are no street lights because we're in the middle of nowhere. Don't worry, you're safe. We pulled over because you were falling asleep at the wheel. I only woke up a half-hour ago."

Nate looks down at Brody and notices the fur that's now covering his clothes. The dog sneezes in his face, making Madison laugh. She's probably relieved. She's witnessed one of his depressive episodes before, and she knows it's not pretty.

His heart rate takes a while to regulate, but he's thankful to be anywhere other than death row. There's no way in hell he'll go back there alive.

couple, Steph was a big part of her life with her son. Saying goodbye is not going to be easy, especially when she feels like she's to blame.

She rubs her neck, stiff from spending so long on the road, but it doesn't help much. It's taken her and Nate a few days to drive to Colorado from northern California—almost thirteen hundred miles—and after she helped him find a girl who went missing from a summer camp, now it's his turn to hold up his end of the deal: helping her to clear her name and find her son. Nate, just two years out of prison himself, was used to being alone after having spent seventeen years on death row for a murder he didn't commit. He wasn't keen on the idea of working alongside a disgraced ex-cop like Madison, but she thinks they're finding their way. She'll always be grateful to him for giving her a trial run as an unlicensed private investigator. It's almost impossible to find work when you're a convicted felon.

Nate slips back into the booth, sitting opposite her, and sips his coffee. Then he fixes her with his serious blue eyes. "Now would be a good time to fill me in on what happened here seven years ago. Because we're almost in Lost Creek and I want to know what we're walking into. So far you've only given me the bones."

She puts her coffee down, knowing he's right. "Well, as you already know, I'd recently been promoted to detective. I loved being a police officer but I worked hard for my promotion. I wanted to do some real investigative work, instead of just acting like a social worker for the locals. But I didn't even get a chance. I was arrested just five days into my new role and not one of my team spoke up in support of me or stayed in touch when I was sent down." She shakes her head, still devastated by how quickly they turned.

"What exactly got you arrested? Who was the victim?" he asks.

"Officer Ryan Levy. He was my coworker but also my friend." She pauses. She can picture Ryan now, clear as day, laughing while they chatted in the police cruiser on the way home from work that afternoon. "It's like I spoke to him just yesterday."

Nate nods. "That's the problem with being locked up: time freezes inside. When you're released, you expect to find everything the same as when you left it, but it doesn't work that way."

He's right about that. "Ryan and I were on shift together the day he was killed. I didn't have a detective for a partner because there was only one other detective in our department—Don Douglas—and he had a thing about working alone. I was asked to attend a residence after we received a call from a guy who said he was being seriously assaulted by his partner, so I requested an officer attend with me for backup. Ryan volunteered."

Nate frowns. "Douglas didn't want to go with you even though someone's life was at risk?"

She shakes her head. "I don't even know where he was that day. He was new to the team and a classic lone wolf, never wanting to tell anyone anything about himself. I expect he didn't stay with the department long after my conviction, as he clearly hated it there." She can feel the old resentments rising. "After that domestic disturbance, which ended amicably because Ryan managed to defuse the situation, he drove us to a coffee shop and treated me to coffee and a slice of cake for my birthday. We were there for less than an hour." She looks up at Nate. "Five hours later, he was dead."

"Were you the last person to see him alive?"

She gives him a stern look. "No. The killer was."

He leans back. "I wasn't trying to catch you out. I may only have known you for a few weeks, but if you've hired me as a PI to look into your conviction after you've already served your time, I'm going to assume you have nothing to hide."

They sit in silence for a while.

"You've had a long time to think about this," he says. "Who do you think killed Ryan?"

The million-dollar question. "I don't know. That's why I need your help."

He frowns as he considers possibilities. "Was he causing problems at the station? Did he have a beef with any of the other officers? Perhaps he was dating another cop's wife and the husband found out?"

She shakes her head. "From what he told me, he was single. And as a team we all worked well together. Until Douglas joined us."

Nate pauses, and she just knows he's wrongly putting two and two together in his head. She's short on patience this morning and it irritates her.

"Were you and Ryan dating?"

"No. We were good friends, but we weren't seeing each other." She doesn't explain how it could have ended up that way, given the chance.

"Sorry," he says. "It's just that I remember you told me previously that you and Stephanie split because you started seeing a guy. I wondered if that was him."

"No. Stephanie and I split way before Ryan was murdered." She tries not to snap at him. It's difficult to relive everything, but she has to remember that Nate's trying to help her. He had a much tougher experience than her and he still manages to stay positive. Well, most of the time, and only when he has enough cocaine to see him through the darkest days.

She wonders whether a crutch like that would help her cope too. She picked up a bad smoking habit in prison, but that's mostly over now. She's intending for the cigarette she enjoyed earlier, before the sun was up, to be her last.

He leans in. "When we first met, in California, you told me you believe someone from your police department must have framed you for Ryan's murder, but why frame *you*? Did you rat someone out? Were you investigating one of them? Or had you arrested a cop's family member? I need to try and understand what their motive would be."

She looks down. "I don't know what they *think* I did to deserve it and I don't know who stood to gain from Ryan's death or from framing me. Trust me, these are questions that plague me, but I wasn't around to do any digging once I'd been arrested."

The waitress brings their bacon and eggs over and refills their coffees without asking.

"What did you talk about in your final conversation with Ryan?" asks Nate. "Did he share any problems he was having?"

Madison waits for the waitress to leave. "I've gone over that conversation a million times in my head." They'd talked about the department, and how Don Douglas had a reputation for being a cold fish. "There was nothing significant. It was just a normal bitch about work. Afterwards, Ryan gave me a ride home and I assumed he was going on to his place from there. He lived alone just a couple of blocks from me."

She sips her fresh coffee as Nate makes notes in his yellow legal pad. She knows he doesn't yet trust smart technology, having spent so long inside.

"Did he actually tell you he was going home?" he asks.

"No, but he was still in uniform and it was early evening by then. There was nothing to suggest he had plans to go somewhere else."

"And he didn't ask you over to his place?"

"No. He knew I had to get home for my son. Owen and I were looking after the neighbor's house that week, while she was on a cruise. We'd agreed to feed the cat every morning and evening and water her house plants."

"Okay. And what do you know about what happened next?" he asks.

Madison pictures the scene. It's easy, because her lawyers showed her the crime-scene photos and they were widely shared during her trial. She's never been able to get those images out of her head. "The TV was on in Ryan's living room, there were candles lit around the fireplace and dinner was in the oven: two frozen pizzas that had burnt to a crisp by the time the police arrived." She pauses. "Ryan was sprawled face down on the kitchen floor with one gunshot wound to the back of his head. The medical examiner determined that his face had hit the stove as he dropped to the floor because his front teeth had been damaged and he had bruising around his mouth." She tries to hide her trembling hands.

Nate raises his eyebrows. "Jesus, he was shot from behind? Isn't that execution style?"

She nods and takes another drink. "Yeah. But Detective Douglas was convinced the scene told the story that he was on a date because of the candles and the two pizzas instead of one. Everyone in town knew that Ryan and I worked together. Team that with the fact that several people spotted us eating cake together earlier that day, like it's some kind of goddam crime, and everyone jumped to the conclusion that it was *me* he was on a date with."

Nate shakes his head and drops his pen. "That's a shockingly lazy assumption. Surely Douglas must have investigated other possibilities? Especially because Ryan was shot from behind."

"No. Unfortunately he didn't."

"But why not? Someone in your department must have spoken up on your behalf. Made them see you weren't capable of murdering a friend, never mind a fellow police officer."

She takes a deep breath and tries to steady her hands. It almost feels like being on trial all over again. Hesitantly she says, "He didn't consider anyone else for the murder once he realized the shot was fired from my service weapon."

Nate's mouth actually falls open. "You're shitting me?"

She shakes her head and sips her coffee. "I shit you not."

CHAPTER FIVE

The breaking news music makes everyone in the diner look at the TV above the counter in unison. A male news desk anchor is talking about a development over in the nearby town of Lost Creek. Madison sits up straight as the anchor cuts to a live outside broadcast and the familiar face of her high school friend, TV reporter Kate Flynn, appears. It doesn't look like Kate has aged a day since she covered Madison's trial, and Madison finds herself feeling sad that their relationship deteriorated when Kate chose her loyalty to her job over their long-term friendship.

"Shocking news coming from the Fantasy World amusement park this morning, folks," says Kate, with a grave look on her immaculately made-up face. "We have unconfirmed reports that a teenage girl has died here overnight. Rumors suggest it could be a suicide, although we've been unable to get hold of the investigating detective for comment."

The camera moves past Kate's shoulder and zooms into a wide shot of the amusement park. The roller coaster and the Ferris wheel are silhouetted against the blue morning sky.

"Jeez, that place is still open?" says Madison.

Nate follows her gaze. "What place?"

"Fantasy World. Owen used to beg me to take him there every weekend in summer. I'd always come away with a headache from all the screaming and loud music." She sighs. "Maybe they'll shut it down completely after this. It's been there over forty years and is long overdue a complete refurbishment, or better still, pulling down altogether. I'm surprised those rusty old rides haven't killed anyone recently."

She remembers a girl from her school who fell off the runaway mine-train roller coaster during its upside-down loop because some idiot didn't secure the safety bar properly. All the boys in her class congregated where the poor girl had landed, silently in awe of witnessing their first dead body. These days they would probably pull out their cell phones and start recording. Stories about the girl's ghost haunting the park were always popular at school.

"You're going to gloss over what you just told me, aren't you?" Nate looks serious. "About your service weapon being at the scene of the crime you were convicted of."

"It's been a long few days, Nate. We have plenty of time to discuss that later." She wants to watch the news report. It's her first glimpse of Lost Creek in a long time.

On screen, the camera operator does a good job of trying to find something newsworthy with his lens, but the police cordon is too wide. All the rides are shut down. Without the colorful lights and loud dance music, the place loses its magic.

"We have unsubstantiated reports that the girl's death took place on or near the park's famous Wonder Wheel, but we don't yet know her identity," Kate continues. "We have, however, managed to find a worker from the park willing to talk."

An older woman with curly gray hair steps into view. She looks a little worse for wear.

"Ma'am, I understand you work here, is that correct?" asks Kate.

"Sure do. I've worked the cotton candy stand for over twenty years."

"And how did you react to this morning's tragic news?"

"I've only just been told!" the woman says, clearly shaken. "I can't believe something like that has happened here, and on July Fourth too!"

"Can you tell me what the atmosphere was like here last night?" probes Kate. "Were there any reports of trouble, or anything out of the ordinary?"

The woman looks shocked at the suggestion, which Madison finds laughable considering that the place breeds trouble. Always has.

"No, ma'am. Everyone was in the party spirit. It was busier than usual, perhaps a little rowdier, but that's to be expected given the occasion. We had a small fireworks display at seven for the little ones, and then the big display at nine for the adults and teens. As far as I'm concerned, everyone was enjoying it." She leans in to Kate. "But truth be told, I was a little wasted by ten o'clock. I can't hold my liquor like I used to and I don't remember getting home." She grins into the camera.

To her credit, Kate keeps a straight face. "I see. And do you know the identity of the unfortunate girl who died here last night?"

The woman shakes her head. "Nope. I just hope to God I don't know her. Working at a place like this, you get friendly with the local kids. And those of us who work here are all one big family. I'd hate to lose any one of them." She starts dabbing her eyes with her sleeve. "Even though it sounds bad, I'd rather it was a customer."

Madison is overcome with a strong feeling of dread as two male cops—one white, one black—emerge from the park. The camera-man signals to Kate and she spins around and immediately runs toward them, forgetting the woman. "Detectives, are you able to give us a statement about what happened here last night?"

Madison thinks they both look like they'd rather be anywhere else than on camera, but when they realize it's probably in their best interests to give Kate something rather than risk her speculating, one of them slows down, signaling to the other to keep walking.

Everyone in Lost Creek knows who these detectives are, because they're the only detectives the town has. And Madison knows them better than most. Mike Bowers and Don Douglas. She's shocked that Douglas is still in Lost Creek and her skin crawls at the thought of inevitably bumping into him.

"Thank you for your time, Detective Bowers," says Kate.

"No problem," says Mike. "We were called out here at approximately six o'clock this morning to a report of a deceased sixteen-year-old girl on the Ferris wheel. We haven't yet notified her parents, so I won't be releasing her name."

"But you do know her identity?" asks Kate.

He nods slowly. "I believe we do, but I want to be sure."

"And how did she die?"

Mike looks uncomfortable now. He's not aged as well as Kate. He's gray around the temples and he looks exhausted. He's gained a little weight too, which is surprising as he was always a keen runner. "Let's wait for the medical examiner's report before we speculate on that, shall we? That's all I can tell you right now." He smiles and walks away to join Detective Douglas in the parking lot.

As the camera follows them, Madison can see that the coroner's van has arrived to transport the girl's body to the morgue.

"That poor girl's mother," says Nate.

She finishes her coffee. "I don't miss delivering news like that." But she'd be lying if she said she didn't miss every other aspect of the job. She's already wondering how the girl died and whether it was a homicide. With Steph being killed nearby only three nights ago, Mike needs to be checking whether the cases are linked. Madison knows she needs to speak to him as soon as possible about what happened to Stephanie.

Nate pulls his wallet out to pay the check, then gathers his things.

Madison stands up. Her heart beats a little faster at the thought of arriving home and facing her past.

CHAPTER SIX

Lost Creek, Colorado

Detective Mike Bowers stares at the dead girl slumped on the Ferris wheel—named by her boss as sixteen-year-old Nikki Jackson. He swallows two pills without water. He's getting a throbbing headache above his right eye. Probably because, like everyone else in town, he was celebrating a little too much last night and now he's paying for it. It doesn't help that the day is already too hot, his cell phone won't stop ringing, and Detective Douglas has left him to do all the work.

"You're saying you don't know the whereabouts of the employee who found her?" he asks the park's owner, Trevor Sanders.

"Afraid not. He obviously called this in to you guys," Trevor nods to Nikki's body, "then called me. He'd already left by the time I arrived. I haven't seen him since and his phone is switched off."

Mike wonders why someone would flee the scene of a suicide. "What's his full name?"

"Ricky Gregor. This is his first summer here."

Mike writes it down on his small pad. "Address?"

"I'm pretty sure he told me he lives in an apartment over the coffee shop in town, but don't quote me on that."

Mike raises an eyebrow. "You didn't get references on this guy?"

Trevor smiles patiently. "Working here doesn't pay that well, so it attracts three kinds of people: teenagers, older women whose kids have flown the nest, and the kind of adults who can't get work elsewhere for whatever reason. That leads to false names and backgrounds, so sure, I ask for references, but I'm willing to bet the majority of them are fake, along with half these people's names." He shrugs as if to say it's not his fault or his problem.

Not for the first time, Mike gets an insight into how so many pedophiles get away with hurting kids. If anywhere should be hot on criminal record checks, it's an amusement park. He doesn't say this, though. He knows from experience it would go in one ear and out the other. "Where was Nikki when you last saw her?"

"She was cleaning up for me. I offered her some extra cash to stay on another hour or two to sweep up all the trash and spent fireworks. Everyone else had let me down, so I gave her the keys and told her to lock up after herself."

Mike raises an eyebrow. "That was trusting."

"Nikki was a good girl. She wouldn't steal from me no matter how much she needed the money." He glances at her slumped, lifeless body, currently being photographed by the medical examiner. "This is so messed up. I had no idea she was thinking of hurting herself."

"Did she seem upset when you left her?"

"No, not at all. But teenagers are good at hiding their feelings."

Mike thinks of his own daughter, who's eleven. Would he be able to spot the signs? He'd like to think so, but he's given bad news to too many parents to know that's not always the case. Besides, she lives with his ex-wife, who has full custody. "Did you touch her body at all? To get a look at her face or check her pulse?"

"No. There didn't seem any point. I mean, it was obvious she was dead."

Mike nods, then looks up at the CCTV cameras and points with his pen. "I'll need to pull your footage from that night."

Trevor shakes his head regretfully. "Sorry, man. They're just for show. I can't afford real cameras in a plot this big." He lowers his voice. "Between you and me, I'm running this place at a loss."

Mike sighs. Luckily this is a suicide and not a murder. "Okay, thanks for your time. If we need a formal statement, I'll be in touch."

Trevor takes one more look at Nikki and shakes his head again. "Can I let the staff know we're closed for the foreseeable?"

"Sure, but I don't want to see anything about this crime scene online, and no one but Lena here, and my forensics guy, are allowed to take photos. You might want to relay that to the guy who found her. If you ever see him again."

He wonders why Ricky Gregor ran when it's clear the girl killed herself. Sure, he could be worried about a shady past catching up with him, but he could also have been doing something to the girl that made her want to kill herself. He'll know more once he's spoken to her parents.

As he watches Trevor walk away to the office, his cell phone rings again. He can't tell who's calling him from the number displayed, so he rejects the call. "Probably another goddam reporter," he mutters.

"What's that?" asks Dr. Lena Scott, the local medical examiner. She's only been in post a few months, since the last ME died on the job.

"Nothing. Looks like an obvious suicide to me." He nods to the dead girl. "What do you think?"

She stands up. "It certainly looks like she bled out from the lacerations on her wrists, I'd guess between midnight and three a.m. I'll need to perform an autopsy and run toxicology tests to see if she was under the influence of anything. Plus, I'll do a pregnancy test to see if that's a potential motive for suicide."

He nods. He doesn't know Lena well yet; this is just the second time they've met. The first time was at Stephanie Garcia's crime scene. All he knows is that she's originally from New Hampshire, but he doesn't know what brought her here. He can tell she's one of the few people who didn't overindulge last night, because she looks like she's fresh out of a salon; her long brown hair is immaculately blow-dried and her clothes are ironed. It probably won't be long before she lets her standards fall, just like the rest of the town.

"If you can prioritize the autopsy, I'd be grateful."

"Sure. The toxicology results may take a while to come back, but I should have a preliminary report ready for you pretty quickly." She looks at the girl as she removes her protective equipment. "Do you know who she is yet?"

"Yeah. The park's owner identified her as Nikki Jackson. Sixteen years old. She worked here for two summers in a row. I'll be visiting her parents shortly to break the news."

Lena makes a note of her name and age. "She was far too young to take her own life."

"You're assuming she did," says a man with a British accent who has walked up behind them. "Perhaps it's not as cut-and-dried as it looks, if you pardon the pun."

Mike turns to see Alex Parker. He's Lost Creek PD's crime-scene technician, and he's an asshole. Mainly because he's like a walking version of Google and has an answer for everything, but also because he contradicts whatever Mike says whenever he gets the chance. Everyone else thinks he's great, which doesn't help.

"Hey, Alex," says Lena.

"Lena thinks it's suicide," says Mike. "And I'd say she's the best qualified out of the three of us. Wouldn't you?"

Alex is unfazed. "Of course, but did she spot the partial bloody thumbprint on our victim's forehead, near her hairline? More specifically, does she know it doesn't appear to belong to the victim?"

Lena immediately kneels down next to the girl's body again and carefully moves some of the red hair away from her expressionless face. Mike can see the blood smeared there, but he can't make out any prints.

"I've taken extensive photographs," says Alex. "Plus, I have her mobile—I mean cell phone—to check. It was in her jeans pocket. I've taken prints from the ride and I've bagged any potential trace evidence I could find: some hairs and fibers from her clothes to see if any of them are foreign. But as she died on a popular ride on the busiest night of the year, these items could be anyone's and they might have nothing to do with her death. I'll examine everything back at the station."

Mike frowns. "The thumbprint on her forehead… The park's owner said he didn't touch her. His maintenance guy found her when he opened up this morning, but I haven't been able to speak to him yet." He looks at his notes. "Maybe he tried to wake her and inadvertently touched her wrists first." If it wasn't Ricky, it means someone else was present when she died. "How do you know it's not Nikki's own print?"

Lena gently lifts the girl's hands. "There's no blood on her thumbs."

"I've taken her prints," says Alex. "So I'll double-check anyway, just to rule it out."

Mike nods. He doesn't want anyone jumping to conclusions about other people being present. The press would be all over it.

"I've also bagged the contents of her staff locker," Alex continues. "There wasn't much inside: just her purse, containing ten dollars in cash and a few coupons and discount cards, along with her house key and a soft toy. It's a unicorn from the shooting gallery." He pauses. "Who has the knife she used?"

Mike looks at Lena, who shakes her head, then back at Alex. "I thought you did?"

"Nope. It wasn't here when I arrived."

"Shit." Mike wonders if Ricky took it with him for some reason—maybe it was worth something—or perhaps he accidentally kicked it out of reach. Either way, they need to find it, and fast.

"I'm sure I don't need to remind you that if it's no longer here, it's already contaminated," says Alex.

"No. You don't." Mike sighs. "I'll get some uniforms to search the park." He looks in the direction of the lake that sits to the right of the park. He really doesn't want to have to send divers down there to look for a knife. It costs a fortune and attracts the kind of media attention he'd prefer to avoid for as long as possible. Because if the knife is down there, it means Nikki Jackson was murdered.

Alex turns to Lena. "I have some more work to do on the scene before you take the young lady away."

"Understood," she says. "Just let me know when you're done." As she walks away, she makes a phone call.

"I know she's both beautiful and intelligent," says Alex. "But it's rude to stare, Detective."

Mike reddens. "Just do your job." He heads to his car. He can't delay any longer. He has to bring Douglas up to speed, then visit Nikki Jackson's parents and turn their world upside-down.

CHAPTER SEVEN

Just after lunchtime, Nate and Madison reach a small town on the outskirts of Lost Creek called Gold Rock. The old wooden buildings look mostly deserted.

"What is this place?" Nate asks.

Madison lifts her sunglasses and sighs. "This is your classic shithole. There's practically nothing here. Nothing of interest, anyway. Just families who have been here generations, probably since the first gold rush. It's dying a slow death, even though the locals try to preserve as much of it as possible. It basically consists of old mine shafts, a few scrap businesses and a handful of stores that remain from the Wild West era. Just drive straight through."

Nate's never been to a gold rush town before, so he drives on slowly. He needn't have bothered; there really is nothing here other than a handful of residential homes, a couple of ranches, and a tiny Main Street that consists of old wooden stores with no sidewalk out front. They come across a pair of large billboards by the side of the road. They look out of place in a town this small, but they're advertising a "Hair of the Dog Festival" that's apparently scheduled for this afternoon and evening. The billboard says the event is sponsored by the "esteemed McCoy family" and is a fundraiser to help restore the old saloon to its former glory.

He keeps driving. "Wow. You weren't kidding when you said it was sparse." He glances at Madison, but she's hiding behind her aviator sunglasses now and sitting low in her seat.

"I always hated this place." She looks like she's trying to go unnoticed, which is easy, as they don't pass a single person as they drive through. Nate half expects to see a cowboy riding into town any minute. The only life they spot is a dog sitting in the back of a Chevy pickup truck outside what looks like a hunting store. Brody barks softly when he notices it.

They carry on to Lost Creek, about a half-hour east. When he finally spots the town sign, Nate slows to read it:

Welcome to Lost Creek
Where the lost are found
Population: 4,566. Please drive safely!

He thinks about that second line but is distracted by the scenery ahead. "Wow. That's an impressive mountain," he says, taking his eyes off the road to try to see the peak.

"It's called Grave Mountain, supposedly because it's killed so many climbers," says Madison. "Numerous people have gone missing up there, presumed dead. Kids talk about sightings of the climbers' spirits wandering the mountain in search of the peak. Or in search of their bodies, depending on which story you listen to."

He smiles. He's always enjoyed horror stories and urban legends. "So why does the town's welcome sign say *Where the lost are found*?"

She laughs. "I guess it's ironic."

In comparison to Gold Rock, Lost Creek is captivating. Nestled in the shadow of several imposing mountains and majestic woods, Nate realizes just how isolated the town is from anywhere but nearby Gold Rock. He spots a railroad track running past the town and wonders if it's still in use. As he drives through a forest of aspen trees, he finds himself wishing he had time to stop and take photos. Their white bark makes them look like ghosts, and he wonders what it's like to walk amongst them in the dark. Having grown up in Kansas, he's used to vast flatlands with extensive, never-ending views. Lost Creek couldn't be more different.

He reaches a rickety covered bridge and notices its name just as he drives onto the structure: *The One-Way Bridge. Take extra care.*

He glances at Madison. "Is it called that for a reason?"

She smiles. "With Lost Creek there's only one way in, and one way out. By car, anyway."

He looks ahead. "Great."

They make it across the bridge and onwards, passing a large white water tower and a smattering of residential areas. When they eventually reach the town center, they're greeted by a busy modern shopping area, though there are no strip malls to be seen. Instead there are plenty of small independent shops. They pass a couple of restaurants and coffee shops, a town hall, a diner, an undertaker's, and he even spots a newspaper office.

"It's bigger than I expected."

Madison laughs. "Don't speak too soon. This is basically it. Let's pick up some supplies before we find somewhere to stay."

He finds a parking spot outside the laundromat and pulls a sweater from the back seat. Unfortunately it's covered in Brody's fur and smells badly of dog.

"I'll do the laundry if you get us some food," he says to Madison.

"Sure." She's looking out the window, craning her neck in all directions.

He knows it must be unsettling for her to come back after all this time. Especially considering the last time she was here she was on trial for murder. "Here." He passes her some cash. She left prison with no money and no family support. They came to an agreement where he would pay her expenses while she was working for him. Technically she's not working for him right now as he's here to investigate for her, but he lets that slide. He's as ready to find out who framed her as she is.

"What about Brody?" she asks as the dog stretches in the back seat, limbering up for action.

He considers what to do. "I'll take him with me." He pulls together their laundry from the trunk while Brody urinates by the sidewalk and then sniffs around the storefronts. One man pats his head as he passes and then nods to Nate.

Madison wanders off toward a coffee shop.

"Brody, come." Nate enters the laundromat and smiles at the only other patron: a cranky-looking middle-aged woman who's reading a newspaper. It must be a late-morning edition, as the headline on the front cover screams: *Fantasy World turns into a nightmare.* Followed by: *A killer on the prowl?*

The woman looks up at him.

"Mind if my dog comes in?" he asks.

She just nods her head and carries on reading.

Brody isn't one of those dogs who has to be petted by every person he meets, and he's not easily distracted either. His police owner died in the line of duty and Nate feels like a poor replacement. After sniffing the entire store, Brody settles in the sunshine by the window, alert and ready for action.

As Nate sits on the wooden bench, watching their clothes spinning in the washing machine, his thoughts turn to Stacey, the woman he wanted to marry. Before he met her, he was studying philosophy at the University of Texas at Austin. Growing up, his life had revolved around the church and he had been working toward eventually becoming ordained. But then he met Stacey—the niece of his mentor, Father Jack Connor—and the unexpected happened. He gradually fell in love with her, and by the time he was twenty he had made the decision to give up the priesthood to marry her. Just a few weeks later, she was brutally murdered and Nate was arrested.

He knows now, twenty years later, that Father Connor was responsible for killing her, but the priest has vanished. Every now and again Nate receives a taunting email sent via a fake account, but he doesn't know where he is. He knows he'll find him eventually, though, and he's ready for the long-awaited showdown. He needs to know why Father Connor killed his own niece, and why he framed Nate for it. He's been feeling lately like the guy is closing in on him. The messages are becoming darker and more frequent, and Nate suspects Father Connor wants to kill him before he finds a way to expose him.

His thoughts are interrupted when the other patron kicks one of the industrial dryers.

"Crock of shit!" She turns to Nate. "Damn thing stole my cash. Can you lend me some change?"

He knows he won't see it again, but it's not like he's stretched for cash since receiving a handsome payout for his wrongful conviction.

"Sure." He stands up and drops some coins into the machine's slots. The woman is staring at him. He smiles and returns to his seat.

"Hey. I know you," she says.

His smile falters. This isn't the first time he's been recognized in the two years since his release. There was so much media coverage about his conviction, followed by his sensational exoneration, that he's surprised it doesn't happen more often.

"You're that killer priest guy!"

Brody looks around at the woman, anticipating trouble. The dog has shown Nate a surprising amount of loyalty in the short time they've been together. Glad that there's no one else in here to listen to her call him by his media nickname, Nate nods.

"I knew it!" she says, clearly pleased with herself. "I saw you on the news. What was death row like? I've got a cousin in San Quentin and it's meant to be the worst death row in the country. Think yourself lucky you weren't in there." She laughs, but it's a mean laugh from an ignorant woman.

Nate doesn't anger easily—he's always been pretty good-natured apart from when suffering one of his depressive episodes—but her flippancy touches a nerve. Maybe it's because he's been on the road too long, with little privacy and the burden of helping Madison weighing heavily on him. He suddenly feels the familiar craving for a couple of lines of coke that overwhelms him in stressful situations.

He smiles at her. "Yeah, I'm one lucky guy alright. Almost two decades on death row in Texas is a breeze."

Her smile falters. She's not sure whether he's making fun of her or not.

To avoid any ambiguity, he adds, "My fiancée was murdered, my youth was wasted in prison, and I'll have people like you recognizing me wherever I go for the rest of my life. But sure, I'm lucky."

He regrets it as soon as it's out, but he can't take it back. Brody must notice that his body language has changed, because he gets up and puts himself between Nate and the woman.

"No need to be a smartass," she says. "I thought you were a man of God. Shouldn't you show more patience to people?"

He laughs bitterly. He's sick of people using his religious background to hold him to a higher standard.

She's angry now. "The way you're acting, I can imagine you're a killer. I think they got it wrong letting you out of prison. You stay away from me." She gathers her damp clothes from the dryer and leaves, letting the door slam shut behind her.

Brody looks up at him questioningly.

"Bet you didn't know I was a celebrity, did you, boy?" He strokes the dog's head and leans back against the wall, wondering how he'll ever stop his past affecting his present.

CHAPTER EIGHT

Mike sits in his car and inspects the mobile home Nikki Jackson lived in. It's in a run-down trailer park on the wrong side of town, but this is the only home with a vegetable garden out front. It surprises him. The lawn is cut too. Someone obviously takes pride in this plot. A rusty bike with a flat tire is propped up against the steps, and there are various garden ornaments dotted around. The trailer itself is clean on the outside and there's an American flag stretched across one of the windows from the inside.

Detective Douglas pulls up next to him. "You ready?" he asks, getting out.

Mike nods as he slams his door shut. "Any calls since the news report earlier?"

Douglas shakes his head. "No one's noticed they're missing a daughter yet."

Mike wonders what kind of parents wouldn't notice that. "You can deliver the bad news."

Douglas doesn't react. He's a man of few words. Mike can't stand the guy, but he keeps the peace because they have to work together. He's betting Douglas didn't celebrate Independence Day yesterday, unlike the rest of them. He doubts the guy has ever touched a drop of alcohol. He's probably too afraid of loosening up in case the stick falls out of his ass.

They climb the steps and Douglas knocks on the closed door.

Mike's dreading how hot it's going to be inside, as all the windows are closed. The trailer is in the full glare of the midday sun, so he can't understand the residents' logic. He spots some fresh tomatoes growing on their vines by the door and wonders if he could get away with eating a couple, since he skipped lunch. Then he spots a pile of empty liquor bottles crushing a cucumber plant and his expectations immediately lower.

A woman opens the door. She doesn't look how he was expecting. She's well dressed and healthy-looking. Clearly worried, she says, "Yes?"

"Afternoon, ma'am. I'm Detective Don Douglas and this is Detective Mike Bowers. We're from Lost Creek PD. Can we come in?"

Surprise makes her open the door to them. Inside, a man is lying on the couch. He's already drinking a beer, and it makes Mike crave one. The place reeks of stale food and cigarettes, but there's something else lurking under that aroma, something familiar. It isn't untidy in here, but the furnishings are well worn.

Mike has to loosen his tie to deal with the heat.

Douglas asks, "Are you the parents of Nikki Jackson?"

The man stands up but keeps his beer in his hand. "She in trouble?" he asks. "She didn't come home last night so I assume she shacked up with some boy and now she's too afraid to face the music."

He's skinny and pale, with hollow eyes. By this stage of summer most people are sporting either a golden tan or scorched red skin, but not Mr. Jackson. Mike can spot a meth user when he sees one. But his wife appears to be his complete opposite, clearly taking some pride in her appearance and with no obvious signs of addiction. He wouldn't have put these two together in a million years. He glances at Nikki's mother, who is strangely emotionless and quiet.

"Have you seen the news yet today?" asks Douglas. "About what happened at Fantasy World last night?"

"We don't watch the news in this house," says Nikki's father. "It's full of propaganda and liberals telling me which way I should vote. I like to make up my own mind."

"What happened?" asks her mom.

Douglas takes a deep breath. "I'm afraid I have to give you some bad news." He pauses. "Your daughter was found dead this morning." There's a softness to his voice Mike doesn't hear often.

Mrs. Jackson takes a seat on the worn couch. "Oh God, no."

Surprise crosses the father's face, quickly replaced with a hardness. "Let me guess. She killed herself?"

Mike shares a look with Douglas but they manage to keep the contempt off their faces. He glances around the trailer while Douglas explains.

"Her injuries would suggest she cut her wrists. She was found on the Ferris wheel at Fantasy World. I understand she was working there?"

"You sure it wasn't a mechanical accident?" asks Mr. Jackson. "Because I could sue the bastards for that."

Nikki's mother remains silent, but her eyes are fixed on the ground and her tears are falling steadily.

"Sir? Do I have to remind you of what's important here?" says Douglas, his tone changing. "Your daughter felt the need to take her own life. Do you know what might have caused her to do that?"

Her father doesn't answer the question. Instead, he sits down and lights a cigarette. His hands are shaking. Mike knows it takes some people longer to react to bad news than others.

"I was just thinking out loud, that's all," Mr. Jackson says quietly.

Mike spots a recent photo of Nikki on the fridge and leans in. She's smiling as she poses outside her school. She has books in her arms and she looks a little bashful, as if she doesn't like having her photo taken. Her clothes are too big for her and he wonders if she has an older sister whose cast-offs get handed down. Judging by the furnishings in their home, it's clear this couple don't have much money.

"Mrs. Jackson?" says Douglas, turning to her. "Is there anything you can tell us about your daughter that could help explain what's happened?"

She struggles to speak. "No."

"Does she have siblings? A boyfriend? Has she fallen out with anyone recently?"

"No to all of those." She pulls a tissue out of a pocket.

Mike tries to get her to open up. "Are those vegetable plants outside your work? You must have green fingers to produce such great tomatoes." He smiles.

She looks up at him. "Nikki likes to grow things from scratch. She uses the seeds from our groceries. Says it'll save us money."

He wasn't expecting that. "She was obviously smart and resourceful." He pauses. "Did she ever mention a guy called Ricky to you?"

They look at each other but there's no recognition of the name.

"No," says her dad. "Why?"

"No reason. I just had to ask."

Mrs. Jackson looks away. "I'm sorry. I'm going to need time to process this. Could you leave us for a while? Maybe come back tomorrow?"

Mike's surprised. He's never had parents of a dead child react this way before. Normally they want answers and information. And normally they want to see the body immediately.

"Sure, we'll leave you to digest everything," says Douglas. "One of us can come back to answer any questions you have, but I'll leave you with our contact details in the meantime." As neither of them offers to take the card from him, he slides it onto the small dining table. "And I'm sorry, but we'll need one of you to identify Nikki. She's currently with the medical examiner. It can wait until tomorrow if necessary, but no longer than that. If you feel you're not up to it, please ask a trusted family member to go in your place."

Mrs. Jackson looks horrified, but eventually she nods.

"Thanks for your time. We'll be in touch."

They let themselves out and walk to their cars. Mike wants to ask Douglas his opinion of the parents, but it'll have to wait until they get back to the station, because Mr. Jackson is watching them from the front window. Mike nods at him as he pulls away, but the guy doesn't respond.

He has to resist the urge to shake his head in disgust as he thinks about the kind of life Nikki must have had with those two as her parents.

CHAPTER NINE

Independence Day

Nikki Jackson is sitting in the stifling hot ticket booth of the Wonder Wheel, anxiously chewing gum and taking money off overexcited kids. It's not even lunchtime yet and she's already tired and hungry. Fantasy World is starting to get busy and tonight is just going to be worse, thanks to the planned firework displays. Although if she's honest, she's kind of looking forward to them. Not much happens around here normally so the Fourth of July is always special.

Her stomach rumbles loudly. It's hard working around the constant smell of meat and sugar. Temptations are all around. Luckily she can't afford to indulge too often. This is the second summer she's worked at the amusement park and she's enjoying it far more than last year. The heat isn't bothering her since she bought a portable fan. And for once, even the messy kids aren't annoying her with their sticky hands and tendency to vomit at a second's notice.

"That's twenty-four bucks, please," she tells the next person in line for the wheel.

The park used to run on token machines but the last one gave up over the spring. The maintenance guy, Ricky, said it couldn't be fixed and they'd all need replacing, so Trevor sold them for scrap metal. He hates running the place with cash as he suspects the staff are stealing from him, but he can't afford to replace the machines. He's right, of course, most of the staff *are* stealing from him. It's pretty easy to do. Although Nikki's never stolen a dime, despite the enormous temptation some days.

"Can I get three for the price of two?" asks the mom holding the Chanel purse. "They're too young to go on the ride alone." She nods to her two children.

"Do you have a coupon?" asks Nikki. They sometimes offer coupons in the local paper during quiet periods.

"No, but you could give me a break. I mean, it's just a piece of paper."

Nikki stops chewing her gum. She glances at the woman's young children who, as well as looking sunburnt, appear unhappy and a little embarrassed. They're not carrying any toys won on the games, or any kind of candy. Looks like their mom prefers to spend her money on herself. Sensing the kids won't get a ride unless she relents, she nods and takes the woman's money.

"Here you go, kids." She hands them each a stick of candy and their eyes light up. The woman doesn't even say thanks.

Next in line is a balding guy with no kids in tow. "Can I get one adult ticket and your number?" He licks his lips as he smiles.

She has to hold back her disgust because she doesn't want to cause trouble, but can he seriously not see she's only sixteen? Forcing a smile, she pushes a ticket his way. "Next!"

The man shakes his head at her. "Ugly bitch. I wouldn't touch you if you were begging for it."

Tears spring to her eyes and she could kick herself for taking it personally. How come he gets to say what he wants to her yet she has to hold her tongue? She turns away from the booth's window to glance at the small mirror nailed to the wall. Her face is a little greasy from the heat and her red hair needs coloring again. It fades faster than any other color she's tried, plus she had to buy the cheapest brand so it barely worked in the first place. She knows she's ugly. She doesn't need creepy old men like him pointing it out to her.

"Come on, lady. I don't have all day," says the next jackass in line.

Her boyfriend, Mason, turns up with Emma, her relief, just as she's ready to run away from the line of people.

"Is it your break time yet?" he asks her.

She nods, stands, and tries to hold back the tears. Emma slips into her seat and confidently yells, "Next!"

Mason takes her hand and leads her out of the tiny ticket booth. She worries that she didn't get a chance to reapply her makeup or brush her hair, but when she looks at Mason, she feels ten times better about herself. He's gorgeous and could probably have any girl he wanted. He wouldn't be with her if he thought she was ugly, would he?

She pushes the thought from her mind and looks around. Between shifts, they become customers, not workers. Normally that means they can finally enjoy the atmosphere of the park and forget about the long shifts they still have to work. But Nikki has had a bad couple of days and she's struggling to get something out of her mind. She has a devastating secret. Something she can't tell anyone. Not even Mason. When she thinks about it, a feeling of dread runs through her body. Her breathing starts quickening now and she has to try hard not to panic. To calm herself down, she focuses on something else, like her therapist taught her to do when she's feeling overwhelmed.

She looks at all the American flags she helped pin up everywhere and notices that a lot of the younger children are clutching the small plastic flags Trevor is selling at the entrance. Everyone looks so happy, but she feels detached from it all. She doesn't know if it's because she works here and seeing behind the scenes makes the park less enchanting, or because of what happened two days ago.

She checks her cell phone. They have forty-five minutes of freedom before starting the afternoon shift.

As Mason leads her along the boardwalk, she jumps in front of him and kisses him on the lips. If she focuses all of her attention on him, she can pretend everything is normal. For the time being at least.

"What was that for?" He smiles, slipping his arm around her waist.

She likes the feel of his strong arm around her. "Just because."

He's been a little distant these last couple of days. They've only been dating for eight weeks, since meeting in her therapist's waiting room, but she'd seen him around town before. Turns out he doesn't go to her school because he's home-schooled. Since he started working here at the beginning of summer, they've spent a lot of time together. He's a year older than her, but he's smart and more mature than the boys at school.

He stops to try to win her a soft toy at the shooting gallery. It takes him numerous attempts and costs him more in tickets than the toy is worth, but she loves him for it.

"Which one do you want?" he grins.

She points to the unicorn she's had her eye on for weeks and then clutches it to her chest with her free hand. Mason leads her away by her other hand. She suddenly feels like she's living someone else's life. That of a rich, popular girl.

He buys them Cokes and hot dogs for lunch, and they find a quiet spot on the grass next to Lake Providence. Nikki sits close to him, their thighs touching, and they both remove their sneakers to rest their feet in the cool, clear water. It feels refreshing and she leans against him as she eats, licking the mustard off her lips and the onions off her fingers. She has to slap away the ravenous flies.

"Holy shit," says Mason through a mouthful of bun. "Derek sure knows how to make good dogs."

She laughs. "Yeah, but that's where all my money goes."

They watch the sun's reflection glistening in the water and the birds and bugs hovering over it. The air is filled with the delighted screams of kids enjoying the rides behind them.

Nikki thinks this might be the best summer she's ever had. Or it would have been. That's when she remembers her secret and the doubt creeps back in.

She should know by now not to trust happiness.

CHAPTER TEN

Madison manages to go unrecognized during her first afternoon back in town. They're even able to eat dinner in a bar without any trouble. As evening advances, she tries to relax as Nate drives them away from the town center. The temperature isn't cooling any but there are rain clouds gathering overhead, increasing the humidity. She glances over her shoulder to check on Brody, who's happily looking out of the rear window at the passing landscape. She likes having him around. Like Nate, he's a good judge of character.

"All I want is a shower, a beer and a good night's sleep without a dog pinned to my chest," says Nate with a smile.

"I hear you."

"Where are we staying tonight?" he asks, before frowning. "Actually, I never asked. What happened to your house while you were in prison?"

"It was just a rental me and Owen moved into after Steph and I split. I lost it after my arrest, but Stephanie agreed to store some of my things at her place. I'm guessing the larger items—furniture, my car and so on—were sold or dumped."

"I know that feeling,' he says. 'I came out of prison owning nothing but Stacey's rosary beads, and I only got them because the officer who booked me assumed they were mine because I happened to be wearing them. I'm guessing there's a hotel or guest house we can book into?"

"Actually, it looks like we'll be staying at Stephanie's place."

He raises his eyebrows. "Really? You still have a key after all this time?"

"No, but Mike Bowers has left her house and car keys for me to find." She looks down at her cell phone. "He messaged me to say they found a copy of her will." Tears take her by surprise, but she manages to stop them from falling. "Apparently she left the house to me, or to Owen in the event of my death."

Nate looks surprised. "You okay?" he asks.

She nods, touched at his concern. "I just can't believe she had no one better than me to leave them to. While I was in prison feeling sorry for myself, Steph was down here all alone. I guess I just assumed she'd be with someone else by now, or maybe even have reconciled with her family."

"Some people like living alone. Families can be trouble." He goes quiet and Madison knows he's thinking of his own family. He hasn't told her much about them yet, but he's alone in the world so they clearly aren't close. All she knows is that his parents are dead and his siblings live back home in Kansas, where they pretend Nate doesn't exist.

"We'll be comfortable at Steph's place," she says. "It's a small farm with three bedrooms, a couple of barns out back and lots of open space for Brody to roam."

"Did she keep animals?"

"Only chickens and goats when I lived with her. She was more into growing her own crops: sweetcorn, potatoes, pumpkins, that kind of thing. She would sell them at the weekend farmers' market to supplement her income. Illustrating children's books doesn't pay well." She sighs. "Once we're finished here, I guess I'll sell up."

She doesn't say it, but she's relieved to have an asset at last. The proceeds from selling the farm could really help her start afresh. Hopefully with her son by her side. She pulls out a cigarette. "Mind if I smoke with the window down?"

"Sure."

The closer she gets to Steph's place, the more she craves a cigarette. Cursing herself for giving in yet again, she lights one. The

first drag is always amazing; it calms her immediately, making her wonder why she keeps quitting. Then she remembers she'll never live to see forty if she returns to smoking the way she was doing in prison. And she has to stay alive long enough to find Owen again.

She looks out of the open window and up at the sky. The rain clouds are thickening. It's been so hot lately they could do with a good downpour. A few heavy spots of water splatter on the window. She watches as a white Toyota overtakes them. It's doing way over the speed limit and nudging everyone out of its way. It's quickly followed by sirens.

As the patrol vehicle speeds by, she can't help but watch, fascinated. It's an LCPD squad car, but it's going too fast for her to identify the driver. That used to be her. She used to chase assholes like that with no regard for her own safety. She'd have to pull them over, figure out whether they were armed and then cautiously approach the driver's window, all the while hoping they wouldn't shoot her dead and leave her son motherless. She takes another long drag of her cigarette and shakes her head at the irony that her son was left motherless in the end anyway. But not thanks to a criminal; thanks to the team who were supposed to have her back.

Her thoughts turn to the long list of things she needs to do now she's home. It's overwhelming. Her first visit has to be to Mike. When he initially called her to say he'd found Stephanie dead at her home, Madison was too distraught and guilt-ridden to ask how it happened. But she wants to help Mike find whoever killed her, and for that she'll need to see his case files and the crime-scene photos. If he'll agree to show her. He may take some persuading, seeing as she's no longer on the force and they haven't seen each other in seven years.

Stephanie was estranged from her entire family, so Madison also has to arrange her funeral. She doesn't want the state to give her a basic burial or cremation with no guests and no minister or words said for her. Even after they split, Stephanie would babysit

Owen while Madison worked the late shifts. He loved her. And Madison did too.

Thinking of Owen fills her with longing. She has to find him. She can't bear the thought of never seeing him again. Child services refused to tell her who he went to live with after her conviction. She knows he was moved away from Lost Creek, because otherwise Stephanie would have spotted him and told her during one of her prison visits. Madison has no idea if she'd even recognize him in the street now he's seventeen.

She realizes then that Owen probably wouldn't recognize her either. Before her conviction she was a little overweight, with dark blonde hair that was always tied back for work and rarely trimmed. After almost six months of waiting tables in California, she's now sporting a golden tan and her hair is more Malibu blonde, thanks to the sun-kissed highlights. As she's been broke for some time, she's also slimmer. Her transformation should buy her some time before word begins to spread that she's back in town.

She sighs. The most logical person to contact about Owen is Kate Flynn, as she has access to all kinds of information in her role as local reporter. But if their friendship can't be saved and Kate refuses to help, Madison has one last resort. Someone she's dreading seeing even more than Detective Douglas.

CHAPTER ELEVEN

Mike hangs his suit jacket on the back of the chair and sits at his messy desk. He'd rather be at home eating a microwave dinner and video-calling his daughter, but he's got reports to file, as always. He checks his cell phone. Madison hasn't replied to his text. He disclosed the contents of Stephanie Garcia's last will and testament and thought she'd reply immediately, considering she's the main beneficiary.

He needs to talk to her as soon as possible to see where her head is at these days. He doesn't know if she's just coming back to say her final goodbye to Stephanie or whether she's holding on to some resentment for what happened in the past. Either way, he knows he needs to keep an eye on her. He's probably her only friend in town.

As he glances around the station to see who else is about this evening, he realizes the place is almost empty. Everyone must be on call-outs. Either that, or they've left early to nurse their hangovers. Even the phones are quiet while the town recovers from yesterday. Then he remembers the McCoys' latest fundraiser was today over in Gold Rock. He was supposed to attend on behalf of LCPD and get his picture taken with them for the paper.

Chief Sullivan wheezes by on his way to his office. He's the same guy who was in charge when Madison worked here, although he's set for retirement in a couple of months. He's only fifty-three and on the outside he looks good for his age—slim, well groomed, sporting an all-year tan—but he's a chain smoker and has some serious lung problems, evident when the whole department has to listen to him coughing violently all day. Tonight, he looks like he's pissed off at something, but then he resents having to leave the building to indulge in a cigarette, so maybe that's it.

Mike wonders how the chief will react when he finds out Madison's back in town. The pair of them never worked well together. Sullivan is full of his own self-importance and Madison was headstrong. She worked hard and outshone most of the department. That doesn't always go down well in law enforcement.

He himself never had any beef with her, though. She could take a joke and she was quick to volunteer for jobs no one else wanted. She also knew how to follow the rules whilst looking for ways to improve them. He expects that helped her get paroled early, as she served just six years of her ten-year sentence. Either that, or it was down to prison overcrowding. More criminals are being released early these days. Makes him wonder why he works so hard to put them away in the first place.

He watches as Officer Shelley Vickers walks up to his desk. Being in her early thirties, Shelley's still enthusiastic about her role. She reminds him of Madison when she first started here, probably because Madison mentored her when Shelley first got out of the academy.

"Hey, Detective. Do you want me to keep looking into that illegal dumping next to the McCoys' ranch?"

He nods. "That'd be good. I've had Wyatt chewing my ear off about it."

The McCoys are one of the few remaining original families living in the old gold-mining town of Gold Rock, located between Prospect Springs and Lost Creek. It's one of those ghost towns you'd see in a Wild West movie, or more recently in one of those shows that hunt for paranormal activity. Wyatt McCoy is a prominent businessman who runs several different operations, including a prosperous scrap metal business and auto repair shop. He's also head of the foundation for the preservation of Gold Rock, and his wife, Angie, is on the board of a number of charities. Everyone in

LCPD knows it's good to keep the McCoys happy as they are well loved in the community and can be relied on to help people out when times are hard.

Mike checks the time and groans. Almost 8.30. There's still time to make it to the fundraiser just before everyone starts heading home. He can't remember what they're raising money for this time, but if he doesn't go, Chief Sullivan will lecture him for the millionth time about how they need to have a community presence at these kinds of events. He never sees the chief attend any, though.

"Check the discarded items for paperwork, stickers; anything that could help identify where they came from. If it's not obvious, we'll just have to arrange for the whole lot to be moved and drop the case. We don't have time for small nuisances like that right now."

"Sure thing."

Shelley walks away just as Detective Douglas arrives. He heads straight to the kitchen, so Mike follows him.

"How's it going?"

Douglas glances at him. "Not good. The knife still hasn't turned up. You need to take over at the amusement park because I have somewhere I need to be and the uniforms are currently there alone."

"Great," mutters Mike. Unlike Douglas, he's been working since the call-out to Nikki Jackson's discovery early this morning.

"While I was there, I was approached by two workers; a couple of teenagers. They seem to think Nikki Jackson's death was a suicide pact gone wrong."

"Really?" Mike doesn't believe it. "Could they just be spreading rumors?"

"They said she has a boyfriend who also works at the park, but they wouldn't give me his name as they didn't want to get him into trouble. We need to check it out." Douglas rubs his face and sighs. "As well as all the other shit we've got going on, Stephanie Garcia's murder and Nikki Jackson's death need closing asap. Let's split them. I'll continue with Garcia; you take the girl."

Mike thinks about it. Knowing Madison is coming back, and assuming she won't want to liaise with Don, he says, "I'll take over with Garcia. I knew her, so it makes sense."

"Fine," says Douglas. "But you still need to babysit the uniforms at the park tonight. We need that knife." He checks his watch. "Shit, it's past eight. I need to get out of here." He grabs his coat.

Mike thinks this might be the right time to tell him about Madison's impending return. He wasn't sure she would actually come back, so he's been holding off. "You remember Madison Harper, right?"

Douglas stops and turns. "Of course. How could I forget a cop killer who shamed our department in the eyes of the community and the media?"

Mike doesn't like the way Douglas stares at people. It's too intense and makes him feel like he's a new recruit in the army, with Douglas the overzealous drill sergeant. Come to think of it, he doesn't remember ever seeing Douglas laugh in all the time he's worked here. The guy needs to lighten up a little. "Well, she's on her way home."

"What do you mean?" Douglas's eyes almost pop out of his head. "It's not been ten years yet."

"I know," says Mike. "She got paroled early. She first contacted me just before Stephanie's death. Said Steph was being hassled by some guys who were looking for her."

Douglas interrupts him. "Hang on a goddam minute. What was our victim doing talking to Madison Harper?"

"They used to live together. They split up a few years before you came to town and they weren't together at the time of Madison's arrest."

Douglas's face is getting redder by the minute. "And you never told me this? Don't you think it's pertinent to the homicide investigation to inform me that the victim's ex-girlfriend was Madison

Harper—the woman who killed her last lover in cold blood? Or have you forgotten that fact, Bowers?"

Mike shakes his head. If this guy doesn't get out of his face he's going to react. He can feel his hands twitching. "I haven't *forgotten*. Unlike you, I worked with Ryan Levy for five years and knew him well, so don't act enraged on his behalf. You barely knew the guy."

Douglas turns away, taking a few steps toward the door.

"Madison wasn't in town at the time of Stephanie's death, so it wasn't her," Mike continues. "Like I said, she contacted me last week and tried to get me to carry out welfare checks on Stephanie before the murder."

Douglas rolls his eyes. "Jesus Christ, Bowers. How can you be so gullible? Just because she told you she wasn't in town doesn't mean she wasn't, and it doesn't mean she didn't hire someone to do it for her. You should've told me who the victim's ex was."

Mike tries to calm him down. "Listen to me. She's coming back to bury Stephanie because there's no one else to do it. She's probably too ashamed to show her face around here for long, so I doubt she'll stay more than a week. She served her time; now cut her some slack."

Looking like he has a renewed enthusiasm in the homicide now he knows Madison's somehow involved, Douglas says, "I'm keeping the Garcia case. You can take the teenage girl."

Mike watches him leave, realizing he's started a chain reaction that's going to have explosive results.

CHAPTER TWELVE

The rain has eased, but it's dark when they reach Stephanie's road. Nate's under strict instructions to turn the headlights off as he drives past the other homes and pulls into Stephanie's driveway. They sit in the car for a minute before getting out. The radio is on low. He's about to switch it off when a newsflash makes Madison stop him.

"We have some breaking news for you now about the deceased teenage girl found at the Fantasy World amusement park in the early hours of this morning. Police have released her name—Nikki Jackson—and confirmed she was a local girl who was working at the park on the night she died. Her death is thought by detectives to be a tragic suicide with no one else involved, but local unsubstantiated reports now suggest the incident may have been either a suicide pact gone wrong or, in fact, a homicide. This is down to reports that the knife used in the incident is missing from the scene. Detectives Douglas and Bowers have yet to respond to these new claims. We'll have more for you as soon as we get it."

Madison looks worried. "Did you hear that? She might have been murdered. Why else would the knife be missing? What if it's linked to Steph's death?"

Nate's not so sure. "Why would they be linked?"

She looks away. "I don't know, but two murders within a few days of each other isn't common around here. Or at least it wasn't. I need to find out the cause of death in both cases to see if there are any similarities."

He stays quiet. He doesn't want to point out that she doesn't have access to case files and witnesses anymore and isn't in a position to interview anyone. Not in this town where people will remember what she was locked up for.

Sitting on her hands and leaning forward, she's having a good look at Stephanie's house. "Ready to face your past?" he asks.

She shakes her head. "Not really. It's been over ten years since Owen and I lived here with Stephanie."

Brody whines softly from the back seat. He's ready to get out, so they open the doors.

Nate looks up at the house Madison has inherited. It's a two-story with peeling white paint on the wooden exterior and a wraparound porch with a couple of potted plants and hanging baskets to cheer the place up. He can't see any of the neighboring houses or farms from here, and with no street lights in the area, it's mostly in darkness except for a single bulb burning orange outside the front door. They retrieve their bags from the trunk and walk up the steps to the porch.

Torn crime-scene tape hangs from the front door and flutters gently in the breeze.

"Wait here a minute," Madison mutters.

Brody follows her around to the side of the house, sniffing everything as he goes.

Nate reaches for the yellow tape and balls it up in his hand.

When Madison returns with a set of keys, she takes one off the ring and gives it to him. "You might need the spare at some point."

She opens the front door, but pauses before going in, then shudders. "It smells of her."

Nate's not sure if she means it smells of Stephanie's dead body, or of their life together. They walk through the door and into the hallway. That's when the smell hits him: stale blood.

He waits for instructions as Madison silently goes around shutting drapes and blinds. Then she switches the overhead light on, illuminating the spacious living room. Nate spots two lamps shattered on the floor and a large potted plant tipped on its side.

The room is nicely decorated, homely, with throws and books everywhere, but it's hard to see past the evidence markers, the carelessly discarded latex gloves and the blood. There's so much blood. It's crusted into the carpet and there's spatter over the upturned coffee table. He knows Madison didn't ask her contact at LCPD how Stephanie died—she said she didn't want to discuss it until she saw him in person—but judging by the amount of blood, he thinks it was brutal.

He glances at Madison for her reaction.

Her face is completely white apart from her red-rimmed eyes. She storms past him without comment and he hears her banging around in what must be the kitchen. Brody enters the living room and heads straight for the dried blood. He sniffs excitedly before sitting next to it and looking back at Nate over his shoulder. He barks once.

"I know, boy. She died in here."

Brody barks again. He's expecting a reward for his find, so Nate pulls out a pack of beef jerky he carries in his pocket as a treat. The dog immediately takes the strip from his hand. "Good boy."

He goes to find Madison. "Are you okay?"

She spins around to face him, clearly angry. She throws the washing-up bowl into the sink. "The assholes couldn't even get the room cleaned before I got here? Mike knew I was coming!"

He moves toward her. He's not a natural hugger after years of solitary confinement, but he wants to comfort her.

She pushes him away and ignores the tears running down her cheeks. "No. I need to clean it up. We can't sleep here with that." She motions to the front room.

"You can't clean it up unless Mike gives you the all-clear. They must still be working the scene."

Madison turns away from him and leans against the sink. Her shoulders dip. She looks defeated.

Brody walks up to her and paws her leg. She pushes past them both and heads upstairs.

Nate fills a bowl with water for Brody, and then pours himself a glass. He knows he needs to give her some alone time. They've been in each other's pocket since they left California.

He walks back to the living room and closes the door on Stephanie's blood. Seeing the crime scene like that makes him more determined to find out what's going on in Lost Creek. Whoever framed Madison for murder must be responsible for Stephanie's death too. The guys who were hassling her a week ago were here to ask about Madison's location; they know that for a fact. So it's all linked somehow.

As he passes the front door, he sees something that makes him want to flee. Brody barks in excitement and runs to the door, trying to peer through a glass panel.

There are blue and red flashing lights right outside the house.

CHAPTER THIRTEEN

Madison is trying to relax, but being here doesn't feel right. It's not just seeing Steph's blood all over the living room—although that's bad enough, because now she knows the killer showed her no mercy—but she has a bad feeling building in her chest in a way she can't ignore. Like that moment when you figure out you can't trust someone close to you, but it's too late because you already have.

She looks at her reflection in the bathroom mirror and isn't surprised to see dark circles under her eyes and scaly skin around her nose. She hasn't bothered with makeup during their journey, as they've been on the road for practically all of it, but it's more than that. They haven't been eating well, relying on fried food from drive-throughs, and she's *got* to give up the cigarettes.

She sighs. All she wants is a hot bath and a comfortable bed, but not here. Not where the ghosts of her past are waiting for her. She needs to listen to her instincts, which are telling her to leave immediately and find somewhere else to stay. At least until the police have a crime-scene clean team clear up the living room and she's spoken to Mike Bowers in person to get some idea of what happened here.

"Goddam asshole," she mutters. Mike should have prepared her for that mess. He knew she was due to arrive today. Is this the department's way of letting her know they're holding a grudge? Washing her hands, she hears Brody bark downstairs. When he doesn't stop, she turns the faucet off and listens.

"Madison?" shouts Nate. "We have a situation."

She hears fear in his voice. Her blood runs cold and she immediately knows she made the wrong decision in coming here. She feels for the cheap Glock handgun she bought after her release, but it's not under her shirt. She left it in the car. "Shit." She flings open the bathroom door and slowly walks down the stairs. "What is it?"

Before Nate can answer, she notices the flashing lights through the door behind him. Clutching the handrail, she stops halfway down the stairs and looks at him.

"Want to leave through the back?" he asks. "We might just make it."

She notices that the blood has left his face. He's as scared as she is. She feels guilty for putting him in this situation, but that quickly turns to anger. "I'm not running. We haven't done anything wrong." She walks to the bottom of the stairs and pulls back the shade on the front door.

When she sees who is standing there staring at her, she takes a step back.

"You know him?" asks Nate.

She nods. Her mouth has gone dry. "He was the arresting officer," she whispers. Her body trembles as she realizes how stupid she's been. She shouldn't have come back here and put herself in the same situation as the one she only recently got out of.

Nate takes charge. He moves in front of her and opens the door, with Brody at his side. Brody appears happy to see cops in front of him. Is he expecting his dead police handler to reappear? Nate has to hold him back by his collar.

"What can I do for you?" he asks.

Detective Douglas looks past him, straight at Madison. "I'm here to speak to Ms. Harper." Apart from more lines around his eyes, he looks exactly the same.

"In relation to what?" asks Nate.

"That's between me and her."

Nate blocks his view of her, forcing Douglas to look at him instead. "Well I'm sorry, but it's late and we've only just arrived in town after a long journey. She'd be happy to stop by the station tomorrow afternoon with her lawyer."

Madison leans in to see Douglas's reaction. He actually smirks at Nate. Then he pushes by him into the house, making Madison take another step back. Douglas has her by the arm before she can get away. "Madison Harper, I'm arresting you for the murder of Stephanie Garcia."

She looks at Nate, who's yelling something at him. She watches two officers she doesn't recognize rush into her house, pushing Nate against the wall and away from her. Brody's jumping up at one of them and she silently prays he doesn't bite anyone. He'll be shot on the spot.

Everyone looks angry. They're all shouting. But she can't hear a word they're saying. All sounds are muffled, as if she's drowning.

How can this be happening again?

CHAPTER FOURTEEN

Mike makes it to Gold Rock in time to see Wyatt and Angie McCoy buttering up the drunk locals. He smirks. They're not stupid; they know a drunk person is more likely to throw caution to the wind and donate more to the fundraiser than they would sober.

Angie spots him first. She's bouncing someone's toddler over her shoulder; a little boy who looks like he's half asleep. "Detective Bowers. Glad you could join us. You missed the journalist, so you won't make it into tomorrow's paper." She winks at him, knowing full well that's the only reason Chief Sullivan sends him to their events.

"Good to see you." He looks around. It's getting dark fast, but there are still a lot of folks here enjoying themselves. The small Main Street has been lit up with party lights, and people are sitting outside on the picnic benches that have been spread around. The local stores appear to be busy with customers. It said on the tickets that a percentage of every ticket sale and of the sales from each shop and stall will go toward the charitable cause. "Looks like you've had a good event."

Wyatt McCoy claps him on the back. "Wish you could've been here sooner. I could've had you blind drunk by now." He laughs heartily.

"Do you think you've made enough money to restore the old Silver Saloon?"

Angie says, "Hopefully. But we'll have to wait until I do the books to find out." She smiles at him. "We've been waiting on you in the hope you'd announce the winner of the craziest moustache competition."

"Sorry, but I can't stay. I just wanted to show my face and pass on Chief Sullivan's message that the police department appreciates your efforts in the community, as always."

He registers Angie's disappointment.

"Perhaps if we didn't have that incident over at the amusement park I could've been here longer. My apologies for that."

Wyatt nods. "We understand. You've got a difficult job, Detective Bowers, and we appreciate you turning up. Here." He hands Mike something warm wrapped in silver foil. "Some hog roast for your dinner. That should see you through a long night."

Mike smiles. "I appreciate it. Have a good evening."

His stomach rumbles loudly as he walks back to his car.

At Fantasy World, Mike watches the officers as they search the amusement park for the missing knife. The park's owner, Trevor Sanders, approaches him after switching on all the lights to make their job easier. The sun has set completely now.

"I was hoping to reopen tomorrow," he says. "I'm guessing that's not going to happen now."

Mike looks at him. "Depends. If we find the knife tonight, we shouldn't need to come back. I'm pretty sure our forensics guy has everything else he needs."

"Good. This is already going to be bad for business, so the sooner I can open, the better." He must notice the look on Mike's face, because he tries to appease him. "I know it sounds harsh when a girl has died, but times are hard, man. There's nothing I can do for Nikki now."

He's right, but it's still callous. "Have you tracked down your maintenance guy yet?"

"No. I doubt I'll see him again, which means I have the added hassle of hiring a replacement."

Ricky Gregor is high on Mike's list of people to interview. "He ever act weird around young girls?"

"No weirder than anyone else. He'd stare at a hot woman, but no one ever complained about him. Not to me, anyway." Trevor shakes his head. "It looked like a suicide to me; I can't get my head around the thought that someone might have killed her."

"Well, we don't know that yet. Do you know who she was dating?"

Trevor looks uncomfortable. "Who knows? The kids who work here are all screwing each other, so I can't keep track. If you need me, I'll be over in the office." He walks away.

Mike sighs. He watches Officer Jim Greenburg lying flat on his stomach with a flashlight in one hand, trying to see into the machinery under the Ferris wheel. That would be the most logical place for the knife to have fallen if Nikki dropped it herself after cutting her wrists. But Jim's been staring down there a while now and not found anything.

Mike turns to see Alex approaching him. "Will my services be needed tonight, Detective?"

"It's not looking that way." He tries to think. "Is there any way to tell for sure whether Nikki made the cuts to her wrists herself? I mean, it must've been difficult to cut the second wrist once she'd cut the first."

Alex considers it. "It would certainly have been uncomfortable, but not impossible. It's likely she took an overdose of painkillers in anticipation, but we won't know that until the results of Lena's toxicology tests are in."

"If she took an overdose, why slash her wrists too? Why not just wait for the OD to kick in?"

Alex looks at him incredulously. "You obviously don't know how painful an overdose can be, Detective. Your organs shut down one at a time. And it's not a quick process. Depending on the drugs used, the victim can suffer seizures, chest pains, bleeding from all orifices, breathing difficulties—"

"Okay, okay, I get it." Mike tries to think.

Jim gets up from the ground and dusts his black uniform off as he approaches them. "There's nothing down there."

Shelley joins them. "We've searched everywhere, Detective. The knife isn't here. My bet would be that if someone did kill her, they've either thrown it in the lake or taken it with them."

Mike agrees. "Okay, guys. That'll do for tonight."

He walks away to his car and checks his cell phone. He has a missed call from Nikki's mother. He decides to pay her a visit before heading home. He needs to update them both on the knife situation.

"Why are we finding out what's happening via the goddam TV instead of through you?" shouts Mr. Jackson before Mike's even through their door.

Mike lets him shout, for now. "I thought you didn't watch the news?"

"Don't get smart with me!"

He knows he needs to calm the guy down, not get him more wound up. "Look, I didn't know someone had leaked it to the press. I came here to tell you myself."

"So what's going on?" asks Mrs. Jackson with tears in her eyes. "You told us she killed herself."

He softens his voice. "The knife Nikki used to cut herself wasn't with her when she was found this morning. That could just mean that the guy who discovered her took it, or it could mean there was someone with her when she died."

Mrs. Jackson sits down on the couch. "Do you mean someone else killed her?"

"I don't know. It doesn't look that way to me, but it's a possible theory."

"Theory?" says Mr. Jackson. "I want more than theories!"

Mike's losing his patience. If the guy wasn't downing shots from a cheap bottle of whisky, he'd have more sympathy. "As part of the investigation, I need a clearer understanding of what happened leading up to Nikki's death." He turns to Mrs. Jackson. "Did you hear from her at all after she left for work yesterday?"

She nods. "She called after the park closed to say she could earn some extra money by working late, but only if her dad would be able to pick her up after."

Mike looks at the father, surprised. "So you went to the park last night?"

"No." Mr. Jackson doesn't offer any explanation.

"No? Why didn't you pick her up?"

He has the decency to look ashamed at least. "I'd had a few drinks. It wouldn't have been safe to drive." He turns away from them.

Mike's gut tells him this guy could be lying. Was he the last person to see Nikki alive? He turns to the mother. "Did he go to the park?"

Her husband spins around and they exchange a look.

Mrs. Jackson is unable to conceal her contempt. "No, he blacked out on the couch. I was already in bed asleep at the time he was supposed to leave, so I didn't know to text Nikki and tell her she'd need to find another ride home. I found him out here in the morning."

"Can't you drive?" he asks her.

"No."

"But you can dial a cab, right? You have a phone."

He sees guilt in her eyes and she looks away, sniffing back tears.

Mike is incredulous that these people wouldn't be concerned about how their daughter would get home after working a late shift. He can't help but shake his head in disgust. It's wrong of him but he does it anyway.

This angers Mr. Jackson. "You can stop judging us. Just because I fell asleep doesn't mean I wanted my daughter to die."

"But weren't you worried when she hadn't returned home? You must have noticed she wasn't here when you got up this morning."

He looks defiant. "Like I told you earlier, we thought she was with some boy."

"But you told me and my partner that she didn't have a boyfriend." Mike's pushing them because he wants one of them to snap. That's the quickest way of finding out whether they're hiding something.

Mrs. Jackson speaks. "We didn't know for sure. We just assumed that if she was starting to stay out later, she must have met someone. Plus, she seemed happy lately."

"For a change," says Mr. Jackson.

Mike doesn't tell them about the rumors that their daughter did have a boyfriend. They clearly have no idea about that, or who he is. He looks at his notepad, but all he's really learned from this visit is that Nikki was waiting for a ride that never showed up. Was that enough to drive her to suicide? Maybe. If she thought her parents cared so little about her that they couldn't even be bothered to make sure she got home safe. It could have been the last in a long line of rejections.

He looks at the father. Or maybe he *did* go to pick her up. Maybe they fought and she killed herself to spite him. He could've brought the knife home with him so the police would never know he was there. There's an easy way to rule him out as a suspect. "I'd like to search this place."

"What?" says Nikki's dad. "For the knife?"

"Yes."

Mrs. Jackson starts sobbing.

Mr. Jackson walks up to Mike, who stands his ground. "If you want to search my home, you're going to need a warrant. Until then, you can get the hell out of here." He points to the door.

Mike turns away from him, determined to obtain that warrant.

CHAPTER FIFTEEN

Independence Day

It's early afternoon and Nikki's turn at garbage duty, which she hates doing. Not only because people stare at her like she's worthless, but also because it gives her too much time to think. She already spends way too much time in her head. Is it normal to overthink things this much? She has no idea.

She watches Mason carrying a young boy on his shoulders as they look for the boy's parents. Kids are always getting lost here, but Mason's great with them. She still can't believe he's her boyfriend. How did she get someone like him to be with her? A terrible thought crosses her mind. What if he's just pretending to like her? Setting her up for some kind of prank? She's never been able to tell the difference between paranoia and reality. Is her anxiety tricking her? She sighs, exhausted with all the thinking.

"Here you go." A guy drops a popcorn carton on the ground in front of her feet instead of placing it in the garbage bag she's holding. He smiles as if he's doing her a favor. She mumbles a thank-you and curses herself for not saying something else.

As she walks past the Brain Drain and Mind Eraser rides, she checks out the groups of teens from her school. Everyone comes here in summer break; the goths, the geeks and even the jocks with their bimbo girlfriends. It's not like there's anything else to do around Lost Creek. The only group she fits into doesn't have enough money to spend at a place like this. Growing up in a trailer park has always set her apart from most of her peers, because she can never afford to do anything with anyone. It costs money even just to hang out somewhere; for drinks, food or weed. Nikki had almost nothing until she started working here last summer. And even now she has to give most of her earnings to her parents for food and bills. Maybe if her mom and dad went out to work, she wouldn't have to support them, but that's never going to happen.

She's suddenly overwhelmed with a feeling of hopelessness. Is she ever going to get out of this shitty town? Thoughts of what happened the other evening flood back and threaten to engulf her. If she could leave town now, she would.

She picks up some empty soda cans and spots Taylor and Mandi from school. They're approaching her with bitchy grins across their faces. She turns away, intending to avoid them, but she hears them call her name. They rush to catch up with her.

"Are you deaf as well as stupid?" says Taylor. She has pink extensions in her long blonde hair that match her false nails. As usual, her makeup looks Insta-ready, and she's dressed in a short skirt and tight tank top. She's everything Nikki hates about girls her age, and Mandi is practically her clone.

"What do you want, Taylor?"

"I want you to introduce me to your *supposed* boyfriend."

Mandi laughs and picks at her pink cotton candy, but she doesn't eat it. God forbid she should put any weight on. Instead she drops it piece by piece onto the ground and then licks her fingers. Nikki realizes why the boardwalk is always so sticky.

"Yeah, right. As if I'm going to introduce you to him." She knows Taylor would love to poison Mason against her.

"I don't believe anyone would date you. I mean, look at your clothes. You look like a boy in those pants. And have you even brushed your hair today?" Taylor laughs.

Nikki hates her for not needing a job in order to buy her clothes. For being able to ask her parents for money whenever she wants. "Fuck off, Taylor. At least I don't look like a Kardashian wannabe."

That angers her. "I'm going to find your boyfriend and tell him he's dating a tramp. And then I'm going to show him what he could be getting instead."

Nikki's so close to slapping her she starts trembling. If Taylor says anything to Mason, she'll die. If she tries to kiss him, she'll kill her. Scared that he might actually prefer Taylor to her, she storms off and doesn't listen to what they're calling after her. There's nothing they can say that she doesn't know already: she's ugly, she's boyish, she's unlovable. Their words are wasted on her.

She fights back tears as she throws the garbage bag onto the ground and runs off toward the Haunted House.

CHAPTER SIXTEEN

Madison's cold, exhausted and running out of patience. An icy shudder tears through her, a result of being locked up almost directly under the A/C vent all night in this holding cell. No one has offered her anything to eat or drink this morning and she's just about ready to rip someone's head off. That's when she hears footsteps approaching.

Officer Shelley Vickers appears with a surprised look on her face that quickly spreads to a warm smile. "I didn't believe it when I heard you'd been brought in." She immediately unlocks the cell and enters, giving Madison the kind of hug you only get from someone who has a genuine fondness for you.

Madison has to hold back unexpected tears. The two of them were close back in the day. "You have no idea how much I need to see a friendly face right now." She pulls away.

"What's Douglas up to?" says Shelley in disbelief. "You shouldn't be in here." But she glances over her shoulder as she says it, as if she's fearful of being overheard.

"I guess I'll find out soon enough." Sensing she only has limited time, Madison speaks quickly. "I don't want to put you in a compromising position, but I need help, and I'm pretty sure no one else in this place is going to want to get involved."

"Of course, what is it you need? Don't ask me to bake a cake with a file in it." She laughs. "I can't bake to save my life."

Madison smiles. "No, nothing like that. I'm happy to face Douglas and Chief Sullivan because I've done nothing wrong. But

I need to know what happened to Stephanie. I need a copy of the crime-scene photos at the very least. The autopsy report would be good too."

Shelley looks doubtful. "Have you asked Detective Bowers for them?"

"I haven't seen him yet—I only arrived back in town last night—but I'm pretty sure he'll say no. Please, Shelley. I think Stephanie's killer could be the same person who framed me for Ryan's murder."

Shocked, Shelley takes another look over her shoulder, but they're the only two people down here. "What happened to you was disgusting. I never believed you killed Officer Levy but I was ordered to present a united front with the department. It was made crystal clear that if anyone spoke out in your defense, all our necks would be on the line. Chief Sullivan told us we were right to be shocked by what had happened but we had to put our friendship with you to one side and believe the evidence. And your gun was found at the crime scene…" She trails off.

Madison takes a step closer to her, disappointed that she clearly has doubts. "Shelley? Give me enough time and I will prove I didn't kill him. All I need is a lead, something that will give me a head start. I think Steph's crime-scene photos will help. I'll be able to see what evidence Mike and Douglas took from the scene and maybe I'll notice something they missed."

Seconds pass and Madison can see her weighing up the pros and cons of passing on inside information. Eventually she says, "Let me see what I can do. Where are you staying?"

Relief washes over her. "Stephanie's place."

"Oh God, Madison. How can you stay there?"

She shrugs. "I have nowhere else to go."

Shelley smiles sadly. "I'll drop by when I have something." She gives Madison a quick squeeze before locking her back in and walking away.

Madison sits on her bunk and tries to think things through. She hears Brody barking in the distance. She can't tell where he's being kept. Hopefully he's being treated better than her.

More footsteps running down the stairs toward her cell make her tense. Mike appears.

"I'm sorry, Madison. I only just heard you were in here."

Seeing him again feels unreal. Their only contact since her conviction has been their recent telephone calls about Stephanie. It's clear he's stressed, as he looks disheveled: his tie is undone, his shirt crumpled, and there's a couple of days' stubble on his jaw. He's starting to let himself go. It's not that surprising: it comes with the job.

She stands up and walks to the bars of her cell door. "What the hell is going on, Mike? Haven't you told Douglas I wasn't even in town when Stephanie was killed?"

"Yeah, I did." He looks around. "As soon as he arrives, I'll speak to him and the chief. I'll get you out of here." He runs his hands through his hair. "For some reason, that guy's gunning for you big-time."

Madison shudders again. She doesn't know why Detective Douglas hates her so much. "There will be absolutely no evidence linking me to Stephanie's murder, so there's no way he can hold me for much longer." Her anger's getting the better of her now. She needs to get out of here. "You're an asshole, Mike! You should never have let this happen to me again."

He holds his hands up. "I don't doubt you're innocent of this. I know you wouldn't have had Stephanie killed."

She hesitates as she realizes what he's implying. "Are you for real? You're suggesting that I may not have been there in person but I might've got someone to do it for me?"

He shakes his head. "That's not what I mean. Calm down, Madison. I'm probably your only friend here, remember?"

She scoffs. They might have been friends once, but that's in the past. "If we were friends, you would have had Stephanie's house cleaned up before my arrival."

He rubs his forehead and has the decency to look ashamed. "Shit, I forgot about that. Douglas is handling her case and I guess I just assumed he'd organized it already. I'm sorry, Madison. I haven't been inside the house since we found her. My last visit was to leave the keys outside for you to find."

She can hear the concern in his voice and realizes she needs to cut him some slack if he's going to stand up for her against Douglas and Chief Sullivan. She looks at him. "I never asked before, but now that I've seen the house, I need to know. What happened to Stephanie?"

He hesitates. "Her throat was slit."

She looks away and imagines how terrifying those last minutes must have been for her. She suddenly wishes she'd never asked.

"She was raped too," he adds.

"What?" Madison feels like she's been slapped. Her body breaks out in goosebumps. The indignity of Stephanie's final hours makes her heart ache for her. "Before or after?" she whispers.

"Before. Someone must have seen her out and about, liked the look of her and followed her home. We're working on a list of recently released sex offenders in the area."

Madison's shaking her head. "No. It wasn't a random attack; it was those guys who were hassling her about me. Come on, Mike. Isn't that obvious?"

He looks doubtful. Maybe he doesn't believe those guys exist. "What exactly did she tell you about them when she called? Were you in touch regularly?"

She looks away. "She visited me in prison for the first few years of my sentence. But we'd split up long before my arrest, so she did it out of pity, I think. Her visits slowly reduced and inevitably stopped. I wasn't upset; after all, it was a long way for her to travel." Madison was incarcerated at the La Vista Correctional Facility, a five-hour drive north from Lost Creek. "Eventually I stopped hearing from her completely. I mean, I knew she would be there for me if I ever

called her, but I wanted her to be able to move on with her life."
She feels deep guilt whenever she thinks of Stephanie. "I got my
first call from her just a few weeks ago, quickly followed by two
more. She said some heavies had turned up at her door asking for
me. They had obviously heard I'd been out for a while, and were
asking her if she knew my location. She didn't know where I was
because I hadn't told her."

Mike nods. He appears to believe her.

"They showed up three or four times, putting pressure on her.
I told her to contact you, but she wasn't convinced you'd help her
because of everything that happened with my unlawful arrest."
She glances at him. He doesn't contradict her. She may still be a
convicted felon in the eyes of the law, but he must know she didn't
kill Ryan. "She said they were both tall and white, possibly brothers.
And one of them was overweight. The last time she called me, she
didn't want to talk for long. But she was genuinely scared and Steph
never scared easy." She pauses. "Did they leave any DNA behind?"

Mike nods again. "The medical examiner found spermicide in
Steph's vagina, meaning the asshole used a condom, thinking he
was taking his DNA with him. But we found semen on her jeans.
Just a small sample, but useable." He pauses, looking concerned.

"What is it?"

"I shouldn't be telling you any of this."

She ignores his concern. "Would you show me the crime-scene
photos? I want to piece it all together and help you find her killer."

He's already shaking his head emphatically. "You know there's
no way I can do that. You shouldn't even ask. And it's not your
case to solve. Take a bit of friendly advice from me: don't get in
the way of our investigation. Douglas will just use it against you."

She feels defeated. Shelley's going to be her only hope for inside
information. "Why the hell am I in here if you know it was a guy
who killed her?"

"I guess Douglas thinks you ordered the hit. I don't know."

She shakes her head, then remembers the girl who died at Fantasy World. "Is there any link to how Nikki Jackson died? Because two unexpected deaths within a few days of each other isn't normal around here."

He frowns. "No. That was a suicide."

She raises an eyebrow. "Really? Then where's the knife? Do you have it yet?"

Annoyance flashes across his face. "Listen, if you saw her body, you'd know it was obviously suicide by the way she'd slit her own wrists." He changes the subject. "Let me go upstairs and find out what's going on with Douglas." He pauses before leaving. "It's good to see you, Madison. Obviously not in here like this, but I'm glad you came back. You just need to tread carefully. People remember what happened and they saw you convicted for it."

"I'll make them see I didn't do it."

He appears surprised. "What do you mean?"

She doesn't want to talk about it with him. "Never mind."

He reluctantly lets it go. "Want a coffee while I'm up there?"

She nods grudgingly and watches him leave.

CHAPTER SEVENTEEN

Nate wakes to the sound of silence. It takes him a few minutes to remember where he is. After Madison's arrest last night, he was ordered to stay away from the police station until morning, or risk being arrested himself.

Forcing himself out of bed, he feels overwhelmed and irritable. More than likely thanks to his unexpected run-in with the cops as well as being seriously worried about Madison. He tries to shake it off, but he recognizes the unsettling feeling that usually precedes a depressive episode. He needs to get busy before it kicks in.

He looks around Stephanie's small spare bedroom. It's pretty sparse: just a single bed, a vanity and a closet. But there's a telltale sign of her life with Madison and Owen: a border running around the middle of the wallpapered walls with trains and a railroad track on it. This must have been Owen's room before the couple split up.

He wonders why Brody hasn't greeted him yet and then remembers he was also taken away last night. Because the dog tried to defend him, he got himself dragged off to the station with Madison. The cops promised they wouldn't destroy him, but Nate doesn't trust the word of anyone in law enforcement. He's sure it was only because he desperately explained that Brody was a former K9 that he wasn't immediately euthanized.

After their long road trip and the stress of last night, he can't resist a shower before getting dressed, even though he has a lot of work ahead of him. The hot water soothes him. He found some shower gel under the bathroom sink and uses it to wash his hair and body, trying not to think about how it belongs to a dead woman whose blood was spilled downstairs. He catches his rosary and it snaps, falling at his feet. "Shit." He can't help seeing it as a bad omen. Is today going to be even worse than yesterday?

Once he's out and dressed, he fixes the beads and slips them back in place around his neck and under his fresh T-shirt. He grabs his cell phone, heads down to the kitchen, and starts searching the internet for local lawyers.

He tries calling the first name that comes up: Darryl Facek.

"Hi, I'm looking for someone to help a friend who was wrongfully arrested last night," he explains. "She's currently being held by Lost Creek PD."

"Is that so? Let me grab a pen." Darryl appears to be chewing tobacco. It makes Nate want to heave. "What's the lady's name?"

"Madison Harper."

Darryl starts laughing down the phone.

"What's so funny?"

"Oh, just that there's no way on earth I would represent *her*. I think you'll struggle to find anyone who would. Anyone from around here, that is. Maybe even from further afield. We don't defend people like Madison Harper."

Nate's grip on the phone tightens. "You're a defense attorney; it's your job."

"Oh sure, it's my job. But I get to pick who I defend and I am *not* working for that woman. Good luck, my friend, but you're backing the wrong horse."

He hangs up before Nate can question him.

"What the fuck?"

The next lawyer he tries sounds nervous the minute he hears Madison's name. "I'm sorry, sir, but I can't work for Ms. Harper. I wish you luck, though."

"Hang on a minute. Just tell me why? You're the second person to turn me down. What's your problem?"

The lawyer hesitates before answering. "All I know is that I came into the office to find an answerphone message telling me I'm not to represent Madison Harper under any circumstances. Not if I want to see my wife and kids when I get home tonight."

Nate's shocked. That's a serious threat. "Who left the message?"

"I'm sorry, I can't divulge that information." The lawyer hangs up.

Nate stares at his phone in disbelief. Someone from her past already knows that Madison's back in town and was arrested last night. They knew she'd be in need of a lawyer this morning and spent the night calling around issuing threats. Because he's not from here Nate has no idea who could be responsible, but it can only be someone with a vendetta and someone on the inside. Detective Douglas maybe.

He tries calling LCPD for an update on Madison, but the woman who answers sternly tells him she'll get someone to phone him back at some point. Not holding out much hope of that, he calls Rex Hartley for help.

Rex is Nate's go-to guy for background information and financial checks. He lives in San Diego on a ranch with a million rescue animals, and he's the only other friend Nate has. Nate has no idea how he gets his information, but he has sources in many different government offices. He's also spent time inside for a crime he didn't commit, and as a result his beef against corrupt cops is even bigger than Nate's.

"Hey, Rex. How are you?"

"Never mind me," answers Rex. "How the hell are you? Have you made it to the Centennial State yet?"

Nate gives him an update on their location. "We're in Lost Creek. But we're also in trouble."

"In trouble already? Jeez, you guys work fast."

"Tell me about it. It's pretty serious."

"Don't tell me you're in jail?"

Nate sighs and uses his spare hand to rummage through Stephanie's kitchen cupboards in a desperate search for some instant coffee. "Not me, although I almost was. Madison's been arrested for murder."

Nate hasn't told Rex much about Madison's law enforcement past, knowing full well his friend wouldn't want him working with an ex-cop, but Rex managed to put two and two together pretty fast last time they spoke in California.

"You're kidding?"

He sighs. His body is craving a line of coke, but he knows to wait it out or he'll be sucked under. "No. I need you to find her a trustworthy lawyer."

"Wow, that might actually be the hardest job you've ever given me." Rex laughs at his own joke. "How long has she been in custody?"

"About thirteen hours. She knows how to play the game, so I'm sure she's kept shtum and is just hanging tight, waiting for an attorney. I tried a couple of locals, but word's out that she's blacklisted and they've all been threatened."

"Holy crap. Sounds like you're messing with something big, Nate."

He nods. "Yeah, I get that impression too. When you find someone, send me their details and I'll call them. I'm heading to Lost Creek PD as soon as I've had something to eat."

"Are you staying in a motel?"

"No, a dead woman's house."

"Wow." Rex pauses. "I'll want full details when things have calmed down."

"Sure thing. Any update on Father Connor?" Nate asks the question every time he speaks to Rex, because he's been helping him track the asshole down.

"Nothing. He's obviously lying low for the time being."

Nate rubs his jaw. "Keep me posted."

He realizes he's sweating, despite having just had a shower and the morning being cool. It's the thought of Madison having to serve another prison sentence. It puts him right back on death row as he imagines how he'd feel in her situation. This morning she's waking up in a cell again through no fault of her own. She must be going out of her mind.

He rubs his nose and thinks of the tempting white powder hidden in his shoe.

For now, he resists.

CHAPTER EIGHTEEN

The time ticks by agonizingly slowly for Madison as she lies on her bunk staring at the dirty white ceiling. She can't shake the feeling that she's never going to be able to clear her name or find Owen. When she hears voices, she sits up. Someone is making a lot of noise as they approach.

"Listen, she's my client and I have the right to talk to her in private, so with all due respect, take a hike, son."

A white-haired guy in a navy suit who looks to be in his fifties is squaring up to a male uniformed officer.

The cop relents. "You have thirty minutes at most." He opens Madison's cell door and lets the guy in before locking the door behind him and walking away with a disgusted look aimed at her. Madison knows that if the cops are still holding a grudge against her, the locals will be too. She tries not to think about what will happen when news breaks she's back in town and has been arrested for another murder.

She stands up as the white-haired guy winks at her.

"Hi. I'm Richie Hope, your new attorney." He holds his hand out and she can't help but smile. When she reaches to shake it, he unexpectedly pulls her in for a hug. It feels strangely reassuring, even though she doesn't know him. It's like being hugged by a father; someone who's going to take control of the situation for her.

"You're a popular lady!" he says, sitting on her bunk and pulling out a laptop from his battered briefcase. "I had two answerphone messages on my office phone this morning telling me I should not represent you under any circumstances." He smiles broadly. "That made me want to sign you up immediately."

She sits next to him, relieved to have a friendly face helping her but shocked that someone's trying to intimidate lawyers. "Do you know who left the messages?"

He waves it away. "Oh please. Who cares? What's important is that they were followed by a call from a guy named Nate Monroe. I take it you know him?"

She nods, and finds herself smiling again. She knew Nate would come through. She realizes it's probably time she started trusting him with some information she's been holding back.

"I don't come cheap, though, and Mr. Monroe is paying me, so you've got a good friend there."

She wonders how she'll ever repay Nate, and not just financially.

"So, Mr. Monroe's clearly worried about you being in here, and looking at your rap sheet, I can see why." He rummages through internet printouts. She sees her name littered throughout. He looks up at her. "I just need to know two things, and time is tight, so give me a yes or a no to both questions. Got it?"

She nods.

He leans in. "That wasn't one of the questions, by the way. So maybe I should've said I had three questions. Sorry."

She laughs for the first time in what feels like ages.

He looks delighted that she's enjoying his sense of humor. "Okay, question one: did you shoot and kill Officer Ryan Levy on the night of September eighteenth 2012?"

Madison doesn't hesitate. "No."

"Good. Question two: did you fatally stab Stephanie Garcia on the evening of July second this year?"

"No."

He smiles. "Phew! Thank God for that." He leans in and winks at her again. "Less work for me. Okay, in that case I need to get you out of here. Nate's filled me in on the background as to where you've been for the last few weeks, and I understand you only arrived in town hours before being arrested."

She nods. "Right. Someone's obviously afraid of what I've come back for if they're willing to frame me for Steph's murder."

He's making notes, tapping away on his laptop. "I agree. You've rattled cages. You need to be careful. Have you got somewhere to stay while you're in town?"

She thinks of Stephanie's house. It feels wrong to go back there, but legally it's hers, and she's guessing that if lawyers are being told not to work with her, other businesses in town will have been told the same, so a hotel is out of the question. "Stephanie left me her house in her will. I have the keys."

"Perfect. They can't argue with a will. Well, unless someone in her family contests it, of course, which they probably will if the media convince them you killed her."

Madison opens her mouth but doesn't know what to say. The thought of the media getting wind of her arrest is horrifying. She's experienced trial by media once; she doesn't need it again. But would news reach as far as Washington state, where Steph's parents live?

Richie sees her fear. "Let's cross that bridge if we come to it. Now, when you get out of here, go straight to your new house and get security." He looks at her over his glasses. "You know what I mean by that?"

She does. "I have a gun back at the house."

"Good. Is it licensed?"

She smiles. "I plead the Fifth."

He laughs.

"Plus, we have a large dog." She remembers that he's here too. "Actually, Brody was seized last night because he was overzealously defending us. They have him here somewhere. Can you get him off too?"

Richie smiles at her. "Ms. Harper, I can get anyone off."

She feels her shoulders relax as she takes a deep breath, feeling better in his capable hands. Until she hears voices approaching.

They both look up and she sees Detective Douglas scowling at her. He looks like he wants to shoot her as he opens the cell door. "Time to go upstairs, Harper. Chief Sullivan wants a reunion."

CHAPTER NINETEEN

Being led through her old police station by Douglas feels shameful. But knowing she hasn't done anything wrong, Madison keeps her head held high and glances around the cubicles to see if she recognizes anyone.

The office is fuller than when she worked here, but most of the staff are busy concentrating at their desks or talking on the phone. Her old desk is gone, replaced with filing cabinets. She spots a large potted plant she bought years ago in order to spruce the place up a little. It's withered and brown, in desperate need of some attention. Seeing that makes her feel strange. She can picture herself as she was when she worked here, enthusiastic and happy. Sure, work was stressful most of the time, but she truly loved her job, and getting a promotion to detective was one of the best things that ever happened to her. It's just a shame it only lasted five days.

The phones are ringing non-stop. She'd forgotten about the constant phone calls: victims wanting updates, families of victims wanting updates, the press and DA's office wanting updates. It never ends. And she'd give anything to be back.

The chief's office hasn't changed much since she last saw it. Although his old desk, which was missing half a leg and balancing on books, has finally been replaced, it's still covered in paperwork, and the same sun-faded and smudged photo of his wife and kids sits facing away from him. The room smells of perfume. Sullivan always liked his designer cologne. Probably to try and mask the smell of cigarettes.

Detective Douglas steps aside as he motions for Madison to sit in one of the seats opposite Sullivan's desk. Mike has joined them.

He squeezes by Douglas and takes a seat off to the left. Her new lawyer sits next to her and pulls out his laptop again.

After a few minutes of awkward silence, apart from the sound of Richie tapping away on his keyboard, Chief Sullivan enters with a coffee in his hand. The strong aroma makes Madison's empty stomach rumble loudly. She'd give anything for a drink of water even. Mike hasn't produced the coffee he promised her.

The chief sits in his chair, sips his coffee and avoids eye contact with her. The smell of tobacco quickly follows him in, making her crave a cigarette. She takes in his sharp suit and navy tie. His dyed black hair is styled precisely and his nails are manicured. She looks more closely at his shiny forehead. Is he getting Botox?

Douglas makes her jump when he speaks from behind her. He's still standing, probably an intimidation strategy.

"I arrested Ms. Harper based on witness testimony that suggests she was in town when her ex-girlfriend was savagely murdered, despite claiming the contrary."

Richie glances at her and rolls his eyes. "What 'witness' would that be?" he asks.

"And you are?" says Chief Sullivan.

Richie half stands, clutching his laptop with one hand and leaning across the desk with the other outstretched. Sullivan is surprised into shaking it. "Richie Hope. Ms. Harper's attorney."

The chief eyes him suspiciously. "Are you local? I don't recognize you."

"I'm not from the good town of Lost Creek, no. My office is based just north of Prospect Springs. Feel free to drop by for a consultation and the best coffee you'll ever have." He grins. "I don't charge for the first hour's advice, but I do charge for the coffee."

The chief rolls his eyes. "Tell him what you've got, Douglas."

Madison's listening, but she's exhausted, and anxious at being this close to her old boss. She just wants to get the hell out of here. She keeps her eyes down.

Douglas clears his throat. "A local person saw the suspect driving away from the crime scene the night Stephanie Garcia was murdered."

Madison shakes her head, then laughs, because this whole situation is just farcical.

Chief Sullivan addresses her for the first time. "Something funny, Detective?"

She looks up at him in shock and watches as he realizes he's addressed her incorrectly.

His cheeks redden and he tries to gloss over it. "Where were you the night Stephanie was killed? I assume you have an alibi lined up?"

She thinks back to when she took the call from Mike. She was sitting in Nate's car with him and Brody. A surge of energy perks her up. "I was in Shadow Falls, California, sir. Thirteen hundred miles away. I believe I was with Trinity Creek PD after assisting them in finding a missing child when Mike called to inform me of Stephanie's death. I'm sure if you call the department they'll verify my whereabouts."

Douglas scoffs. "As if a police department would hire a convicted cop killer to help them with a case."

She has to resist the incredibly strong urge to verbally attack him. "Ask for Chief Hennessy. The facts don't lie. Also, I don't own a vehicle, so I don't see how a witness could have seen me drive anywhere. Plus, I don't have a penis, so I clearly didn't rape Stephanie."

Richie looks over his reading glasses at her with bemusement before glancing at Sullivan for his reaction.

Sullivan looks to Douglas.

"Then whose car was that at the house last night?" asks Douglas.

"My employer's. You met him when you arrested me. I haven't owned a car since I was framed for Officer Levy's murder."

No one says anything for a minute, but Chief Sullivan gives Douglas a pissed-off look. It's painfully clear that there was no witness and Douglas is just a bent cop.

Richie claps his hands together and closes his laptop. "Okay then. That's all cleared up, so my client and I will get out of your hair and leave you to work on finding Stephanie Garcia's actual killer."

He stands up, but Madison stays where she is. Surely they won't let her go this easily? They must have something more than that. Richie makes eye contact and nods to the door. She looks at Chief Sullivan for permission.

Sullivan looks away and shuffles papers on his desk. "We'll be checking your alibi. If we find anything else, you'll hear from us."

She shakes her head in disgust and is about to tell him they can't get away with pulling her in every time they come up with a new lie, but Richie gently tugs on her arm.

"What about Brody?" she asks as she stands.

Douglas gives her a look of pure hatred. "That dog is dangerous."

"If you have evidence the dog harmed anyone, I'd love to see the photos and medical reports," says Richie. "Otherwise, we'll be taking him with us."

Sullivan glances at Douglas, who gives a barely perceptible shake of his head. The chief sighs. "Wait out front. I'll have an officer bring him out."

Madison smiles at Richie and follows him out of the office. Douglas has to lead them through to the front desk area, but he doesn't say a word as the door slams shut behind him.

"Well, he's a pleasant guy," says Richie.

Madison laughs. She hasn't felt this relieved since she left prison.

CHAPTER TWENTY

Nate pulls up outside the police station, which is smaller than he expected. He sees Madison walking toward him. She looks tired, but she's beaming, something he hasn't seen her do much. As he gets out of the car, she comes straight in for a hug.

"Thank you so much for hiring Richie," she says into his neck. "I promise I'll repay whatever he costs." She pulls away.

"No problem." He knows she won't be able to repay the lawyers' fees, but he goes along with it. "Rex found him."

A suited older man leans in for an enthusiastic handshake. "Richie Hope. Good to meet you, Mr. Monroe."

"I told you on the phone, call me Nate."

"Then call me Richie. You did the right thing contacting me. There's something going on with them," he nods to the station, "that I don't understand, but if it gets any worse, you could both be in need of a lawyer."

Nate frowns. "Why would I need one?"

"For helping your friend here. Make no mistake: if a cop wants someone behind bars, they'll make it happen one way or another. Believe it or not, they're not all good guys."

Nate looks at Madison and they smile. Richie means well, but he has no idea they've both already learned that lesson the hard way.

The door to the station swings open and he watches Brody excitedly run out, pulling an officer behind him. The officer gives up and lets go of the leash.

"Brody!" calls Nate.

The dog notices them and runs up to him, jumping up with his front paws on Nate's chest. When he jumps down, he enjoys a back-scratch from Madison.

"What a handsome dog," says Richie. "Looks like a wolf. I've heard about this mix. They call it a shepsky; half German shepherd, half Siberian husky."

Nate smiles at the word.

Madison stands up. "I can't thank you enough for today, Richie. If you hadn't ignored the phone threats, I have no doubt I'd still be sitting in that cell."

Richie waves away her thanks. "That's my job."

"I'm dying to know," says Nate. "Is Richie Hope your real name?"

Richie winks at him. "That's between me and my lawyer."

Nate suspects it's not, but it doesn't matter because he's clearly good at what he does. Checking his watch, Richie raises his eyebrows. "I have to be in court soon, so I'd best be off. It was a pleasure meeting you both."

Nate stops him. "Are you not concerned that the person who left the messages is going to make good on their threats?" He doesn't know how this good-natured middle-aged lawyer would defend himself if someone turned up at his office to hurt him.

"Oh, I get death threats almost every day. It's part of being a lawyer. But so far no one's been crazy enough to follow through."

Nate almost winces at his blasé attitude. He believes in tempting fate, and Richie just did exactly that. He watches as the lawyer waves goodbye and pulls out of the station's parking lot in a brand-new Mercedes.

Madison turns to him. "I seriously need to eat."

He notices a satellite truck over her shoulder. It's pulling into the parking lot, fast. "Shit."

She turns to see what he's looking at. "News trucks? Already?"

He touches her arm to get her attention. "Madison? Someone in there must have tipped them off."

The satellite truck pulls up alongside them and the smartly dressed female reporter they saw on the news earlier doesn't even wait for it to stop before she's out and running toward Madison. Only seeing Brody step forward makes her back off slightly.

"Madison," she says. She has a mic in her hand. "I've only just heard you're back. Someone tipped us off that you'd been arrested again. Is it true?" She shakes her head as if forgetting her manners. "Oh my God, I'm sorry. First of all, how are you?"

Nate looks at Madison. These two obviously know each other. Perhaps the reporter covered her last arrest.

Madison goes in for a hug. "I'm doing okay. How are you?"

"I'm good, but what are you doing here? Is it true you were arrested?"

Madison glances at Nate to explain. "Kate and I are old friends from high school."

The reporter looks at him and holds out her hand. "Kate Flynn. I work for the local news station." She has the look of a TV reporter: a clear complexion, perfect white teeth, her wavy brown hair perfectly styled. She's wearing a pant suit, but instead of heels she's sporting sneakers for comfort.

"Nate." He's wary of reporters, so he doesn't give her his full name, but he does shake her hand.

"Are you two…" Kate leaves the rest of the question in mid-air, but he knows what she's asking.

"No," says Madison. "I work for Nate."

He's surprised she doesn't say they're friends. Maybe he's misjudged their relationship, or maybe she doesn't want this reporter to make any more assumptions.

"I was surprised to learn you're still in Lost Creek," Madison continues. "I thought you had bigger aspirations."

Kate screws up her face. "I moved away after your conviction. I just felt horrible about the whole thing; it didn't seem right what they did to you. It was all so… rushed. Anyway, as you know, I'd been wanting to get away and work at a bigger news corporation, so I moved to Denver and settled there. But Patrick contacted me on social media—you remember Patrick, right?"

Madison smiles. "Sure I do. You used to make me stalk him with you when we were teenagers."

Kate laughs. "It's embarrassing how obsessed I was! Well, he divorced the perky cheerleader and eventually tracked me down online. We met up and ended up getting together."

"Finally!" Madison laughs.

"I know, right! All that work I put in during high school finally paid off! Anyway, we lived in Denver for a while, but almost a year ago he decided he wanted to move back here to be closer to his family." She waves her wedding ring finger. "Married for four years. We have two kids aged five and three. And yes, before you do the math, one of them was out of wedlock." She smiles.

Nate finds himself smiling too. He can see how she's perfect for TV, as she has a way of setting people at ease, making them drop their guard before she goes in for the real story.

A guy hauling camera equipment joins them and gets ready to record. "Are we covering the story or not?"

Nate looks at Madison, whose smile has vanished.

"If you give me exclusive access to your story, I'll make sure the audience knows what really happened." Kate lifts her mic.

Madison shakes her head. "There's no story here. I'm just back to bury Stephanie. Please don't announce my return on the news. I don't need everyone in town gunning for me. Plus, I don't want to upset Ryan's parents."

He can see that Kate's conflicted. She looks at the police station and then back at Madison, sensing that something interesting just went down. "Fine. Put the camera away, Bob."

Madison steps toward her. "Do you know where Owen went after my conviction?"

Kate looks taken aback. "You mean you don't?"

Shaking her head, Madison explains that child services didn't tell her anything. "It's like they were paid off to keep quiet. Have you seen him around?"

"No, I haven't. But I don't know if I'd even recognize him after all this time. I'm sorry. I can ask around for you?"

Madison smiles. "That would be amazing. Thanks. I'm staying at Stephanie's place. She left it to me in her will."

Kate looks surprised. "I'm so sorry about what happened to her. It was such a shock to the community. And now we've got a dead teenager at the park. People are starting to worry something sinister is going on." She reaches into her pocket and pulls out a card with her contact details. "Let's catch up soon, okay?"

They hug goodbye and Nate leads Madison and Brody to the car. He notices Kate watching them as he speeds out of the parking lot.

CHAPTER TWENTY-ONE

"What the hell was that?" shouts Chief Sullivan, slamming the door of his office shut behind Douglas. He bursts into a coughing fit.

Mike could really do without being yelled at for someone else's stupidity.

"A witness came forward last night," says Douglas defiantly. "Was I supposed to ignore him?"

Mike looks at the chief. He won't like Douglas's attitude.

"Who was the witness?"

"Brad Skelton, a contractor. Said he was working on a neighboring farm when he saw the car speed by and he recognized Harper from the media coverage of her trial."

Mike frowns. He knows that name. "He's not reliable. He has a record."

"You were supposed to check the validity of his claim before arresting someone for murder!" Chief Sullivan glares at them from behind his desk. "You can't just bring someone in because you have a beef with them."

Douglas remains calm. He's always calm. That's what freaks Mike out about the guy.

"I don't have a *beef* with her." He pauses. "Sir, with respect, Madison Harper killed her former lover, so when someone comes forward to tell me she was in the vicinity when another of her lovers is murdered, I'm going to go with the evidence and act fast. If that's not something you agree with, then I might not be the right fit around here anymore."

Mike's eyes widen. Douglas is going to talk himself out of a job at this rate.

The chief waves a dismissive hand. "Stop being dramatic. I know you hate being told what to do, but just stop harassing Harper. She's done her time. If it turns out she did kill this woman, then be my guest: arrest her and build an ironclad case. But it's highly unlikely if she was working with another police department at the time."

Clearly annoyed, Douglas says, "I don't believe that. I'll contact them to verify it. And I need to look into her companion. Never seen him around here before."

"Could he be a boyfriend?" asks the chief. "I mean, it would appear she's happy to sleep with anyone."

Mike winces. They can't be talking like that. "Let me speak to her," he says. "I'll catch up and find out what she's planning once she's buried Stephanie. Maybe she'll leave just as quickly as she arrived."

Douglas turns to him. "Stephanie Garcia was cremated yesterday."

Mike opens his mouth but doesn't trust what he'll say. He looks at the chief, then back at Douglas. "What do you mean?"

"The coroner's office released her body and I managed to get in touch with her mother up in Washington state. She showed no emotion when I told her of her daughter's death; she just asked where the body was and if we were done with it so that she could get it cremated." He shrugs. "It's done."

Mike shakes his head in disbelief. "Madison was going to arrange a burial."

Chief Sullivan speaks up. "Jesus, Douglas. You've just caused me a massive headache. She's going to be pissed, and rightly so if you ask me."

Douglas remains defiant. "The victim's body was autopsied with a conclusive cause of death. It was photographed and analyzed by forensics, and released by the coroner. Plus, her mother gave permission. Are you saying you think I should have left her lying in a morgue for no reason?"

"Listen," says Sullivan. "If she was nothing to do with Madison Harper it wouldn't be an issue. But you should have waited."

"I didn't even know Harper was on her way here, plus Bowers only told me yesterday that the victim was her ex-girlfriend."

Mike feels like he's being thrown under the bus yet again. "Don't pin this on me. You can be the one to break the news to Madison."

Douglas shakes his head. "I don't answer to cop killers."

"It's done now; there's no changing it. Let's move on." Sullivan rubs his jaw. "So apart from Madison, who else is a suspect for Garcia's murder?"

"I'm waiting for Alex to process the evidence found at the scene," says Douglas. "Then I'll go where that takes me."

Sullivan looks at Mike. "And what about Nikki Jackson? Is that ready to be closed yet?"

"Maybe," says Mike. "I'm heading to the morgue as soon as Lena's autopsy report is ready. But Alex doesn't agree with the cause of death being suicide because he found a thumbprint on her forehead that doesn't belong to her. Plus, the knife is still missing."

Chief Sullivan raises his eyebrows. "Well that's not good. Any leads on where it could be?"

"Not as of this moment, no. But I'm working on it."

Douglas turns to him. "You need to react to the reports in the news. It's getting out of hand. They know the knife is missing, so they're suggesting it was murder."

"What's that?" says the chief. "Should I be watching the news now, Bowers? You know how much I hate watching the news. Especially when we're on it."

Mike takes a deep breath. He could do without Douglas ratting on him. "No, sir. I'll handle it."

"Good. Get on top of it quickly." Sullivan points at them both. "You two need to learn to communicate more effectively. I'm sick of babysitting you." He turns to his computer screen, signaling that the meeting is over. "Keep me updated. Now get back to work."

They leave his office like scolded schoolboys.

Outside, Mike stops Douglas. "Listen, Don, we're meant to be on the same team. You should have spoken to me before you arrested Madison and before you had Stephanie cremated."

Douglas shakes his head in disgust. "What's she got on you? Were you two fucking back in the day or something? Are you hoping she'll pick up where she left off now she's back?"

"Don't push me, buddy. That's out of line."

"Then stop protecting her. In my eyes she's the most likely suspect for Garcia's murder. And I need to be able to talk to you about what I find without worrying you'll tell her everything I say."

Mike crosses his arms. "I've seen her for all of five minutes since she's been back. How can I be protecting her?"

Douglas starts walking away. "Just remember who you work for."

Mike's fuming. He doesn't need this asshole telling him how to do his job. He storms out of the station.

CHAPTER TWENTY-TWO

As Madison enjoys a scalding hot bath, she stares up at the shelf above her, which holds a range of succulents happily absorbing the steam from the hot water. She's too exhausted to feel weird about being back in Stephanie's house. Instead, her thoughts turn to the happier times she had here. She remembers the brightly colored plastic boats Owen loved playing with in this bath when he was a toddler. She tries to remember what happened to them. They must have gone to someone else's kids when he outgrew them. There's a selection of half-burnt candles dotted around too. They remind her of the times she and Stephanie would share a bath. There were always candles and a glass of wine each.

She looks at the cracked tile above the faucet and smiles. Owen did that with his basketball. She's surprised Steph never got it fixed. Maybe she liked the reminder of him. Child services didn't ask Stephanie to care for him when Madison went to prison, despite Madison's request and despite the fact that she and Owen had spent almost five years living with Steph as a family. It made her life in prison hell, not knowing who he'd gone to live with.

"I'm back!" shouts Nate from downstairs, making her jump. "Don't be too long, it'll go cold."

"Roger that," she yells. He sent her upstairs almost two hours ago, instructing her not to come down until he was ready. From the sound of all the running water, she's assuming he's been cleaning. Then he stationed Brody outside the bathroom door to protect her and said he was going out for pizza. If it was anyone else, she'd be offended that they thought she needed protecting, but Nate means well. Although he's only thirty-nine, he's a little old-fashioned, undoubtedly because he missed the advances in society while he was on death row.

She pulls the plug out, dries off and steps over a sleeping Brody in order to get to Steph's bedroom. The room they shared. She doesn't focus on that right now. Instead, she rummages through her bag looking for some sweats to pull on. Keeping her damp hair tied back, she heads downstairs, with Brody beating her to the bottom.

She checks the front door is locked and latched and then peeks out through the blinds to make sure there's no surveillance outside. Nothing yet. She would bet a hundred dollars Detective Douglas drives past at least once tonight.

Nate approaches her and nods to the living room. "It's all clear in there now."

Her eyes water at the fumes coming from a mix of strong bleach and too much vanilla air freshener. Nate's overdone it a little. There's a large patterned rug in the middle of the room that wasn't there last night. But the evidence markers, latex gloves and shattered lamps are gone.

"I managed to clean up most of the blood, but it left a stain on the carpet," says Nate. "So I cut it out and covered the hole with the rug from the spare room. It stands out like a sore thumb, but hopefully it's better than what was there."

He has a way of making her feel better, even when he's talking about something as horrific as Steph's crime scene. She didn't realize until meeting him just how much she misses being cared for. Taking a deep breath, she says, "Please tell me you also got wine? Because this is nice and all, but it's not going to get me drunk."

He smiles and heads to the kitchen while she opens the windows.

Brody sniffs the new rug and whines softly. He's not fooled by the bleach, the air freshener or the rug. He knows what happened in here. She goes to him and strokes his head. "It's okay, boy. We know. But we can't go anywhere else at the moment, so we'll have to pretend it isn't there. Okay?"

Nate returns and holds a bowl of cooked chicken pieces under Brody's nose. "This will help him relax."

It certainly distracts him. Madison sinks into the couch and switches the TV on low. She got used to it being on almost 24/7 in prison, so it's a habit now. Brody eats loudly as Nate fills two glasses with white wine.

"Douglas and Chief Sullivan will probably accuse me of covering up my DNA if they find out we cleaned this up." She takes a long sip of her drink. It tastes good. She sits back, pulling her feet up under her.

Nate sits in the armchair opposite the couch. "I called Richie Hope first and asked him to check whether the cops had got everything they needed from the house. They had, so they were just being lazy by not getting a clean team in here."

"More like vindictive," she says. Again she wonders why Mike wouldn't have thought of her. She wants to give him the benefit of the doubt and assume he would've got someone in eventually. "Thanks, Nate. For cleaning it up. That can't have been pleasant."

He waves a hand. "I cleaned up far worse in prison."

She raises her eyebrows. "What could be worse than someone else's blood? Actually, you know what? Pretend I never asked."

Nate relaxes back in the chair. "I know I only met him for a few minutes last night, but Douglas seems like a regular asshole. The type of cop who arrests guys for domestic violence in the daytime and then goes home to beat his own wife."

She grimaces. "Surely no one would marry him?"

Nate doesn't smile. He's looking serious now. "Madison, I have to ask. How did your service weapon end up at Officer Levy's crime scene?"

She swallows hard. It's time to tell him everything.

CHAPTER TWENTY-THREE

Madison tenses. Nate's not going to like what she's about to tell him.

"Did you know your gun was missing?" he probes. "And if so, how long had it been missing for? Had you reported it?"

She takes a sip of wine. "It was never missing. As soon as Ryan dropped me home that evening, I locked it in my gun safe, the same as every time I finished a shift. When you have a child in the house, you can't leave a gun lying around; locking it away is always the first thing you do when you get home. It becomes automatic."

Nate is clearly confused. "So how did it end up at Ryan's house?"

She shrugs. "That's what you need to find out."

He leans back in his chair and cocks his head while he thinks out loud. "Someone took it from your safe, killed Ryan, left it at the scene to be found, and then… what? Called the shooting in to the cops?"

Madison can't help feeling relieved that he's not even considering that she might have killed her friend, despite how it looks. Her department knew her a lot longer than he has, yet they immediately suspected her, and that hurt. Hell, it still hurts. "Douglas got an anonymous tip-off."

His eyes widen. "Did they trace the call?"

She nods. "It was from an old phone booth in Prospect Springs—a large town north of here—that wasn't covered by CCTV and that had been wiped clean of prints. My defense team got a hold of the 911 recording but no one recognized the voice, including me. So the prosecution concluded I'd paid a random bum to make the call."

"Okay…" He's thinking. "I assume your prints were the only ones found on the gun?"

She nods. "The perp must've worn gloves."

Nate looks so eager to solve the riddle that she feels a wave of appreciation wash over her.

"So who had access to your gun safe?" he asks. "Who knew where you kept the key?"

She repeats what she told her lawyers and what she told the jury. "No one had access. I deliberately had just the one key for it so there was no chance of Owen ever getting inside, and that was on the same chain as my house keys. Stephanie obviously knew about the safe and where I kept the key, because we previously lived together and she knew my routine."

"Anyone else?" he asks.

"Well, anyone who has ever been to my house and seen my gun safe, I guess. My coworkers, Owen's friends' parents, my decorator. The list is endless. But my house keys were always with me and the safe wasn't damaged. It wasn't broken into."

"Was your house broken into?"

She shakes her head. "No. And Owen and I were only out for an hour that evening—we went to spend time with next door's cat. Owen wasn't feeling well, so when we returned, we went to his room to watch a movie in bed."

Nate leans back, clearly frustrated. "Did the gun safe also have an electric key code?"

"No. The only way to access it was with the key, which I still had in my possession after the shooting."

They sit in silence, eating pizza. Nate stops every now and then to make notes.

Madison smiles. He's clearly desperate to solve this for her. "I know cold cases are notoriously difficult to investigate, so I just want to tell you how grateful I am that you came all this way with me when you could've worked on something fresher."

He looks up and drops his pen. "To me, cold cases are the same as regular investigations except they're frozen in time because someone gave up on them. They just need a fresh set of eyes to defrost the evidence." He smiles at his cheesy analogy.

"And that would be you, of course," she says, happy to play along.

"It would. You're not the right person to solve your own case. You've had too long to think about it and you're too close to see the overall picture."

She nods, knowing he's right. She's so sick of thinking about it all and is happy to let him do the investigative work on her behalf. But that doesn't mean she can't look into Stephanie's murder to see if there's a link. "How much am I going to owe you for all this when the time comes?"

He smiles wider. "Oh, it'll be a lot. My skills don't come cheap."

She laughs, knowing he's joking. Or at least hoping he is. "You'll have to take it out of my future earnings."

Brody sits up, sniffing the leftover crusts in the pizza box. Nate's about to hand him one, but the dog steals them all in one bite.

"Tell me about your history down here," he says. "About your family."

She tenses. She hates talking about them, because there's not really anyone left. "I have a so-called sister who I haven't seen or spoken to in about eighteen years because we have absolutely nothing in common. But my wider family are dispersed across the country: aunties, one uncle, and grandparents, although they might be long gone by now. I wouldn't know. My mom kept in touch with them all, but she passed away when I was in my twenties, and communication with the rest of the family just kind of fizzled out after that. I wasn't able to let any of them know I'd been arrested because I didn't know how to get in touch with anyone by then." Something she bitterly regrets, as it would have been nice to have some family support over the years. "My dad moved to Alaska after leaving my mom for another woman when I was still in high school.

Last I heard he worked for the Alaska Bureau of Investigation, but he's probably retired by now."

Nate raises his eyebrows. "He was a fed? Is that why you became a cop?"

"What, to gain Daddy's approval?" She laughs. "Please don't try to psychoanalyze me. We'll be here all day."

Nate smiles.

"After Steph and I split, my family consisted of just me and my son."

"Were you still able to see Owen after your arrest?"

"Rarely. He came for a couple of supervised visits while I was being held at the police station, but I could tell he found them upsetting so I made the decision that he shouldn't come anymore. That kind of thing can scar a kid for life. He wrote me lots of letters at first, when he was still in the care of child services. I kept every single one of them, but Troy stole them from my cell the night before I was released and burned them."

"Troy Dunn? The guard who raped you?"

She nods and takes a mouthful of wine. "I put in an official complaint to the Department of Justice about his abuse of power once I was released, but I never heard anything. No one cares about the accusations of a convicted felon."

Nate nods sympathetically.

The fact that he's experienced similar injustices is one of the reasons she thought he would be the right person to help her. No one else can appreciate how it feels to want justice after a wrongful conviction. When they first met, she told him how she deliberately sought him out to help her with her case. It made him uneasy, which was understandable. But she'd watched his battle for exoneration play out on TV while she was incarcerated, and cheered for him when she saw the footage of him emerging from the prison, dazed and fearful. It gave a lot of her fellow inmates hope that they might get their less serious sentences overturned. Madison, although determined, was a little more realistic. It's not an easy process, which is why she needs help.

"Once you were convicted, what happened to Owen? Did child services keep you updated?"

She leans back in her chair and tries not to get emotional. "They were a massive disappointment. They should have facilitated more communication between us, but they didn't tell me anything. It was like there was a conspiracy to keep his whereabouts from me. My lawyer told me at the time that I had a legal right to know whether he was being fostered or adopted, but not who by, and child services should have been providing me with regular updates. But I was told nothing until the decision was made that I couldn't see him anymore. That was decided by a family court judge, who said it wasn't in Owen's best interests to stay in touch with a murderer. My legal team were looking into whether he was going to be adopted, but I couldn't afford to keep paying them and I couldn't find anyone to take it on pro bono."

Nate appears angry on her behalf. "Was his dad ever in his life?"

She shakes her head. "No. His father never knew I got pregnant; Owen was the result of a one-night stand." She looks him in the eye. "I genuinely believe this was about me, not Owen. Someone hated me so much they wanted me out of town."

She goes back to watching the news. It looks like they're analyzing the Nikki Jackson case. If Nikki's supposed suicide is headline news, Madison knows the knife must still be missing. If she were in Mike's shoes she would have stepped things up a gear by now and started treating it as a homicide investigation while the trail is still hot.

Nate clears his throat and suddenly looks on edge. Before he speaks, she already knows what he's going to say.

"It's time for you to level with me, Madison." He leans forward. "I think you're holding out on me. Would that be a fair assumption?"

She takes another sip of wine and then places her glass on the side table. "I don't know anything for sure, but I may have brought you here under false pretenses."

He clearly wasn't expecting her to say that, because he suddenly looks like he's been badly betrayed. "In California you told me you had nothing to do with Officer Levy's murder and that you suspected your police department framed you for it. That's why you wanted my help in particular: because you know I hate corrupt cops."

Brody sits up. He's licking his lips but he's alert to the change in Nate's voice. He looks from Nate to Madison and then back to Nate again.

"Have you been lying to me this whole time?"

Madison's worried about his reaction, but she has to tell him everything. He's done so much for her that she can't mislead him anymore. She pulls her feet out from under her and straightens up. "Kind of."

CHAPTER TWENTY-FOUR

Nate's anxiety is kicking in. Has he really travelled all the way to Colorado for nothing? Did his judgment fail him in taking a chance on Madison and trusting her when she was at her lowest? He can't imagine what part of her story is a lie, but if she's about to tell him she *did* kill Officer Levy and he's been helping a bent cop, then he's going to drive right on out of here. "What did you lie about? Are you just like all the rest?"

His words clearly sting her, as she looks crestfallen.

"No, Nate. I didn't kill my friend. Everything I've told you is true except that… well, I don't really believe I was framed by someone from my police department." She looks sheepish as she says it.

"Then why the hell did you tell me that?"

She sits forward in her seat and pushes her hair behind her ears. "Listen. Detective Douglas certainly jumped to the wrong conclusion and rolled with it, which isn't unheard of for a detective who wants a one hundred percent success record, but do I think he'd frame a fellow detective for murder? My instinct says no, because that means he would have had to kill Ryan himself, and I don't think many cops would be able to do that. Even him. There was just no motive. His general attitude toward me could suggest he's homophobic, but is that reason enough to target me?" She rubs her face. "I don't know who killed Officer Levy; I just know it wasn't me. If I thought I could find the real killer on my own, obviously I would have preferred to do so. But I was practically fresh out of prison with no money, no means of transport and no support. And you'd been through something similar so I thought you'd have the motivation to want to help me, but only if I told you I thought the cops were involved somehow."

"How are our stories similar?" he says angrily. "Seventeen years on death row is a lot different to six years in a women's prison, Madison."

She looks down, her cheeks burning red. "I know, I didn't mean that. I just meant that we'd both been framed."

"You've basically been using me as a free investigator, haven't you?" He's bitterly disappointed. "That crap you told me when we met about wanting to work with me on other cases was all a lie to get me down here."

She looks up at him. "No, it wasn't. No one else would hire me in any job that I could feel proud of. I helped you find the missing girl in California, didn't I?"

She looks miserable but he's not sure he cares. He doesn't know if he can trust her anymore.

"I didn't think you would travel all the way to Colorado with me for a cold case I couldn't pay you for. When I first approached you, you didn't seem keen until I mentioned the possibility of the police being involved, so I guess I played that up a bit. I know you believe all cops are bad because of your terrible experience, but that's really not the case, Nate. I'm sorry for misleading you. And I'm so appreciative of you coming here and helping me. I promise I *will* pay you for your time."

He looks away from her. His craving for a line of coke is overwhelming right now. He feels like he's been duped. Trust is so important to him, but she's broken it.

Shaking his head, he stands up. "You were out of line. How can I believe a word you say after this? I need to get out of here."

She jumps up and blocks his exit from the living room. "Please don't leave, Nate. I still need you. And where would you go? You don't even know this town."

"Move out of my way."

Brody barks at her.

She ignores the dog, but she must see the disappointment in Nate's face because she visibly slumps. "Fine, but please don't do anything stupid."

He pushes past her, into the dark, slamming the front door behind him before either she or Brody can follow.

CHAPTER TWENTY-FIVE

Mike wakes up in a foul mood. His headache from yesterday is still lurking and the local news is repeating the speculation around Nikki Jackson's death. That means the whole town will have seen it by now, and after Stephanie Garcia's murder, they're going to assume there's a killer on the loose. It's his job to quash the rumors before they gain traction, and the best way to do that is to close the case as fast as possible. With that in mind, his first job is to visit the morgue.

When his garage door opens, he sees Kate Flynn waiting on the road outside, next to her car. He rolls his eyes. "Great."

There's no sign of her satellite truck or camera guy. She's looking at her cell phone when he pulls up next to her.

"Morning, Mike. Any update for me?" She leans in to his open window.

"I was about to ask you the same thing, seeing as you're reporting things I've not confirmed. Who's been telling you the knife is missing?"

She shrugs and then pulls out a compact to check her makeup. She doesn't need it; Kate always looks camera-ready. "What can I tell you? People like talking to me."

"Only because they think they'll be on TV." He sighs. "Just level with me. Do you actually believe there's something in the suicide pact theory, or are you just trying to fill airtime?"

"I'm repeating what I've been told by Nikki's coworkers." She flips her compact closed and looks at him. "Where's her boyfriend right now? Have you tried tracking him down? Have you had the results of her autopsy? You're not giving the press much to go on."

"Listen. To me, all signs point to suicide and you and the other media people are upsetting the parents by suggesting otherwise. I'm heading to the morgue next. As soon as I can confirm this *was* suicide, I'll let you know. Just stop stirring trouble in the meantime."

She stands up straight. "I'm not stirring trouble, Mike. I'm doing my job. Let's not have the same argument every time I try to report the news and hold the police accountable." She spins around, gets in her car and drives off ahead of him.

His cell phone rings before he can pull away from the house.

"Detective Bowers."

"Mike? It's Davis Levy."

Just when he thought his day couldn't get any worse. Davis is Officer Ryan Levy's father, and owner of the local shooting range. He has a domineering personality and friends in high places. If Mike never had to speak to him again, he'd be happy. Their conversations always leave him feeling emotionally drained. He leans his head back against the rest.

"What's this I've been hearing about Madison Harper being back in town?"

"Who told you that?" asks Mike.

"Doesn't matter. Is it true?"

He sighs and rubs his temple. "Yeah, she's back."

"When my wife and I were told she was being released early, it made me want to vomit. It's disgusting that she only served six years and now she's back in town to flaunt her freedom."

"I hear what you're saying, Mr. Levy. But a voluntary manslaughter conviction doesn't carry the same sentence as murder." Mike's starting to feel like all he does lately is defend Madison.

"She executed my son!" Davis's voice is rising now. "How is that *manslaughter*? I don't care what the jury decided; they were wrong.

And now she has the audacity to return here. How dare she? Does she have no shame?"

Mike takes a deep breath. There's no point trying to appease the man. They've had this discussion many times before, and Davis has every right to be upset. Mike feels deep sympathy for what he and his wife went through, but he can't give them what they want, which is for their son to be alive. Ryan was their only child. "Don't worry, I'll make it clear she needs to stay away from you and Jane."

"You should know that if I bump into her, I won't be holding my tongue. And I'll be armed, seeing as she likes to play dirty."

Mike hopes it's an empty threat, but you never know in this town. Gun ownership is on the rise. So is vigilantism. "Don't be making threats, Mr. Levy. You have to remember who you're talking to. Just steer clear and leave her to me. She only came back to bury Stephanie Garcia." He suddenly remembers that he has to break it to Madison that Stephanie has already been cremated. "I'm sure she won't stay for long."

"She better not. Jane doesn't need a daily reminder of what happened to our son. And Garcia got what was coming to her for associating with a cop killer." He hangs up.

Those last words are chilling. Could Davis have killed Stephanie in retaliation for Madison being released early? As a warning that she shouldn't come back here?

Mike slips his phone into his pocket. Things are getting way too heated around here, and everything appears to revolve around Madison Harper.

When he arrives at the morgue, Lena offers him a coffee.

"Thanks, but it would be weird."

"Why?" she asks, bemused.

"Eating or drinking anything in a morgue feels wrong." He looks around the room. It's sterile and clinical. It's cold in here too, for obvious reasons, although that's a welcome relief from the temperature outside. "It just feels like this place is riddled with the germs of dead bodies. You know, maggots and shit."

Lena laughs. "If you say so, Detective. But it's actually clean enough to eat your dinner off any surface."

She walks him over to Nikki Jackson's body. Lowering the sheet that covers her, exposing her head and shoulders, she says, "Okay, so here's a copy of my report."

He takes it off her. He can never understand all the medical terminology in these things.

"To summarize: I found fourteen hypertrophic scars on her thighs and six on her stomach, all consistent with self-harming behavior. But they were faded, which suggests they're old, maybe over five years old, which further suggests she'd sought help for her issues and stopped using cutting as an emotional release. Having said that, I believe she died from self-inflicted lacerations to her wrists. We call it suicidal DWI—deep wrist injury. She bled out after severing the radial artery in both wrists." She crosses her arms. "I would estimate she slipped away between midnight and two a.m."

Instead of looking at the report, Mike glances at the girl. Her eyes are closed but she doesn't look asleep. The gray, mottled pallor of her loose skin ensures no one could make that mistake. Her head is intact, so Lena didn't check the brain. The blood that was previously smeared across her face has been cleaned away. "Could it have been a self-harming incident that went wrong, or do you think this was intentional?"

She pulls out Nikki's left arm from under the sheet and points to the wound. "I don't think it was an episode of self-harm, because there are no old scars on her forearms or wrists, and she pressed hard enough to reach the artery. That would have been extremely painful for her, so to carry on and cut the second wrist after experiencing that level of pain and nerve damage suggests to me that it was an intentional act."

Mike winces as he leans in for a closer look. "What about toxicology? Was she under the influence of anything?"

"I'm still waiting for results, so it'll be a while longer before I know what was in her system."

He nods. "Was she pregnant?"

"No. There were also no signs of sexual assault or any recent sexual activity."

"That's something, I guess." He sighs. "So you'd conclude this was a suicide?"

"That's what her body tells me so far. But Alex might disagree, depending on the forensics."

So why is the knife missing? "Have the parents been in to see her yet?"

She nods. "Mrs. Jackson stopped by yesterday and gave a positive ID. She had to be comforted by my assistant."

He's not surprised Nikki's father didn't come with her. He still needs to figure out how to obtain a warrant for their place.

"Thanks, Lena. Keep me updated."

"Sure thing."

He heads to his car and drives over to the station, where Douglas is leading a man through to one of the holding cells. Mike follows them and looks in at the guy he's brought in. White, tall and heavy-set. He's seen him before. The guy gives him a deadly stare. "What are you looking at?"

"Shut up," says Douglas. "I'll be back to interview you later."

The man laughs. "There's no point. I'm saying nothing. Get me my lawyer."

"Why do you need a lawyer if you're saying nothing?"

He looks at Douglas like something he's stepped in. "Fuck off."

Mike follows Douglas back to his desk. "What's going on?"

"Looks like this guy killed Stephanie Garcia."

"Who is he?"

"Paul Harris. Lives near Prospect Springs with his brother. Doesn't have a credible alibi for that night." Douglas is typing into his computer, searching for priors. "Bingo. The asshole has already served time for rape and aggravated assault."

Mike has a bad feeling about this. He pulls his tie away from his neck and undoes the top button of his shirt. He wishes the weather would break; this humidity is killing him. "Did you get some kind of tip-off?"

Douglas stands up straight and nods. "Anonymous caller. I'm going to get him processed, then obtain a warrant to search his house. Didn't you say Harper told you the victim complained about being hassled by two guys leading up to her death?"

He nods. "Yeah. She said one was overweight."

"And what did the other one look like?"

"I can't remember. But I still haven't caught up with her properly yet. That's my plan for this afternoon."

"I'll go with you."

Mike shakes his head and laughs. "There's no way you're coming. She won't talk to you. I'm not even going to entertain the idea, so you can forget it."

Douglas glares at him but he doesn't push it. "Good luck telling her Ms. Garcia was cremated yesterday."

He walks away with a smirk leaving Mike fuming.

CHAPTER TWENTY-SIX

Madison feels like she's hung-over, but it's not alcohol-induced. Last night she was frantic with worry. Since Nate shot out of the house, there's been no word from him, though she's tried calling him countless times. He doesn't know the town, and if he ends up in the wrong place, he could find himself in trouble.

She has to assume he's high on cocaine somewhere and will return when he's ready, but she can't shake the feeling that she might not see him again. Especially if he spirals into a depressive episode.

As she eats breakfast, her thoughts turn to Steph's murder. If she could just see the crime-scene photos, she would have a place to start investigating. It suddenly dawns on her that she's *living* in the crime scene. Okay, it's been cleaned up now, thanks to Nate, and the police would have taken any obvious evidence away with them, but she could find something here that they might have missed.

She starts in the living room by trying to identify anything that might be out of place, or that doesn't belong to Steph. But it's been so long since she lived here and everything has changed. She goes to check the front door to see if it shows any signs of a break-in. There are no scratches or damage to the locks on either side. She tries the back door, but that's in good condition too. The downstairs windows don't open wide enough for someone to crawl through, and they're not damaged either. So Steph must have either left a door unlocked or she knew her killer. Did she voluntarily let him in? Or did she open the door before she realized who was there and he pushed past her?

If it was the heavies she had told Madison about, she wouldn't have voluntarily let them in. But they could have taken her by surprise.

She walks around the downstairs, but nothing seems out of place. Upstairs is as tidy as it ever was. She spots the trains on the wallpaper in Owen's old room and her heart skips a beat. He used to count them to help him fall asleep. She tries to focus.

By lunchtime she's none the wiser, so she goes outside into the hot sun. Brody's busy investigating the outbuildings. She notices there are no chickens or goats here anymore and wonders when Stephanie stopped keeping them. She takes a second to listen to the collection of wind chimes in the tall fir tree.

Stepping into the hay barn that Steph used to store mowers, tools and animal feed, she notices some boxes stacked up in the far corner. Her stomach flips as she approaches them and sees her name scrawled across a couple. She'd wondered if Steph had kept hold of her belongings after she cleared her house for her, but as so much time had passed, she'd assumed it had all been dumped by now.

Touching a box with her name on, she notices there are six with Owen's name. These have been here since her conviction and they contain belongings from her past life. An overwhelming sadness envelops her and she can't bring herself to open any of them. The boxes will have to wait until she finds her son. She wants to be able to open them with him by her side. She has to push away the thought that it might never happen.

It's humid inside the barn, so she moves on to the vegetable patch. It's overflowing with ripe tomatoes, peas, salad leaves and berries. Spending a pleasant ten minutes picking them makes her feel normal. Like there's no cloud hanging over her. It makes her wonder if she could stay here now the property is hers. It always was a great place to live.

She spots a wicker basket stacked full of fruit and vegetables going moldy in the sun. They must have been here a few days.

There's an envelope on top. She gasps when she reads who it's addressed to: *Nikki*.

Could it be for Nikki Jackson?

She opens it and finds fifty dollars inside along with a note.

Thanks so much for mowing the lawns and harvesting the veg yesterday. Take these with you but watch out for the chilies—these ones are extra hot! S.

Madison tries to think. Could Nikki Jackson have been helping Stephanie out with garden chores? That could be the link between their deaths. Adrenaline kicks in as she realizes the implication. Could Nikki have seen who killed Steph? She feels a level of satisfaction that she might be one step ahead of the police and decides to keep it to herself for now.

She needs to visit Nikki Jackson's parents to see if they can confirm the note was meant for their daughter. The local news showed the trailer park they live at, so they shouldn't be difficult to find if she starts knocking on doors.

Brody walks up to her and she remembers that Nate is probably wasted in a ditch somewhere. But she can't wait here any longer for him to show up. What was at first concern turns to frustration. He should have blown off enough steam to be back by now. She heads inside to fetch Steph's car keys. She finds the navy Honda in the garage and quickly searches it to see if there are any more clues inside. There aren't. It's almost spotless, like the house.

She calls Brody to her, but before she can leave the house, there's a knock at the door.

"Oh, thank God." Nate must have left the spare key here. "He's back, Brody!"

Brody beats her to the door.

Experience makes her check who's standing outside before she opens it. She spots the police cruiser first and her heart skips a beat, but then she's pleasantly surprised to see Shelley smiling at her. And she's holding what looks like a case file.

"Hey, Madison. Mind if I come in?"

She opens the door wide. "Of course not."

They hug, and Madison has to drag Brody away from Shelley. He really does have a thing for cops.

"I can't stay long; I shouldn't be doing this." Shelley hovers inside the door and looks at what's in her hands. "These are copies of Stephanie's crime-scene photos and autopsy report. If anyone at the station finds out I gave them to you, I could be fired."

Madison can't wait to read the file, but she also feels a tinge of guilt for putting Shelley in this position. "I promise I'll burn them as soon as I've finished with them. I'll never tell anyone who gave these to me. I know how it works."

Shelley searches her eyes for reassurance and then finally hands the file over.

Madison leans in for a hug. "Thank you so much. Maybe it will come to nothing, but she was part of my family so I need to know what happened." She steps back. "There's just one other thing. Do you know anything about Nikki Jackson's death?"

Shelley looks confused. "Yeah, why?"

Madison doesn't want to tell her the cases might be linked. She needs time to check it out for herself. "I just keep seeing it on the news and they're saying it could have been murder rather than suicide."

"Yeah, well, the medical examiner says it looks like suicide, but we still haven't found the knife, so Alex is convinced it's murder."

"Who's Alex?"

Shelley smiles. "Our new forensics guy. I forgot he wasn't here when you worked in the department."

"Wow, Chief Sullivan has finally invested money in something useful. Sounds like things are improving."

Shelley scoffs. "If only."

Madison isn't sure what she means, but there's something more important she needs to ask. "I don't suppose you know what happened to Owen after my conviction, do you?"

"I thought he was adopted by someone out of state. That's what Mike said at the time. He thought it might have been Montana." Shelley frowns. "Or was it Utah?"

So why didn't Mike tell *her* that? Madison's heart sinks. She's never going to find her son unless someone from child services tells her what happened.

Shelley's radio crackles into life with a call-out over at Ruby's Diner. "I have to go. Here's my number. Call me if you need anything else. Don't send a message, as I don't want anything being traced back to me."

"Of course."

Madison watches her drive away and then looks down at the file in her hands. It's time to see for herself what happened to Stephanie.

CHAPTER TWENTY-SEVEN

Madison sits outside in the sunshine. After taking a deep breath, she opens the file Shelley gave her.

Immediately she's confronted with Stephanie's dead body. At first she gasps and looks away, letting the tears fall. Eventually she steels herself and looks back at the top photo. It's a full-body shot of Stephanie lying face down, with her shirt pulled up covering her head and her jeans and underwear roughly tugged down to her ankles.

Madison looks up at the sky, letting the sun dry her tears while she tries to deal with the horror of what she's seeing. Could she have prevented this? Should she have raced back to Lost Creek after that first phone call from Steph? She'll never know, but she'll always feel guilty for not doing so.

She leans in and tries to view the rest of the photos with the detachment of a homicide detective. There's one showing Stephanie on her back, presumably turned over by the forensics guy. It reveals a deep gash to her throat. Her face is covered in blood and her eyes stare through the camera's lens.

"I'm so sorry," Madison whispers.

She continues to the close-up photos of the neck wound, then looks around Steph's body at the rest of the room. She can see no murder weapon or clue as to who did this.

Wiping her nose, she stands up and lights a cigarette with shaky hands. She gets through it in less than a minute and finds herself wishing it was weed, or something even stronger. But the nicotine helps her relax slightly. Her thoughts turn to the type of funeral she wants to give Stephanie. She'll need to find out which funeral home has her body and start organizing it as soon as possible.

The autopsy report is next, but it just confirms what the photos show. Madison skims the graphic details about the intimate wounds caused by the vicious rape. She checks the toxicology report: no alcohol or drugs were found in Stephanie's system. That doesn't surprise her. Steph was never much of a drinker, and used natural remedies for things like headaches or anxiety.

One detail makes her smile faintly.

The deceased has green grass stains around her fingernails and compost beneath.

She looks up at the vegetable patch and remembers the note left for Nikki. That's the only lead she has.

She uses her cigarette lighter to burn the documents, then walks through the house to Steph's car, with Brody following her excitedly. As she starts pulling out of the driveway, Mike appears. If he had arrived any sooner, he might have caught her with the photos.

He swings his car in next to hers and walks around to her open window. Spotting Brody in the passenger seat, he says, "Nice dog."

"What do you want?" she asks. Last time she saw him was in Chief Sullivan's office. He didn't even follow her out to apologize for what happened.

"Can we go inside? I want to catch up properly, away from the station."

"I'm on my way out; you'll have to speak to me here."

He leans against the car, pulling his sunglasses off, and she notices sweat patches under his arms. Is that down to the rising temperature or because he's nervous around her? He rolls his shirtsleeves up.

"So how long did it take before you got my job?" she asks, deliberately trying to provoke him.

He looks surprised. "Come on, Madison. Give me a break. It wasn't like that. And to be honest, I wish I hadn't bothered. I preferred being a sergeant."

The look on his face does suggest he's had it with being a detective. He seems harassed, with heavy bags under his eyes and messy hair. It makes her feel better about the situation.

"What's it like being back here after all this time?" he asks.

It's the kind of question a friend would ask, and she remembers that he was her friend once. "It was horrible at first. I don't know if I'll get used to it, but needs must."

He nods as if he knows exactly how she feels, but how can he?

"This is probably the wrong way of wording it, but I hope prison wasn't as bad as you were expecting."

She breaks eye contact and looks out through the windshield. He thinks he wants to know what it was like for her, but he doesn't. Not really. If she tells him she was raped by one of the guards, or that she found cellmates hanging from their bunks, or that she was targeted for being a former cop, he'll just shake his head in sympathy and then forget all about it the minute he leaves. She told Nate all those things, but he understands. She suddenly finds herself missing him. She needs to find him before he does anything stupid. He became suicidal on their last investigation, and she's worried it could happen again after she broke his fragile trust.

She looks back at Mike. "It was worse than I expected. I shouldn't have been put in that situation, Mike. Someone has to pay for that."

He looks wary. She doesn't blame him. She's clearly here to upset the status quo, and that will affect him too.

He glances at his cell phone, then back at her. "I have some news for you, and then I have some questions. That okay with you?"

"News first."

"We have a suspect for Stephanie's murder. Douglas brought him in for questioning this morning. He's not under arrest yet, so it's early days."

Goosebumps cover her arms. "Who?"

"I can't tell you that as we're not releasing his name just yet. As far as I know, he was mentioned in a tip-off, so I'm not sure how

Wendy Dranfield

credible it is. Don't get your hopes up, but he fits the description of one of the heavies you told me she was complaining about."

Madison lets go of the tension in her shoulders. That's the best news she's had in a long time. "I'm guessing you can't keep me updated?"

"No."

"Has he denied it or tried to blame anyone else?"

A pause. "He's not exactly in the mood for cooperating."

She rolls her eyes. "Does he have an alibi for the night Nikki Jackson died?"

He frowns. "Why would we ask him that? You can't think these two cases are linked?"

She doesn't reply. He obviously doesn't think they are. And just because they might have found the guy who actually slit Stephanie's throat doesn't mean they have the person behind it. "Anything else, or are we done here?" she asks.

He shifts position and focuses on the ground. It makes her nervous.

"Just tell me. I'm used to getting bad news."

He clears his throat and looks up at her with regret on his face. "I know you came back to bury Stephanie, but her mom has already had her cremated."

Madison is so angry she gets out of the car. "What? How dare she? How fucking *dare* she?" Her voice rises and Brody barks. "Mike, that woman hadn't spoken to her daughter in twenty years! She kicked her out of the house at eighteen!"

Stephanie was disowned by her family for coming out. Neither her parents nor her brother ever contacted her once she left home. It was a sore point for her and it knocked her confidence, making it difficult for her to get close to people. Madison always felt like Steph was waiting to be dumped, whether by friends, lovers or employers. It wasn't surprising. If your own parents can disown you, it must feel like anyone could.

"She never heard from her family in the five years we were together. Not even a goddam Christmas card! She tried several times to reach out to her brother on social media, but he never responded. Instead, he made his accounts private. Can you imagine how that felt? To be rejected by your family for no logical reason? To feel like you're invisible to them? So how do *they* get to decide what happens to her remains?"

Mike is nodding, agreeing with her.

Madison can't believe she won't get to say goodbye properly. She won't have a grave to visit. And Stephanie didn't get the send-off she deserved. She's so angry she could cry. "When did it happen?"

"Yesterday, apparently. Douglas only told me afterwards."

She sees red, suddenly understanding. "He let it happen to piss me off. That son of a bitch! He probably talked her mom into rushing it on purpose." She puts her hands on her hips. "That's it. I want to make a formal complaint against him." She's starting to seriously wonder whether Douglas *could* have been the one who killed Ryan Levy. He obviously has it in for her. She needs to dig into his background, and she thinks Nate and his friend Rex could help her with that.

"I don't think he did it on purpose, Madison."

She scoffs. "You would say that."

He looks at her. "No, I wouldn't. Trust me, I'm not exactly his biggest fan either. The guy's an asshole and not easy to work with. But the coroner released her body. Douglas tracked down her family and they wanted her cremated. If he'd told me, I would have made him put a hold on it, but we're not exactly working well together, so I never know what he's up to. I'm sorry, I've been distracted by another case."

She takes a deep breath. Once she's calmed down, her interest is piqued. "Nikki Jackson? Do you have the knife yet?"

He shakes his head. "I can't talk about that."

They're both silent for a while, and Madison wonders what he wanted to ask her. "You said you had questions."

He avoids eye contact, looking at Brody instead. She used to be able to read him so well, but he's changed since they worked together. Instead of the light-hearted person she knew, he looks like he's carrying a heavy burden. She wonders if he ever remarried after splitting from his wife. Then it occurs to her that she hasn't asked him anything about himself or his daughter. She's been too absorbed in her own problems. He's probably thinking how much she's changed too.

"I just want to know what your intentions are now you're back." He looks at her. "Because sooner or later it's going to make the news, and Ryan's father has already called me, which means someone's told him."

Her heart sinks. She's still hated here.

"I assumed you were only coming back to bury Stephanie, but now that you own this place, I'm guessing you might plan on staying a little longer, which would put you in a precarious situation with the locals."

"Screw the locals, Mike. I can live where I want." She realizes she's being too harsh with him, but it's frustrating to be treated like a killer. She leans against the car. "I don't know what my intentions are anymore. I guess I thought I could find out who framed me, but that's not looking likely now Nate's gone AWOL."

"Is Nate the guy you travelled here with?"

She nods. She doesn't want to tell him too much. "He's a friend. Maybe I'll just stay long enough to find out what happened to Owen."

She sees trepidation in his eyes and wonders why. She leans forward. "You could help me with that."

Mike's shaking his head. "No, I can't. His child services record is sealed until his eighteenth birthday. I don't have access to any of that."

He could call in a favor if he wanted to. She looks away, disappointed that he's not willing to help her. Just like when she was arrested. She knows he'll be conflicted because of his badge, but it still hurts.

She opens the car door. "I have things I need to do."

He moves away slowly. "Sure. Keep in touch."

She waits for him to drive away before she leaves to find Nikki Jackson's parents.

CHAPTER TWENTY-EIGHT

Madison gets lucky at the trailer park. An elderly woman with a bad wig and no qualms with gossiping about her neighbors points out the home of Nikki Jackson's parents. Brody explores the area while she heads over there. The minute she spots the vegetable patch outside, her stomach flips. It could confirm that Nikki Jackson was the intended recipient of Steph's note, but she still wants to speak to the parents to make sure. She walks up the steps and gently knocks on the door, wiping the sweat from her brow as she waits. With not a cloud in the sky, the direct sunshine is intense.

When the door opens, a woman who looks slightly older than her appears.

"Sorry to bother you," says Madison, "but I'm working with the police and I just have a few questions about your daughter. Do you have a minute?" She holds her breath, praying the woman doesn't ask to see her badge.

Mrs. Jackson steps out and quietly closes the door behind her. "My husband's asleep."

Madison wonders why he's asleep in the afternoon, but then she spots some empty liquor bottles spilling out of a garbage bag to her right that answer her question. "This won't take long." She gestures to the vegetable patch. "Am I right in thinking Nikki planted those?"

Mrs. Jackson frowns. "What's that got to do with anything?"

"I'm just trying to find out if she ever worked for a woman called Stephanie Garcia. Helping her mow lawns and maybe doing some basic gardening."

"She was doing some garden-related chores for someone, but I can't remember the woman's name. She did tell me." Mrs. Jackson tries to concentrate, but gives up. "Whoever it was, they taught her all about how to grow fruit and veg, and she'd come home once a week with a fresh box of it. It certainly saved me some money." She looks down at the vegetable patch, misty-eyed.

"Do you know where this person lived?"

"No, just that it was the other side of town. Nikki needed to cycle over there because it was too far to walk."

That sounds like Steph's place.

"It helped her mentally, I think. Being outdoors and growing things stopped her obsessing over high-school dramas."

Madison tilts her head, trying to figure out what the woman isn't saying. "Was everything okay with Nikki before this happened? Was she getting bullied at school, perhaps?"

Mrs. Jackson chews her lip, clearly reluctant to say too much.

"I know high school is awful for a lot of kids her age," says Madison. "I have a son just a year older than Nikki, and I worry about him all the time. Some kids cope well, but not everyone. Was Nikki sensitive to that kind of thing?"

Eventually Mrs. Jackson nods. "She didn't have a lot of friends and she suffered with bouts of depression. It meant she sometimes cut herself."

"She was self-harming?" Madison's surprised. Then again, that might be why Mike is so insistent on treating her death as a suicide. "Is that something she did often?"

"She used to, before she started going to therapy. But she didn't like her new therapist, Dr. Chalmers, so I was worried she'd start doing it again. It was her way of coping with her anxiety and depression. But helping out with that woman's garden really seemed to settle her mind." Mrs. Jackson pauses, clearly putting two and two together. "Isn't that Garcia woman the one who was murdered recently?" She suddenly looks horrified. "Did she get my girl killed?"

Shaking her head, Madison tries to calm her down. "There's no evidence to suggest your daughter was murdered, Mrs. Jackson. These are just some leads we're working on to get some background information, that's all." And now she has a new lead: Nikki's therapist. She knows Dr. Chalmers: he worked with her on the case of a sexually abused boy they were trying to get removed from his parents. She doesn't know if he'd talk to her now she no longer works in law enforcement.

"Did you tell the detectives about her history of self-harm?"

"They never asked."

The door behind them opens and a skinny white guy appears. He looks annoyed. "What's going on?"

"This woman is just updating me on Nikki's case," says his wife.

He eyes them both suspiciously. "Why are you doing it out here?" He stands to one side, indicating they should go in.

Madison considers whether it's safe. She looks around for Brody, but he's vanished. Some police dog. She has no choice but to follow Mrs. Jackson inside.

Her husband closes the door behind them and stands in front of it, arms crossed. "You trying to have a discussion without me?"

Madison tenses and immediately understands that he runs things around here. The resigned, slightly fearful look on Mrs. Jackson's face confirms it. "Not at all. Your wife didn't want to wake you, that's all."

"So what's going on? Can we have her back yet?" he asks. "I never realized how much caskets cost. Our girl's got to be cremated instead of buried because some asshole businessman wants to turn a profit from her death."

Or you could get a job to pay for your daughter's funeral, Madison thinks. She'd never say that, though. She has to be careful, as she doesn't want him to find out she's not a cop. "Not yet, I'm afraid. But as soon as you can, the office will let you know. Now, I need to be going."

"That's it? You didn't tell us anything."

His cell phone rings and he rushes to take the call. When he looks at his screen, he disappears to a bedroom for privacy. No doubt it's his dealer.

Madison looks at Nikki's mom, who relaxes ever so slightly when her husband leaves the room. She knows she should just leave right now, but something compels her to speak up. "There are ways of getting away from him, places you can go."

Mrs. Jackson's eyes widen in horror at discussing this out loud. Then she checks over her shoulder to make sure he's still out of earshot. "Not without money there aren't. It's not like you think. He doesn't hit me. He controls me financially and…" she hesitates, "psychologically. I don't know why he has a hold over me, but he does. I can't explain it to someone like you. Someone with bags of confidence and who probably has a whole family to support them. I have no one else. Especially now Nikki's gone."

Madison tries not to comment on her own situation. "There are shelters to give you a head start. It doesn't have to be in Lost Creek; in fact it's better if you go further afield. If you have any distant relatives in another state who might help you, try asking them. If Nikki was your buffer, now's the time to go, because he's only going to get worse." She can tell from the look in the woman's eyes that she already knows this.

Mrs. Jackson opens the front door and composes her face so that Madison can't read her expression. "Thanks for stopping by."

Brody's waiting for her at the car, and she scratches behind his ear as she googles the number for Dr. Chalmers. A receptionist answers and surprises Madison by agreeing to put her straight through to him.

"Detective Harper, what a pleasure. How are you?"

"Well I'm not a detective anymore, I just want to make that clear from the start."

"Yes, I remember what happened. How can I help you?"

He's probably wondering if she's after some therapy to help her deal with the repercussions of serving her sentence. "I'm unofficially looking into Nikki Jackson's death, and I understand she was a patient of yours."

He doesn't reply immediately, and when he does, he sounds guarded. "She was, yes. But as you know doctor–patient confidentiality remains after death, so I'm afraid I can't tell you much."

She opens her car door and gets in, switching on the A/C. It's too hot to stand outside. Brody jumps in beside her. "What if I get her parents' permission?" She thinks she might be able to talk the mother round if she could catch her alone.

"That's not enough. And Nikki would not have wanted to give them that choice."

Madison wonders what he means. Is it because Nikki's dad is an alcoholic? Maybe he was abusing her in some way. Could he be a suspect? Maybe for his daughter's death, but not for Steph's. Stephanie would have been able to overpower a scrawny guy like that. "How about a court order?"

"Well, yes, that would be one option. But since you're no longer a detective, how are you going to obtain that?"

She resigns herself to the fact that if she wants answers, she'll have to tell Mike about Nikki's therapy sessions and get him to take over. But there's no guarantee he'll tell her any of what he discovers.

"Are you able to just tell me when your last session with her was?"

He sighs. "I suppose that won't do any harm. I saw her on the afternoon of July fourth."

"The day she died?" She's surprised. That might suggest Nikki needed to talk to someone urgently.

"That's right."

"Dr. Chalmers, can you at least tell me whether, in your professional opinion, Nikki was suicidal the last time you saw her? I wouldn't ask you if it wasn't important."

He remains silent for a minute, and Madison thinks he's not going to reply. Then he says, "She was perhaps a little more emotional than usual, but she didn't mention any intention to harm herself. The fact is, she didn't ever really open up to me about anything. Just snippets here and there. I always felt she was holding back, and even cynical about therapy in general. But I was under the impression she was not at risk when she left my office. If she had been suicidal, I would have taken the necessary action." He sighs down the phone. "I can't disclose any more than that, but put it this way: I was shocked when I heard the news."

Madison nods slowly. It's looking more like someone else persuaded Nikki to harm herself, or her death was a murder staged as a suicide. "Thanks for talking to me, Doctor. I appreciate it, and I won't repeat anything you told me."

"No problem at all. Before you go, can I just ask out of professional interest how your reunion with your son went?"

She's taken aback. "What do you mean? I don't know where Owen is."

He hesitates. "I, er, I just assumed with you being back in town that you'd reunited, but maybe I've misunderstood the situation."

The hairs on her neck stand up. "Are you saying Owen is in Lost Creek?"

He answers too quickly. "No, not at all. I'm sorry, I just thought…" He stops. "I have to go; my next appointment has arrived. Don't listen to me, I'm easily confused the older I get. Goodbye, Ms. Harper." He ends the call before she can react.

"What the hell?" Looking at her phone, she tries to figure out whether he was just jumping to the wrong conclusion, or whether he knows where Owen is. Maybe she's wishing for the latter so much that *she's* the one jumping to conclusions.

It's exhausting being back and not knowing who to trust, or where to turn. It's so different to when she was on the force. Before her arrest she had a mostly supportive team around her, and if she called someone for information, they'd give it willingly, knowing they could trust her with it. But now she feels like an outsider who has to fight for every small detail. The community feels closed off to her.

She sighs and thinks about what Dr. Chalmers told her about Nikki's appointment. She can't shift the feeling that the girl wanted a session that day to discuss something that had recently happened to her. One thing is certain: the link to Stephanie is too important to ignore.

CHAPTER TWENTY-NINE

Independence Day

At mid afternoon, Nikki slips away from the park without anyone noticing. She has a therapy session with Dr. Chalmers at the medical center, and even though she doesn't feel like he's helping her much, if she misses just one session he'll stop seeing her. And if he stops seeing her, she can't get her prescription. She's lucky to get free sessions thanks to the principal at her high school. He referred her after she disclosed to the school counselor about a year ago that she was starting to have distressing thoughts again.

Instead of wasting money on catching the bus, she cycles to the medical center, but gets a puncture just as she's arriving. She curses as she realizes she'll have to leave her bike locked up out front until she can persuade her dad to pick it up for her. It'll probably be stolen by then. This is turning into the worst day ever. A flashback to two days ago makes her take that thought back immediately. Nothing could be worse than that day.

She catches her reflection as she approaches the glass doors to the center. Her face is bright red thanks to the heat, and her hair is sticking to her face. She can see her makeup has melted away from her latest acne outbreak. Basically, she looks gross.

"Hey, Nikki," says the receptionist. "You can go right in. His previous appointment didn't show up. I think everyone's gone to a party but us." She smiles, then waves a small plastic flag unenthusiastically, obviously bummed that she has to work today.

Nikki walks into Dr. Chalmers' office, where he nods to the couch as he finishes typing something at his desk. Even though today is a public holiday, he's on duty for emergencies. She knows he always volunteers to cover public holidays and emergency referrals because he once told her he doesn't celebrate anything and he doesn't drink. He just likes to work. He sounds like no fun at all. Today, she's considering telling him what happened the other day. But she's not sure whether that's a good idea. She starts shaking just at the thought of it.

She sits on the leather couch directly under the cool breeze from the A/C and checks out his many house plants, which are all wilting from a lack of water. She can't help thinking that if he can't even take care of his plants, how can he take care of his patients?

As the minutes tick by, waiting for him to finish what he's doing makes her anxious. Her breathing becomes fast and shallow and she still can't decide whether to confide in him about what happened. She could find herself in trouble for not telling anyone sooner, but she was scared for her life.

"So sorry about that." He takes a seat opposite her with a notepad balanced on his knee. "I know we're leaving longer between sessions now—is it a month since I last saw you?"

She nods, pushing her trembling hands into her lap.

"How have you been?"

"Fine. I'm working a lot."

"At the amusement park?"

"Right, mostly."

"And have the intrusive thoughts been bothering you lately?"

She looks away. Even though he's her therapist, she doesn't always tell him the truth. She only gets fifty minutes with him, and that's just not long enough to explain what's going on in her head, so she doesn't bother starting anything that won't fit into their time together. "I'm still with that boy I told you about last time. He makes me feel much better."

Dr. Chalmers crosses his legs. "Now, Nikki, I can tell you're evading the question." He smiles at her. "But remember what I've told you before: we can't rely on others to make us happy, even though it feels like the easiest solution. Ultimately you have to find happiness within."

She's so confused. If Mason makes her happy, isn't that enough? It's like she's always being told she has to be comfortable with herself, but if someone else helps her feel that way, isn't that still a good thing? This is why she clams up when people ask her how she is. She has no idea how to answer correctly.

"How are things at home? Is your father working yet?"

She avoids the impulse to roll her eyes. "You don't understand. That's not his plan. He doesn't *want* to work. He likes living off the state. My mom wants to get a job, but he won't let her."

"And how does that make your mom feel?"

She has no idea. Her parents' relationship confuses the hell out of her. Her mom is intelligent and hard-working, but she chose to marry a guy who brings her down. She lets him waste their limited income on liquor and drugs, and she allows him to verbally and emotionally abuse their daughter. Why doesn't she leave him? "My mom would never say anything bad about him to me, so I don't know. I wish she'd leave him and take me with her. I want her to choose *me* for once." She has unexpectedly let her guard down, and tears quickly follow.

Dr. Chalmers looks sympathetic. "It's difficult to understand someone else's choices sometimes. What to us looks inexplicable can make perfect sense to them. That doesn't help you, though." He pauses. "Perhaps you could try telling your mom how you feel. I'm sure she'd be receptive to hearing it."

Nikki shakes her head and laughs at the idea. "They're too close. She's always with my dad and she takes his side in every argument. I get no alone time with her at all. I think that's why he won't go out to work: because it would give us a chance to talk about him.

He probably knows we'd come to realize we both hate him and that he'd come home one day and we'd be gone." The tears start again. "But it's not like he shows us any affection, so why does he want us there at all?" She's sobbing now. She just doesn't understand how someone can hate you but want to keep you chained to them at the same time.

The doctor rises and hands her some tissues, which for some reason makes her feel dirty. Like she's a mess that needs to be cleaned up. She decides, not for the first time, that this will be her final session. It's probably not his fault; she just doesn't think therapy is for her. It always feels like it's all about her finding solutions rather than someone else trying to help her. She's just a teenager, so how is she supposed to solve her own problems? Anyway, maybe she'd be okay without her medication. It's not like she cuts herself anymore.

Dr. Chalmers is flicking through her record. "It looks like you've had quite a few therapists over the years."

"What's that got to do with anything?"

He leans forward. "It just seems to me that you don't want to truly open up, and I'm wondering if it's because you don't feel comfortable with me. I could find you a female therapist if you'd prefer."

She doesn't answer. Is he actually trying to get rid of her?

"I only ask because to get the most out of these sessions you have to feel comfortable and you have to trust the person in my seat. I'd love for you to trust me, but tell me what you want and we'll always do what's best for you."

Her heart sinks. He doesn't get it. None of them do. They don't know what it's like to return home to a toxic household where she has no control over anything: no money, no say in the food she eats, no relationship with her own mother. How does anyone solve that through talking? Feeling despondent, she decides to leave. "I'm going to think about what you said." She stands up. "I'll let you know what I decide."

He stands up too. "Okay. That's probably for the best, I'll check in with you in a week's time to see how you are. Does that sound okay?"

She nods and forces a fake smile.

"Well, happy Independence Day, Nikki. Take care of yourself."

She follows him out of his office. She can't help feeling that he wants rid of her, same as everyone else. That's okay. She won't be seeing him again.

CHAPTER THIRTY

Madison glances at her phone, but there's still no word from Nate, despite all her messages.

As someone blasts their horn behind her, she realizes she's got a green light. The other drivers join in. "Shit." It's been too long since she last drove. She needs to learn to pay attention to the road again. Brody barks in the seat next to her.

"Yeah, I know. I'm an embarrassment." She strokes his head. He's been whining since they got in the car and she thinks it's because he's hungry. They don't have any dog food at the house and Steph's kitchen cupboards aren't well stocked, so she has no choice but to stop by the grocery store for supplies.

In the parking lot, she slides her sunglasses on as she gets out the car, hoping it will reduce the chances of her being recognized. She tries to get Brody to sit outside the store and wait for her, but he runs off to survey the parking lot instead.

He always seems to come back, so she lets him go.

As she pushes a small cart around the store, scanning each aisle for people she might know before turning into it, she tries to pretend it's perfectly normal to be back here, but the truth is, last time she was in here, she would have been buying food for her and Owen. Rice Krispies, pasta and plenty of milk and coffee were always the staples. She smiles at the memory of Owen in his pajamas watching cartoons while dropping cereal everywhere. She used to find it all around the house; crunched into the carpets.

Turning around to add some bread to her cart, she jumps as she comes face to face with Jane Levy, Ryan's mother.

Jane looks her up and down, her face pinched like she's chewing a wasp. "I knew it was you as soon as I saw you. Your sunglasses can't fool me." She leans in close and Madison wants to flee. "I think it's *disgusting* they let you out early. And how do you even have the nerve to come back here? You bitch." She grabs a bottle of ketchup from her cart and squirts it all over Madison's shirt.

Madison turns away just as someone walks up and grabs the ketchup bottle from Ryan's mom. She has to fight back tears of humiliation. She can feel some sauce on her face. As she turns to leave, the other person steps in front of her. Unable to see clearly past a dollop of ketchup, she removes her sunglasses. When she looks up, she sees that it's Ryan's father.

He leans in. "You need to leave town."

She has to stand up for herself, despite wanting to get out of here before anyone notices what's happening. "Look, I understand why you're upset at seeing me back." Her voice is shaky. "But I did not kill Ryan. He was my friend, and—"

"You don't understand a goddam thing!" shouts Davis Levy. His fury makes her back away, but she's been cornered against the shelves. "Our son had a fantastic career ahead of him. He was an excellent police officer."

"I agree."

"No! You don't get to agree. You murdered him!"

She notices a man behind Davis pointing his cell phone at her. Her heart sinks as she realizes she's being filmed. She needs to get out of here.

"Let me by."

"You won't understand how we feel until someone murders *your* son. Until you attend *your* son's funeral. Only then will you appreciate what you did to us."

His words chill her. She looks him dead in the eye for the first time. "Don't you dare mention my son."

He leans back with a satisfied smirk. "Hurts, doesn't it? Imagine how much worse it is when he's dead. If you stay in town much longer, you won't have to imagine."

Anger wipes out any sympathy she once had. "Are you threatening my son, Mr. Levy?"

His wife tries pulling him away. "You stay away from us," she says. "You need to do the decent thing and leave Lost Creek. I mean, you haven't even apologized to us!"

Madison doesn't look at her. There's something on Davis's face she doesn't like. "You know where Owen is, don't you?"

He smirks at her. "I hear your girlfriend was killed last week. You know how I can be sure it wasn't you who killed her?"

It takes everything Madison has not to punch him, but she's transfixed.

"She might have been a lesbian, but at least she got to experience a man before she was—"

Madison doesn't let him finish. She slaps him across the face so hard his head snaps sideways. Her hand stings.

His wife gasps. "How dare you?"

Madison leans in close. "What happened to Ryan was despicable. He was my friend and I will miss him every day. I know you miss him too, but that's no excuse for threatening to kill my son. I had nothing to do with Ryan's murder and I'm going to prove it to you." She looks at Jane. "And then *you'll* apologize to *me*."

She pushes past them on shaky legs, trying to leave the store with some dignity intact, but Davis follows her. As she reaches the exit, he grabs her by the arm and spins her around, but before he can say anything more, Brody runs in through the entrance and hurls his full force against the man, knocking him into a stacked display of tinned soup and onto his back. He barks over him until Madison pulls him away.

"It's okay, boy."

She runs to the car with Brody behind her and pulls off her sticky shirt, glad that she's wearing a T-shirt underneath. After wiping her face with it, she throws it in the back, then gets inside and locks the doors just as the familiar sound of police sirens reaches her. Some asshole has already called the cops.

With shaking hands, she pulls out of the parking lot before they can arrive.

On the radio, she hears Kate's voice talking about Nikki, so she turns it up as she drives, trying to calm her breathing and checking the rear-view mirror frequently in case she's being followed.

"We have a surprising development in the Nikki Jackson case for you now, folks," Kate is saying. "Two workers from the amusement park have come forward to suggest Nikki had a boyfriend, who has finally been identified by locals as seventeen-year-old Mason McCoy. And what's odd is that no one has seen or heard from Mason since his girlfriend's tragic death. His only social media account that we know of—Facebook—has been recently deleted. His disappearance certainly suggests he might have been involved in Nikki's death. We're waiting for the Lost Creek Police Department to comment."

"Oh my God." Madison's blood runs cold and she almost hits a sedan when she hears that surname; McCoy.

Last time she was here, the McCoys were childless. And Kate said Mason is seventeen. Her mind is in overdrive. Could the couple have taken Owen in and renamed him? She tries to think rationally. They can't have him. Stephanie would have told her; of that she has no doubt. Maybe this Mason kid is a nephew who came to live with them to work at the scrapyard.

Pulling into a random parking lot, she grabs her wallet and finds the business card Kate gave her. She phones the number, and eventually Kate answers.

"Hey, it's Madison."

"Hey, how are you?" The tone of her voice gives away her surprise.

"I just heard the news. Who the hell is Mason McCoy?"

"I've been trying to find out." Kate seems as confused as she is. "Has Angie never mentioned him?"

"I haven't spoken to Angie in years."

"Oh, sorry. I didn't realize. She won't speak to me either. They declined to comment when I went to their place. All I can gather from asking around is that he works at Fantasy World part-time. I haven't found a birth certificate, so he must have been born elsewhere, and he didn't go to the local high school. He's not on social media anymore, which is weird for a kid of his age, although he could be using a fake name. None of the McCoys' staff will talk to me either."

Chills run down Madison's arms and she feels like heaving. Her hands are sweaty but she's shaking with cold. "Do you have a photo of him?"

"Not yet, but I'm working on it."

She tries to think, but she doesn't want to believe where this is leading.

"Madison? You still there?"

"Yeah, sorry. Let me know if you find anything out, or if you locate the boy. I want to see him before the cops get to him."

"Sure." Kate sounds wary. "Let's catch up soon, okay? I don't want you to leave town without telling me."

Madison agrees. Leaning back against the headrest, she tries to focus.

She knew the day was coming when she'd have to visit the McCoys, but she didn't know it would be for this. She needs to see this boy for herself.

CHAPTER THIRTY-ONE

Angie McCoy places her cell phone on the dinner table and sighs. The clock above the sink, which was a wedding present that's managed to outlive the love in the marriage, says it's almost six, and Mason's been out all day. Fantasy World has reopened, so she can only assume he took a couple of day shifts, which surprises her. She thought he wouldn't be ready to go back yet after what happened. Not that he'll talk to them about it.

She's learned that teenagers have their own secret lives where they do things they'd never want their parents to know about. Mason's at the age where he desperately wants to be an adult, but she knows he's not ready yet.

The computer screen is making her eyes ache. She's been working on the monthly accounts for their scrap metal and auto repair business. It brings in peanuts compared to their financial loan business and fundraising endeavors, but it keeps Wyatt busy and out of her hair. He works there part-time knowing he can afford not to. Probably because he hates spending time with her as much as she does with him.

As Wyatt slurps an early supper of soup and bread at the dinner table, she fixes herself another vodka. Car tires crunch their way toward the house. Mason's back. She can relax now. Wyatt won't be worrying like her, of course. He's planning to eat supper, grab a bottle of whisky and spend the evening upstairs watching crappy black-and-white Westerns in bed, and she's glad. It means she can talk to Mason alone. He spends all his spare time out of the house these days, so she's looking forward to getting him to herself and finally having a proper conversation.

When he walks in, Mason ignores them.

"Where have you been?" she asks, trying to keep her tone casual. "Haven't seen you since breakfast." They've kept him on a tight leash over the years, for his own benefit. Allowing him to work at the amusement park this summer was a decision she's starting to regret. But he's getting older, so the leash is becoming slippery.

He brushes his hair from his sweaty forehead. "What does it matter? I'm here now, aren't I?"

He has a little attitude going on, but that's okay. She'll forgive him that after the week he's having.

"Answer your mother," says Wyatt, watching him carefully. "She worries about you."

Mason grabs a soda from the fridge. "I'm almost eighteen. I can take care of myself."

That makes her sad. She knows she's going to have to let go of him at some point, but if he would stay in their lives and work in the family business, he'd always be close. And he'd be that important buffer between her and her husband. Unfortunately, for the last few months she's had a horrible suspicion he has no intention of doing either.

She places a bowl of soup and some bread in front of him and is surprised when he sits next to his father to eat. She joins them at the table with just her vodka. Her appetite for food isn't too good lately. Her throat is always stinging with the acid she gets from heartburn, making her nauseous. She's constantly on edge, and even the blazing hot summer sunshine can't put her at ease.

Wyatt's a noisy eater, slurping his soup like he has no teeth, wiping his mouth with his sleeve and tearing his bread apart with his oil-stained hands. She's been married to him since she was eighteen; twenty-four long years. It's not just his noisy eating that bothers her. That's actually the last thing she'd complain about if she were compiling a list.

She tries not to think about her husband's faults and instead watches Mason eat. He looks like his dad, but that's where the similarities end. Mason has always been a good boy, studious and kind. The first time Wyatt took him hunting when he was eleven years old, he cried for a week. He hated the idea of killing animals. She had to explain they weren't doing it for the sport; they ate every bit of what they killed.

Slowly, over time, he's got used to going out with Wyatt and coming home with something for dinner, but she can tell he still hates it. He just pretends not to in order to keep his dad happy. Wyatt has a fast temper that they would both rather avoid wherever possible.

Her husband wipes his mouth and looks at his son. "I have a long list of jobs for you to cover in the scrapyard with Brad tomorrow."

Brad Skelton has worked for the family for twenty years and is still loyal. Although they can never be one hundred percent certain of anyone. He mainly works at their scrapyard but can be useful for other jobs too. Angie watches Mason's face, but if he's annoyed, he doesn't show it, which is wise.

"Sure."

She wants to ask him if he's okay, but she knows he won't open up in front of his father.

Wyatt gets up and pours himself a whisky. Taking the bottle with him, he leaves his dirty bowl and plate for her to clean up and heads upstairs without a word.

She resists the urge to shake her head. They never had children together. Mason is the result of an affair. She hates to think how many times Wyatt has cheated on her over the years; she'd bet he has more kids floating around out there, but she'd rather not know about them.

She and Wyatt did try for their own children as soon as they were married, but they quickly learned that Angie was infertile, so that was the end of that. Until Mason came to live with them, which turned out to be a blessing in disguise. She's loved every minute of mothering him and considers him her own. Not that he'll ever call her Mom.

"How is everyone at the park?" she asks. "Are they upset about the girl?"

He stops eating and pushes the bowl away. "I guess."

He's so closed off to her now he's getting older, and she can't understand why he won't trust her. The sun is beginning to set, and where it hits his face through the kitchen window, it bathes him in an orange glow, highlighting the bags under his eyes. Is it normal for teenagers to be so tired all the time? Could it be depression, or drugs? Having had no previous experience of parenting, she'll never know. She does know the smell of weed, though, and she's never caught it on him or his clothes.

"Mason? Are you ever going to tell me anything about your friends? Or do I have to stalk your Facebook account?"

His head snaps up and he gives her a look to suggest there will be repercussions if she does. He looks like his father for a minute, making her shudder.

"Don't be one of those people," he says.

She leans against the kitchen counter and sips her drink. She knows she should hold her tongue, but her fear of losing him, mixed with her third large vodka, gets the better of her. "It's about time you were a little more appreciative of what your father and I have done for you. It's time to stop pretending you're going to be a goddam lawyer or whatever you've got in your head, and come to the realization that you'll be working alongside your father in the scrapyard. Then, once you've proved yourself, you can take over from him in our other business. You'll be set for life."

He stands up, pushing the chair away with his calves. "You can't tell me what to do once I turn eighteen."

She leans forward. "You really think your father is going to let you go? You're more intelligent than that, Mason. He didn't take you in just out of the kindness of his heart. He expects a return on *all* his investments. Besides," she pauses to laugh, "you know too much."

Mason starts pacing the kitchen, back and forth and she worries she's taken it too far. Scared him off. She walks over to him and grabs his arm. "Mason? Please don't leave for college next year. Your father's an asshole, but I care about you. I need you here. Doesn't that mean anything? Haven't I been good to you?"

He collapses back onto the chair and runs his hands through his hair. "I have no idea what to do about anything right now."

His eyes give away his fear and she genuinely feels sorry for him. "What's going on with you? You can tell me anything and it won't leave my lips. I can guarantee you that."

To her surprise, Mason breaks down. His head is in his hands and he's sobbing. She's never seen him like this before.

"What's the matter?" She goes to him, rubbing his back.

He looks up through his tears. "I was there that night!" He tries to catch his breath. "At the park! Nikki is my girlfriend. *Was* my girlfriend. And my name has just been mentioned in the news! It's only a matter of time before I'm arrested."

She's stunned. She didn't even know he had a girlfriend, despite scouring his Facebook account regularly. She realizes how good he is at keeping secrets and it unnerves her. How could he have been there when Nikki Jackson died? She knew he was working that day but thought he'd finished well before it happened. She takes a step back and thinks about how best to deal with this.

Mason's looking at his cell phone. His face goes white. "Holy shit. My name's all over the internet already!"

Alarmed, she glances over his shoulder.

Mason McCoy named locally as the deceased's boyfriend. Does he have the missing knife? Did he trick Nikki Jackson into killing herself?

"Why didn't you tell me you were there?" she says, panicked. "Did you see anything?"

He doesn't respond; he's too busy scrolling.

"I wish you'd told me sooner. I could have handled the situation before the press got wind." It's too late now. She downs her drink and puts her glass on the counter. "Mason, listen to me. You need to get away from here, otherwise the cops will try to pin this on you. I want to protect you, and we both need to protect the McCoy name."

A look of shock passes across his face, but he quickly realizes she's right. "But where do I go?"

She thinks about it. "Grab some things—clothes, a sleeping bag, a flashlight—then meet me out front. We'll take my car."

He just stares at her.

"Now, Mason!"

He turns and runs up the stairs while she collects some food and drink. She has to take control of the situation and make sure no one can find Mason anytime soon.

CHAPTER THIRTY-TWO

Independence Day

Nikki screams as if she's being attacked. Then she spins around and giggles in relief as Mason comes in for a kiss after tickling her.

"You've got to stop doing that! I'm nervous enough without you creeping up on me, especially at night!"

He laughs. "Sorry, I'll stop. I promise."

The glint in his eye tells her he's lying, but she doesn't mind really.

She's taken over at the runaway mine-train roller coaster and a woman in line for the ride clears her throat to get their attention. It's dark outside now and the big firework display is about to start. The lines for the rides are reducing, as everyone wants to film the display on their phones.

"Sorry," says Nikki. "That's fourteen bucks."

The woman slides the money over as her child cries loudly. Nikki slips the little boy a stuffed animal from the lost-and-found box. "Mr. Lion's lost his owner. Would he be able to stay at your house with you?"

The boy's cries reduce to sniveling. His chubby hand reaches out for the lion as he gulps back his tears. "Okay."

His mom nods her thanks and leads him away to the ride. When they're safely harnessed, the ride assistant starts it up with only them and one other family on it.

"I take it you want kids someday?" asks Mason.

She's surprised by the question. He looks at her so intently, like she's the only person in the park. Is he asking about kids because he sees a future with her? The thought makes her hopeful, but at the same time a feeling of dread runs through her, like it always does when she considers anything that might make her happy.

"Maybe." She's hesitant because she doesn't want to risk passing down her mental health issues to a child. She'd hate for them to have to go through years of therapy and anxiety, never mind the dark days that seem never-ending.

It's like Mason knows what she's thinking. He puts the *Be right back!* sign in the ticket booth's window and pulls her up from her seat.

"I can't just leave," she says.

"It'll be fine; everyone's going to be watching the fireworks. Come with me." He takes her hand and leads her away from the rides and up the hill to the staff parking lot. "Sit up there." He lifts her onto the hood of his car.

It's quiet here, with a great view of the park. Sometimes they come here to listen to music on their breaks.

"Turn toward me slightly." With the amusement park lit up behind her, Mason pulls his cell phone out and backs away. "Stay there," he says. "You look great with the rides as a backdrop."

She smiles self-consciously as he snaps away.

"I can't see your face, so I'm going to try the flash."

When he has what he wants, he sends her the best photo and climbs onto the hood next to her, wrapping an arm around her shoulders as they wait for the display to start. It's so warm out she can smell his anti-perspirant working hard. The screams from the rides are loud, but she finds the sound comforting. She prefers being around large groups of people; anonymous. It's when she's alone that she spirals.

Suddenly the first firework shoots up into the sky above them, exploding into a shower of flashing bright colors. It's followed by more, and the sky turns wild.

"Wow!" She can hear the customers whooping and whistling in the park, equally enthralled as her. She pulls her phone out and snaps some photos, then decides to just enjoy the moment.

She rests her cheek against Mason's and they take it all in. Nights like this make her feel invincible, but they're so rare.

When the fireworks start to wind down, she notices he's staring at her.

"What do you want to do next year?" he asks as he entwines his fingers with hers.

It's a strange question. She still has two years of high school left. "I'm going to school."

He sighs. "Once I graduate, I'm out of here."

She turns to face him. Their hands drop to his lap. She wants to ask, "What about me?" but instead she says, "Where will you go?"

He smiles. "You mean where will *we* go?"

She doesn't know what to say.

"You could finish your final year of high school online, or somewhere else," he says. "I've worked for my dad's business since I was eleven and I've saved everything I've earned, except for buying my car. I'm thinking of heading to New York City. Somewhere we could get lost. Somewhere my fucked-up family can't find me."

She looks away to the water. Mason won't talk about his family so she doesn't know why he wants to get away from them, but she knows who the McCoys are. She doesn't know why he's so unhappy with them. They seem nice from the interviews she's seen on TV. They're always raising money for one cause or another and she knows they gave a neighbor of hers a loan when times were tough. But she also knows Mason's been struggling for a long time and that's why he was in therapy.

As for her own parents, well, they wouldn't miss her but they'd miss her wages. Her dad always accuses her of eating more food than she pays them for and running the shower for too long. But he literally sits on the couch all day drinking vodka. More than once she's wanted to point out that vodka costs a hell of a lot more than a cheese sandwich. But she never would.

"What's your dream, Nikki?"

She clears the image of her parents from her head. She doesn't want to spoil tonight. "What do you mean?"

"What are your hopes and ambitions?" He's looking into her eyes. "What do you want from life?"

She shrugs. "All I know is surviving day to day. That's enough for now."

He smiles sadly and kisses her forehead. "Ever been to New York?"

She laughs. "I've never been anywhere."

He whispers into her ear, "Come with me. We'll start afresh, with no adults to mess us up."

Looking into his eyes, she feels like he means it. Like he would rather she joined him than go alone. Her heart feels like it might burst. If this were her last day on earth, this is how she would choose to spend it. "Count me in."

He hugs her to him and they sit that way, listening to the screams of children mixed with the heavy beats of their own hearts.

CHAPTER THIRTY-THREE

It's only 6.30, but Mike's eyes are heavy, and rubbing away his exhaustion isn't working. He glances at the coffee mug on his desk. It's empty again. He takes that as a sign that it's time to finish up for the evening and head home. By the time he switches off his computer, Alex is hovering behind him. "What is it?"

"I have an update on the forensics from Nikki Jackson's investigation if you have a minute."

Mike sighs, then reluctantly follows him.

"And I just saw on the news that someone is saying our victim was murdered by her boyfriend."

Mike stops in his tracks. "What? Who's saying that?"

"Kate Flynn."

"Goddammit."

Alex leads him through a dark corridor where a flickering light tries its best to make up for a lack of windows. He opens the door to his makeshift lab—it was an evidence storage room before they hired him—and points to the wall-mounted TV, but the news anchor in the studio has moved on to a different story.

"She said Nikki's boyfriend has been named as Mason McCoy," says Alex.

"Shit," says Mike. A feeling of unease creeps over him. Why did her boyfriend have to be Mason McCoy? He shakes his head. "How come everyone talks to Kate Flynn but no one tells me anything?"

Alex raises an eyebrow. "I guess she comes across a little friendlier than you."

Mike shoots him a warning look, but Alex is unfazed.

"The thumbprint from our victim's face doesn't belong to her or the employee who found her."

"How do you know? I thought Ricky disappeared."

"I lifted fingerprints from his staff ID badge."

Although Alex is annoying, he does use his initiative.

"Turns out his name isn't Ricky Gregor; it's Marty Baker, and he's wanted in four different states for robbery."

Mike sighs. The guy will be long gone by now. "Any offenses against kids?"

"None. I checked Trevor Sanders' prints too—the guy who owns the park. Again, no match."

For Mike, Trevor was never really a suspect as he'd have the most to lose. If he was going to kill someone, he wouldn't do it on his own premises. "Have you run the thumbprint through the database?"

"Of course. No match."

"Great." Mike shakes his head. Along with the missing knife, this confirms they're looking at a homicide now. "Is that everything?"

"No. I have some fibers and hairs I've sent to the state lab for analysis, but it could take a while for the results to come back. Should now just say: I also went through Nikki's cell phone. She really only ever messaged two people regularly: her mom about mundane things like when she'd be home; and her boyfriend. His number is stored under 'Mason', adding weight to Kate Flynn's version. She has a few social media apps installed, but she logs out after each use, and without the passwords I can't gain access to check her private messages."

Mike rolls his eyes. "Great. Getting access to any social media accounts is almost impossible without passwords."

"I'm aware. Also, there's a photo on the phone of Nikki taken on the night she died."

Mike's eyes widen. "Show me."

Alex opens the photo on his computer. "Mason sent this to her at nine fifteen."

He leans in to get a good look. It shows Nikki sitting on the hood of a maroon Dodge Ram with the park behind her. The flash from the camera is lighting up her face. She looks a little tired and disheveled from a long shift in the hot sun, but the bashful expression on her face is similar to that in the photo he saw on her parents' fridge. Is that doubt he sees in her eyes too? Her arms are folded self-consciously and her smile doesn't reach her eyes.

"What were her exchanges with Mason about?"

"Just the usual," says Alex. "What shift are you on, want to get lunch together, I miss you and so on. But on the night she died, she texted him at eleven thirty and asked him to meet her at the park."

Mike remembers Lena concluding that the girl died sometime between midnight and 2 a.m. "Did he reply?"

"Yes. He said, 'On my way. Is everything okay?' She didn't reply. Which means he was likely the last person to see her alive. Which could also mean her death was a suicide pact like someone on the news suggested, or perhaps Mason killed her and made it look like a suicide. If his prints match the thumbprint found on her face, you have a lead."

Mike nods. Normally he'd be annoyed at Alex for telling him how to do his job, but he's distracted. He's starting to get a bad feeling about this case, because if Mason McCoy is implicated in the girl's death, things are about to get complicated.

CHAPTER THIRTY-FOUR

Nate's tired, hungry and ashamed. He regrets storming out on Madison but he didn't know what to think when she told him she'd been misleading him all this time.

He's been questioning whether it was stupid of him to agree to investigate her cold case and travel all this way for her. She's meant to be just an employee, but he's taking massive risks for her and so far she's brought him nothing but trouble. And if he's honest, from an investigator's perspective it doesn't look good for Madison to be the sole beneficiary of Stephanie Garcia's property. If he were a cop, he'd be looking into whether she could have hired someone to kill Stephanie in order to benefit from her will.

Madison told him she wanted his help solving her cold case, but was that just a lie? Could she be using him for his money; as a free ride from California to Colorado, where she perhaps always intended to claim Stephanie's property and then find her son? Knowing now that her service weapon was used to kill Officer Levy—something else she held back—he's realizing there's a lot he still doesn't know about her. But from what he does know, he can't believe she's capable of murdering anyone, despite how it looks on paper.

He spent last night alone in a nearby church. Well, almost alone. He thought he'd find solace in either the church or the cocaine, and it was peaceful watching the sun set behind a stained-glass window. The organ music filled his soul with hope. He was able to imagine he was young again and still training to become a priest, before he fell in love with Stacey Connor. Before she was cruelly taken from him. It made him question whether it was time to return to the church. He could find a town to settle down in and blend into the community, helping out at Sunday school and surrounding himself with people he could support. Being a PI doesn't help as many people as he expected. But on the other hand, those who hire him have far more serious problems than anyone he ever met at church.

He ended up passed out near a statue of Jesus. He only woke up because some homeless woman was rifling through his pockets, trying to steal his phone and wallet. She ran off after he opened his eyes and grabbed her wrist. Ashamed of his behavior, he left the church feeling like he wasn't good enough to ever return.

As he drives, he wonders what to tell Madison when he sees her again. Should he be honest, or pretend he stayed at a hotel, seeking alone time? He's being stupid, of course: he can't fool her. She'll know exactly what he was doing.

He takes a deep breath. He's been off death row for two years now and can't understand why he still uses drugs to cope with being outside. The thought of attending Narcotics Anonymous enters his mind, but he dismisses it. He's not that bad. It's rare that he lets it get out of control.

He shakes his head at his own excuses.

His morning has been spent on and off the phone with Rex, trying to track down some background information on Officer Ryan Levy and Detective Don Douglas. Because regardless of what Madison says, to Nate, Douglas is the most logical suspect in Ryan's murder. They knew each other, and it could be said that Douglas benefited from his death because he secured a conviction for it. That's the only possible motive Nate's been able to think of: that Douglas is some hotshot who needs a one hundred percent success record to feel like a tough guy or to progress up the ladder of law enforcement. Rex is going to look into whether he's been the subject of any internal affairs investigations. Perhaps he's done something similar before.

Nate's phone buzzes. Rex has sent him the address of Ryan's parents. He punches the zip code into his sat nav and heads over there.

When he pulls up outside the house, he's surprised by how big it is. Ryan's parents clearly have money. There's one car on the large driveway, which has room for three. He spots a woman walking toward it from the house.

"Excuse me, ma'am?" He approaches her.

She's well dressed in a silk blouse and navy slacks. "Yes?" She doesn't look fearful of a stranger approaching.

"My name's Nate and I'm a private investigator." He holds his hand out but she doesn't take it. Instead she looks at him as if he's some foul mess she's stepped in. "I'm looking into a potential corruption case at Lost Creek PD and I wondered if you'd take a few minutes to answer some questions about how your son's murder was handled?"

She takes a step back and looks surprised. "Are you investigating Madison Harper again?"

"No, this relates to someone else." He can't tell her he's trying to clear Madison's name, as she'll ask him to leave immediately and probably call the cops, so he has to mislead her a little. "Am I right in thinking your son was an outstanding officer who never had any conflict with his coworkers?"

She relaxes slightly and even smiles. "Ryan got on with everyone. One of his strengths was his ability to defuse tense situations. He wanted to become an FBI hostage negotiator in the future." Her smile fades. "But thanks to that woman, he was robbed of the opportunity."

"So there was no one in the department he might have had trouble with?"

"Not that he ever mentioned. And he would have mentioned it. We saw him regularly."

Nate strikes that off his list of potential motives for the killer. "Could he have been investigating someone from his department? Maybe undercover, for internal affairs?"

"What do you mean?"

"Well, if he knew a coworker was breaking the law, would he report them to his superior?"

Mrs. Levy eyes him suspiciously. "What did you say your name was again? And who are you working for?"

He smiles. "I'm not at liberty to offer that information."

She folds her arms. "Perhaps you should be asking my husband these questions. I'm sure he'd be very interested in talking to you."

Sensing he's not going to get anything else from her, he takes a step back.

"Madison Harper killed my son," she says. "My husband and I have no doubt about that, because her weapon was used and only her prints were on it. So I don't know why you would come here and ask me these questions. If anyone in Ryan's department was corrupt, it was her."

"I'm sorry for bothering you, ma'am. Thanks for your time."

He feels her eyes on his back as he walks away. His instinct tells him the answer to who killed Ryan won't be found by asking about motive. He needs to start thinking about the method instead.

Something that's been bothering him is how the killer gained access to Madison's locked gun safe. He googles a local locksmith and keeps walking as he calls the number. He watches Mrs. Levy drive away from her house as he nears his car.

A woman answers.

"Hi," he says. "I'm just after some hypothetical advice. I have a riddle to solve and need an expert locksmith to humor me for a moment."

"I like a riddle," she says. "Go ahead."

"Great. How would someone gain access to a locked gun safe if they didn't have the key and there's no key code?"

She hesitates before answering. "You're not trying to rob a bank, are you?"

"No, nothing that stupid!" He laughs to set her at ease.

"Well, I guess you could find out online anyway, so I may as well tell you what I'd do. Depending on the brand and type of safe, you could pick the lock with any number of instruments—a screwdriver or a sharp-tipped knife, for example—or you could use a drill to—"

He interrupts. "There was no damage at all to the safe in question. Yet someone got into it and removed a gun that was then found in a different house."

"Hmm."

"Would a locksmith be able to open it without damaging it?" He doesn't for one minute think a locksmith was hired to get into Madison's safe—they'd be a potential witness linking the killer to the crime—but he's got to at least know whether it's possible.

"Not without a key. You sure whoever did it didn't have the key? Maybe a spare one the owner forgot they had?"

Madison was adamant there was only one key. "I'm as sure as I can be."

Silence. Then, "Well the owner must have left it unlocked by mistake. It's the only other logical explanation."

Nate nods. He wonders how Madison would react if he asked whether she'd neglected to lock it. It would be easily done with all the distractions of being a working single parent, but she'd be mightily offended at the suggestion. "That must be it. Thanks for your time, I appreciate it."

"Not a problem."

He can't delay it any longer. It's time to face Madison.

CHAPTER THIRTY-FIVE

Angie's back home, in the paddock next to the house, and she'd bet Wyatt doesn't even know she and Mason went anywhere. She'll have to fill him in eventually and he probably won't be happy with her, but she had to make a fast decision for the sake of their family. For now, she needs some alone time, and grooming her horses at the end of each day always relaxes her. She gently pulls the brush through the thick black mane. She's read somewhere that stroking a dog or a cat can reduce your blood pressure, and grooming her horses does the same thing. They seem to enjoy it too.

She thinks of Mason and of how frightened he was when she left him. She couldn't think of a single thing to say that would make him feel better. It hurts to think of how much they've gone through in order to be a family and how quickly it can be shattered.

She hears the sound of car tires on gravel. She pats the horse's glossy hindquarters and walks toward the porch, where her half-empty bottle of vodka awaits. As she sits in her rocking chair, she listens to the approaching footsteps. She's expecting someone from LCPD to come by looking for Mason, and she has it all figured out in her head what she's going to say.

She waits to see who appears. A blonde woman comes around the corner and stares at her. It's been so long since they last saw each other that it takes a full minute before Angie recognizes her sister. She tries not to give away her surprise, but truth be told, she's stunned. She'd heard of her early release from prison but hoped she wouldn't be stupid enough to return home.

Madison's looking better than Angie would have expected considering where she's been. "Well, well, well. Look what the cat dragged in."

"Can we talk?"

Angie thought she'd be angry if Madison ever dared to come here, but now Mason's gone, she feels like she has the upper hand. "Well, I suppose our catch-up is long overdue. Pull up a chair."

Madison perches on the other rocking chair, the one that's stained with engine oil. She looks nervous and angry.

"So how was prison?" Angie asks, trying to provoke a reaction.

"I'm not here to talk about that. Tell me about Mason McCoy." She pauses. "He's my son, isn't he?"

Angie takes pleasure in confirming it. "He is."

She watches as Madison looks up at the sky with tears in her eyes. She should be relieved that family stepped up to look after him, but when she makes eye contact again, she looks angry.

"Why did you take him in?"

That annoys her. "He's Wyatt's son. I had no choice." She sips her vodka. "I think *I* should be the one asking the questions, seeing as you slept with my husband. Were you ever going to tell me, or did that slip your mind?"

Madison looks away. "How did you find out?"

"What does it matter?"

"I want to know."

"I don't give a shit what you want!" Angie's losing her cool, but she doesn't want Madison to know how much it bothers her. "It's none of your goddam business."

"It is when my son's involved."

"Well maybe if you didn't sleep with married men and get pregnant with their babies, you wouldn't have ended up in this situation, sis." Her eyes narrow. "You ever think about that?"

Madison's shaking her head. "You don't know what you're talking about."

"Like hell I don't. Wyatt told me everything."

The look on her sister's face has turned to surprise. "Really? Everything?"

Angie turns away from her and takes a deep breath. "The stupid asshole got so drunk one night that he let it slip. Told me you begged him for it. Imagine that: my little sister lusting over the man she pretended to hate." She turns back. "You made such a big deal about what a bad guy he was and how I'd end up miserable and lonely if I married him. Is that because you wanted him for yourself? Because according to Wyatt, you were infatuated with him."

Madison's shaking her head. Her hands are trembling. "It was nothing like that. Look, I didn't come here to fight. I just want to know about Owen. It's been so long since I've seen him, Angie. Where is he?" She looks around.

"He's not here. You can't see him."

Disappointment makes her shoulders slump. "If he's not here, then where is he?"

Angie remains silent.

"He's my son, you can't stop me from seeing him! Does he even know I'm back?"

"Wouldn't matter if he did. He's not here."

"Angie, he's in trouble. The press have named him as Nikki Jackson's boyfriend. I need to protect him."

Angie sees red. "I've already taken care of it. I've already protected him. *I'm* the one who's been his mother for the last seven years, since you went and got yourself convicted. You should be thanking me, but of course you won't, so I'll never tell you where he is."

Madison looks away and Angie realizes she'll stop at nothing to find him.

"Can't you at least tell me how he is? What he's been doing all this time?"

Angie has no sympathy for her. The bitch is a hypocrite. She can't resist the urge to rub it in. "He's special, that's for sure. A natural hunter, too. We didn't think he would be at first, 'cause he cried every time Wyatt took him out, but until recently he was hunting almost every morning with his dad." She takes another sip. "He's academic, like you were."

Madison smiles for the first time.

"Wants to be a lawyer, can you believe that?" Angie scoffs. "A McCoy practicing law? Maybe he wanted to get you out of prison or something, I don't know."

Madison looks surprised, and Angie can tell she's trying to control her emotions.

"Did he ever ask about me?" There's a hunger in her eyes. She wants every detail of her son's life.

"Sure he did, at first. But he hasn't done for years. To be honest, he asked after your girlfriend more. He was pretty upset when Stephanie died."

Her eyes widen. "Did she ever visit him here?"

"God, no! I wouldn't have had her in my house." Again, no reaction from Madison. She's not as hot-headed as she used to be when they were kids; she's harder to provoke. Maybe prison teaches you patience. Or maybe she's just lost all her fight. "Your son needed a fresh start. He was being bullied at school because of what you did to that cop. So we took him out of school and changed his name. We kept him close those first few years, away from Lost Creek and the media. After a while, people forgot he even existed. The press quickly assumed he'd been adopted out of state so they lost interest. Your friend Kate might have been more persistent, but I heard she moved away after your trial. Only the locals here in Gold Rock remember Owen Harper, and most of them work for us. No one else put two and two together. There was no reason to: you were incarcerated and the town moved on to the next scandal. Those who might have thought they'd figured it out were persuaded to mind their own business."

Madison's jaw is clenched with the effort of controlling her reaction. Finally she says, "Do you think he could have been involved in Nikki Jackson's death?"

"Well I never thought *you* would have killed anyone, yet here we are. Maybe he gets it from you." Angie smirks.

Madison look like she's going to slap her.

Angie stands up. "Time for you to leave, Madison. I don't want to see you around here again. I'm done with you."

But her sister doesn't move.

CHAPTER THIRTY-SIX

Madison can feel the tension gripping her shoulders and can't imagine it easing until she sees her son again. Seeing Angie after all this time is disorienting. They haven't had a one-on-one conversation like this for eighteen years. And they wouldn't be having one now if her sister hadn't taken Owen in. Madison would have stayed well away, knowing they were incapable of a normal sibling relationship.

She recognizes that on some level she should probably be grateful to Angie, but she can't find it in her. Not whilst knowing her son has been exposed to Wyatt for seven years. "I need answers before I leave. You owe me that much."

Angie looks incredulous. "I don't owe you anything! You owe *me* answers."

Madison can't understand the hateful expression on her face. The resentment she's been harboring has clearly aged her: her hair is sprinkled with silver and the bags under her eyes are heavy. Something is keeping her up at night, that much is obvious. Is it her loveless marriage to a dangerous man, or resentment that her own sister could betray her in such a way?

If Angie knew what really happened, she'd realize Madison is the one who should be bitter and angry.

"Are you sure you want answers?" Madison says. "Because I don't think you really do. I think you're hiding from the truth."

Angie looks like she might throw the glass at her. Madison intended to keep this non-confrontational, but there's no reasoning with her older sister. There never was. That was half their trouble growing up. Not for the first time, she thinks how crazy it is that you can be so different from your sibling when you were both raised the same way.

"I already know what happened," Angie says with venom. "You fucked my husband because you were jealous that I was happy. You wanted to split us up. Then you had his baby and hid that from him so he never even knew he was a father."

Madison's shaking her head. "No. You're wrong. I wasn't jealous of you. I pitied you."

Angie isn't listening. "You told me and Mom that Owen was the result of a one-night stand with a cop. I had no reason to doubt you. Turns out Wyatt had his suspicions all these years that Owen was his, but he kept quiet, not wanting me to know what the two of you had done. It was only because he got wasted one night that it slipped out. Told me there's a chance the boy might be his. And the thought of *you* having his child instead of me made me sick to my stomach. Still does." She shakes her head in disgust. "The minute he told me, I knew my sister was a whore as well as a killer."

Madison springs up and slaps her hard across the face.

Shocked, Angie holds her cheek, but her eyes burn. "You're going to regret that."

"How dare you call me a whore! You want to know the truth, Angie? You want me to spell it out for you? Because I think you already know, but you're too afraid to admit it."

Angie turns away and downs her drink.

"You know full well that I'd never stoop so low as to sleep with Wyatt McCoy. You knew I hated him." She pauses. Suddenly the words feel too big to get out of her mouth. "He *raped* me, Angie. Your ugly, arrogant monster of a husband raped me when I was just twenty years old."

Angie scoffs. "You would say that."

Madison pulls her sister by the arm, spinning her around to face her. "I'm telling the truth. He followed me out of a bar and coaxed me into his pickup truck by offering me a ride home." Her eyes fill with hot, angry tears, but she wipes them away. They won't help her. It's already done. But she needs to set this awful secret free at last. Angie should have known what he was capable of. She should have known Madison would never betray her sister like that, even if she could stomach the idea—which her loathing of him would never have allowed.

"He drove me to the woods, pulled out a shotgun from the back seat and made me walk toward the creek. I thought he was going to kill me."

"I'm not listening to this." Angie tries to get away, but Madison holds onto her arm.

"You *are* listening to this, because I had to *live* it!"

"I don't believe you."

Madison ignores her. "Your husband took me to the darkest part of the woods and threatened to shoot me dead unless I undressed for him."

"You would have told someone afterward!" shouts Angie. "You would've called the cops."

The adrenaline rush is making Madison dizzy, but she needs to fight back. Because she didn't fight that night, and telling her sister about it feels like being violated all over again. "He made me lie on my front while he pointed the gun at my head."

Angie pulls free of her. She looks wild. "You would have told Mom."

Tears are streaming down Madison's face. "You don't get to say what I *would* have done or what I *should* have done. Not until you've lived it. I was frightened for my life. He told me he'd hurt Mom if I ever told anyone. And he said he'd tell you I seduced him if you ever found out." She wipes her face. "You know the worst part about that for me? I knew he was right. I knew you would have taken his word over mine. And today you've proved that."

She sees something in Angie's eyes. Is it regret? Sympathy? Belief? Is there hope for them? It clears before she can tell.

"You need to get off my land. And if you ever tell your crazy story to anyone, Wyatt will kill you. With my blessing."

Madison's heart sinks. Angie has made her choice. They don't have anything binding them together anymore. The woman in front of her is a bitter stranger.

Someone creeps up on them.

"Angie? I need to speak to you."

Madison looks up in surprise to see Mike turning the corner. When he spots her, he almost turns back, but then realizes it's too late.

"Madison? What are you doing here?" he asks.

She wipes her face again. She's drained and shaky and she just wants to get the hell out of here, but Mike's reaction confuses her. "I could ask you the same question."

He looks at Angie. "I came to speak to Mason."

"You mean Owen," she says through gritted teeth.

He looks confused for a moment, then comprehension dawns.

"You asshole!" she shouts. "Why didn't you tell me?"

He takes her arm and leads her away from Angie.

"Listen to me: I didn't know for sure. Owen disappeared after you were sent down. You think child services tell us anything? You know better than that. When I asked about him, the social worker said they'd managed to track down his father. How was I supposed to know you screwed Wyatt back in the day?"

She shakes her head. She feels like killing him for keeping this from her. She's wasted two days when she could have been with her son.

"They took him out of school and I didn't see him around Lost Creek at all," Mike continues. "I only started seeing this Mason kid around when he was older, and I never asked them outright who he was because it was none of my business. You've got to remember that until recently I hadn't heard from you for seven years!"

"Yeah, well, I was a little busy serving someone else's sentence. You kind of slipped my mind. Apologies for the lack of Christmas cards." She knows her attitude stinks but she doesn't care.

"Where's Owen now?" he asks. "Douglas is trying to get a warrant for his arrest and it's in Owen's best interests to give himself up rather than be brought in. You know that, Madison."

She looks him in the eye as she realizes what he's saying. "Why are you assuming he had anything to do with his girlfriend's death?"

Mike takes a deep breath and folds his arms. "Because we still don't have the knife, and there's evidence on Nikki's cell phone to suggest he was with her when she died. On top of that, he hasn't contacted us despite his name being all over the media. That's why I'm here, so I can question him before Douglas assumes control. So tell me: where is he?"

"If I knew where he was, I wouldn't be wasting my time talking to you. You need to speak to Angie. She's hiding him. She clearly doesn't want to give him back to me, but he was never hers in the first place."

"Don't be stupid, she wouldn't hide him from you."

Madison goes quiet.

"Madison?"

"How can you say that? You know as well as I do she's never liked me."

"She's allowed to be disappointed in you after learning you slept with her husband. And don't forget you were convicted of killing a cop. Angie's had to bear some of the burden of that."

"But I didn't kill Ryan!"

He sighs. "I'm sorry, but that's not what the jury decided."

She gasps. "You asshole. I'm going to find my son before you let Douglas do to him what he did to me."

Just then, Wyatt appears from the house. Her stomach leaps at the sight of him.

"What the fuck's going on here?" he says. When he recognizes Madison, he looks over at Angie. "What's your cop-killing sister doing on my property?"

Madison can feel the tension rising. She needs to get away before Wyatt finds out what she told Angie. She doesn't know if Mike being here is enough to protect her.

She walks silently away from them all, down the steps and toward her car. She tenses as she walks, not trusting she won't get shot in the back.

CHAPTER THIRTY-SEVEN

It's after eight by the time Madison arrives home. She's completely drained from seeing her sister, but when she spots Nate's Jeep in the driveway, she relaxes. Finally he's back.

He must have been waiting for her, because he and Brody greet her at the front door. She left the dog at home this time. She ignores Nate's smile and walks straight past them both to collapse onto the couch in the living room.

Nate hesitantly joins her, looking as drained as she feels.

"You're an asshole."

He nods. "I am. I'm sorry. I didn't know what else to do. I guess I need to make some changes in my life."

She looks away from him, out of the front window. The sun is starting to lose its intensity, but the sticky feeling under her arms tells her there's no sign of the day's humidity reducing as the evening advances.

"I promise I won't disappear like that again."

"You can do what you want. You're a free agent." She turns to him. "You don't answer to me. Especially after I brought you here under false pretenses."

She must look pathetic, because he moves closer and places a comforting hand on her back. "You shouldn't have led me to believe you suspected the cops were the ones who framed you. But after disappearing on you last night, I guess that makes us even."

She squeezes his other hand and leans back, silent. She doesn't have the energy to explain everything that occurred while he was off on his coke binge. Brody sits between them on the floor.

Eventually Nate says, "Has something else happened?"

She turns to him and takes a deep breath. "I've found Owen."

His mouth opens in surprise, which quickly turns to excitement. "What? Where is he?"

She has to hold back tears. "I don't know. Still! All I know is that he's changed his name. He's the Mason McCoy kid everyone's talking about in the news."

"Nikki Jackson's boyfriend?"

She nods. "Apparently his name was changed after my conviction to give him an easier time."

"But who adopted him?"

She tenses. "He wasn't adopted. He went to live with my sister and her husband."

Nate frowns. "I didn't realize your sister still lives here."

She pushes her hair behind her ears and pulls her feet up under her on the couch. "We hadn't spoken for eighteen years. Angie's older than me and we had a terrible relationship growing up. When she was a teenager, she started hanging out with the troublemakers from high school and joining in with their drinking and shoplifting, that kind of thing. She eventually married a complete asshole by the name of Wyatt McCoy. After that she distanced herself from me and Mom. I think she realized she'd made a terrible mistake in her choice of husband but would never admit it, so she stuck by him and pretended she was happy. That's how stubborn she is. Mom and I told her how we felt about Wyatt before they got married, but she didn't want to hear it. And she was never an aunt to Owen."

"So how come she took him in?" he asks.

Madison takes a deep breath. "Because her husband, Wyatt, is Owen's biological father."

She can see him putting it all together in his head; to say he looks surprised is an understatement.

"Did you sleep with Wyatt while your sister was married to him? Because I'm guessing that would be a good enough reason for not wanting to speak to you again. She must have been angry at both of you, but I guess especially you, being her sister and all."

Madison feels the shame reddening her face. "They were married at the time, yes. But Angie never knew it happened and neither she nor Wyatt knew Owen was his. Angie never cared enough to ask me for details when I fell pregnant; we were barely in contact by then anyway. And I never told anyone who his father was. I still wouldn't if I had my way. When I fell pregnant, I told my mom and Angie that it was the result of a one-night stand with a cop."

"But she obviously knows Wyatt's his father now," he says.

She nods, imagining how livid Angie must have been when Wyatt let it slip. "Wyatt told her, presumably after I was arrested. I expect he didn't want his son living with strangers."

"How come Stephanie never told you they had him? Wouldn't she have spotted him around?"

That's something Madison has been thinking about too. Stephanie must have known all those years. "I can only think of two reasons: to let Owen have a fresh start in life without living in my shadow, or to save me from worrying about where he was. She would have known I wouldn't have been able to sleep knowing he was with the McCoys." And she'd have been right. A family of strangers would have been better.

"But what's so bad about them?"

"Wyatt's a monster." She glances at him. "I didn't voluntarily sleep with him, Nate." She pauses. "He raped me. That's how I got pregnant."

Nate shakes his head. She doesn't have to worry about whether or not he believes her, because his face says it all. He takes her hand, but she pulls away after a minute or two. She doesn't need to be treated delicately. It's better if she's not, or she'll break down. Instead she needs to focus, because her son's freedom is at stake.

"Owen wasn't at their place earlier. Angie's taken him somewhere to lie low, under the guise of protecting him, which is only going to make things worse with the cops. It's making him look guilty."

"So we need to find him," says Nate. "Find out who his friends are. He could be with one of them."

"I agree. The best place to start is Fantasy World. Apparently he worked there alongside Nikki Jackson, so all the teenagers will know him and who he hangs out with." She stands up, but notices the look on Nate's face. It suggests he was hoping to wait until morning.

"I can go alone."

He gets to his feet. "Don't be stupid. Let's go."

CHAPTER THIRTY-EIGHT

It's past eight o'clock before Mike can finally get his things together and go home. His cell phone rings as he washes his stained coffee mug in the station's tiny kitchen and his daughter's smiling face pops up on the screen. Instead of delight, he feels dread. He takes the call in an empty interview room.

"Hey, Dad! Are you still taking me to Fantasy World next weekend?"

He sighs. That place will never be the same for him after witnessing Nikki Jackson's lifeless body on the Ferris wheel. "Sure, if you still want to go. Aren't you getting too old for amusement park rides and cotton candy, though?"

"Dad, I'm eleven, not *your* age."

He laughs. Sally's the only good thing going on in his life.

"I've got birthday money to spend, so it won't cost you too much."

"Oh sure. I'll believe that when I see it."

She giggles and the sound tugs at his heart. "How's your mom?" he asks.

"She's good. Her new boyfriend is annoying, though. I've told her he's not allowed to move in until I'm old enough to move out."

Mike didn't know Viv was dating someone new. It's none of his business, but it still stings. "I like that idea."

Detective Douglas pokes his head into the room, gesturing for Mike to join him. Mike sighs. He was so close to getting out of here.

"I've got to go, honey. I'll see you next weekend."

"Do you promise this time? Because last time you had to work."

She's right; Stephanie Garcia's murder got in the way. "I promise that nothing will stop me from taking you to Fantasy World this time."

"Even if your boss tries to make you work?"

He laughs. "If that happens, I'll play hooky and we'll still go. I might have to wear a ski mask so no one from work recognizes me, but I'd do that for you."

"Yay! Bye, Daddy."

He leaves the interview room with a heavy heart. He doesn't see her enough. He doesn't know whether that's because there's never enough time, or because being with her makes him feel like a bad father. A bad person.

Douglas is waiting for him. "I've charged Paul Harris with Stephanie Garcia's murder."

Mike smiles. "Good work. Based on questioning or because of the evidence?"

"He didn't have an alibi, and Alex is collecting his DNA so he can check it against the semen found at the scene. But I have a positive ID from one of Garcia's neighbors, who saw Harris loitering in a car near the house at least three times in the weeks leading up to her murder. On two occasions he had another guy with him, presumably his brother, but he's not giving up any names and is still denying he was there."

Mike nods, relieved that they have someone in custody. "So Madison was telling the truth when she said Stephanie had been calling her about getting unsavory visitors. I take it she's no longer a suspect in your eyes?"

Douglas looks away. "Unless she ordered the hit."

Mike scowls. "Come on, Don. You need to let it go. She's not stupid enough to turn up straight after ordering a hit on someone! Besides, earlier today I broke the news that Stephanie's been cremated. She was devastated."

Douglas appears to consider it. "Fine. But I need to figure out what Harris's motive was. If he was one of the men hassling Garcia about Harper's whereabouts, then he must know her in some way. Otherwise why would he care where she was?"

"Maybe Davis Levy hired him to keep track of her after her release? He called me earlier. He's pretty pissed now she's back in town."

Douglas nods. "I'll look into it. Have you heard from the McCoys or their boy since he was named by reporters?"

"I spoke to them earlier and they said he's gone camping, but they're going to get him to call me as soon as they can reach him on the phone. Cell service is bad where he's gone."

"They expect us to believe that?" Douglas is shaking his head.

Mike shrugs. "Sullivan says we have to tread carefully because it's the McCoys and we wouldn't want to wrongly arrest their son. Wouldn't be good for community relations, apparently. We're to give them an opportunity to bring the boy in themselves. If he's not here by mid morning tomorrow, he'll let us go get him."

Douglas looks annoyed. "I swear that couple have got half this town in their pockets."

"All the more reason to tread carefully."

"I've already put out a BOLO in case he's skipped town, but the McCoys don't need to know that yet."

Mike's alarmed. That won't go down well with Angie and Wyatt if they find out.

"Why are you so worried?" asks Douglas. "No one's above the law, Bowers. Not even the McCoys."

Mike nods. He knows Douglas is right. He just can't help feeling that nothing good is going to come out of arresting Mason McCoy.

CHAPTER THIRTY-NINE

Madison drives to the amusement park in Steph's car while Nate fills her in on what the locksmith said about her gun safe.

She responds before he's even finished. "I didn't leave my safe unlocked. I can see why you would think that was possible, but it was still locked when I was arrested and the key was in my purse with no one else's prints found on it."

He nods, then runs her through his conversation with Jane Levy. "She was adamant you were to blame for her son's murder."

The thought of Jane Levy bad-mouthing her pisses her off. "I had the misfortune to run into both of Ryan's parents in the grocery store earlier. The hatred they had for me was shocking. I'm pretty sure they threatened to kill Owen to show me how they feel about losing their son."

"You're kidding?"

"No." She sighs and watches the sun setting behind the mountains ahead of them as she drives. Her heavy eyelids are fighting to stay open. She needs caffeine as soon as they reach the park.

"In that case, could they have been behind Stephanie's murder?" asks Nate.

She hadn't even considered that. "Jesus, that would be messed up: killing someone I loved in the mistaken belief that I killed their son. How will they react when they find out I was wrongly convicted?"

He thinks about it. "Hang on. What if it was them who killed Ryan? I mean, we've been working on the assumption they were a loving family, but could one of them have wanted him dead for some reason?"

She cocks her head, mulling it over. "You know, I never once considered them as suspects. His dad does have an awful temper, from what I saw today, but Ryan never mentioned any rifts between them. He didn't talk about his parents much at all. I mean, he was a thirty-year-old guy living his own life, so why would he?"

"I'll get Rex to check whether the father has a criminal record. What's his name?"

"Davis Levy. He owns the shooting range in town, so he'll have a business registered to him. Maybe he had an insurance policy out on Ryan and needed the payout to stay afloat."

"It's a possible motive." Nate's taking it all down on his phone in a message to Rex.

Madison pulls out a cigarette with her free hand and lights it, blowing the smoke out of her window. "On the face of it, Detective Douglas is still the most obvious choice to frame me, but he barely knew me so I'm really struggling to come up with a credible motive."

"Me too," says Nate. "But what if he got into a fight with Ryan for some reason, killed him, and then needed a fall guy to take the blame?"

"I guess it's possible. Maybe they were up to something and Ryan wanted out."

"What about your friend Mike?"

She shakes her head. "I've thought about that a lot, but again there's no motive. He eventually got my job while I was inside, but I could tell from speaking to him that he's not enjoying it. I think he's out of his depth. Besides, who would murder someone just for a promotion? He didn't even apply for the vacancy when I did."

Nate nods. "Yeah, that's not a strong enough motive for murder. Were you two ever intimate?"

She laughs. "God, no. I never screwed anyone from work. I've seen it go wrong too many times."

They're silent for a few minutes, then Nate says, "Let's look at this another way. Could it have been more about wanting Ryan dead than framing you for murder?"

"What do you mean?" She glances at him.

"Well, we can't find a motive to frame you, so maybe you *were* just the fall guy. Maybe Ryan was investigating someone, or owed money to someone."

"But then why use my service weapon to kill him? Why not just a random gun and take it with them after?"

He frowns. "That's a good point. I'll ask Rex to do a full background check on Ryan's dad, see what he can find out."

"While you're at it, get him to look into the police records of Detective Don Douglas too."

"Already done."

She smiles. "Great. And you know what? Give him Mike's name too—his last name is Bowers. Hell, throw in the chief as well—Charles Sullivan. For all we know, they could all be involved." That's a depressing thought, as it would prove Nate's theory about most cops being crooked.

She can see the Ferris wheel in the near distance as they draw closer. "By the way, I did get one piece of good news today."

He raises his eyebrows and glances at her.

"Mike told me they're questioning someone for Stephanie's murder. Sounds like it's one of the heavies she was complaining about, so they might actually have the right guy."

"Depends on whether he was put up to it by someone else."

"I know. Mike wouldn't tell me his name, so I'll have to wait to see whether I know him or not. But I also found out today that Nikki Jackson was working for Steph."

"You're kidding? Doing what?"

"Just garden chores. But it's a link between the two of them. I'm working on the theory that Steph was killed for not giving up my location and Nikki might have witnessed what happened. She could have been out back picking vegetables when the killer arrived."

"Do you know for sure yet that Nikki was definitely murdered?"

"Mike wouldn't tell me anything, but Kate said on the news that the knife used to slit her wrists is still missing. If it wasn't, they'd have closed the case as a suicide by now to shut down the media speculation."

"So she could have been killed to keep her quiet about what happened to Steph."

She nods. "And if I was a teenage girl who'd witnessed something like that, the person I'd most likely confide in is my boyfriend."

Nate looks at her. "Owen."

She nods. "Exactly. He could be the key to both Stephanie and Nikki's murders. And if anyone in my police department *was* responsible, they'll come to the same conclusion and will want to pin the murders on him."

"Or worse."

She looks at him.

"They might not bother framing him. They might silence him so he can never speak out."

The thought of it makes her accelerate. She has to find her son before it's too late.

CHAPTER FORTY

Independence Day

"Hey, Nikki?"

She spins around. The park's owner, Trevor, is standing there.

"How about earning a bit of extra cash tonight?"

She's already exhausted and was looking forward to going home now the park's closed for the night, but it's hard to turn down extra money. "Doing what?"

"I need someone to clean up. The rest of the clean team has let me down. They've probably gone to some after-party or something."

Her heart sinks. Cleaning up? Everyone takes a turn, one week out of four, at cleaning the park while it's closed overnight. It's mainly just picking garbage from around the rides, wiping down the fun houses, and putting stray shoes and wallets in the lost-and-found box. Ricky, the maintenance guy, catches whatever they've missed when he arrives in the morning, and he's always bitching about how they leave the vomit for him.

On a humid night like tonight, she doesn't fancy being inside the Haunted House or the Ghost Train. They have no windows, so it's hard to breathe in there after a full day of high temperatures.

He must see the lack of enthusiasm on her face. "Okay, I'll give you double pay for the whole of today. How about it?"

Her eyes light up. They've already been promised a bonus for working Independence Day, but double pay will mean she can replace her old sneakers at last. She checks the time. It's almost eleven. "Okay, but I need to make sure my dad can come collect me after. My bike's got a puncture so I was just about to catch a ride home with some of the others."

"Go ahead."

She walks away, pulling out her phone. Her mom answers. "Hey, Mom. I've been offered double pay to work late. Can Dad pick me up at about twelve thirty, as my bike's screwed."

"Let me ask him."

Her mom relays the message and she hears her dad cursing her. But she knows he won't turn her down if it means she'll be bringing in more money. Eventually her mom says, "He'll be outside at twelve thirty, so don't be late. He's been drinking all day, but I'll make him some coffee. He's not too bad yet."

Nikki feels a flush of sadness. Even though her dad's an embarrassment, the thought that alcohol is one day going to kill him is hard to stomach. On some level she does care about him. She's not concerned about him drink-driving, because that's what he's always done. The alcohol doesn't affect him too badly until he combines it with the meth. His body has got used to the amount he drinks. "He's not using tonight, is he?"

"No. Not yet."

"Mom, you need to learn to drive. We can't rely on him anymore."

"Don't speak poorly of your father, Nikki. He's doing the best he can. You ought to be more grateful that you have someone to collect you."

Nikki shakes her head. Yet again her mom has taken his side. "Okay. Bye, Mom." She walks back to Trevor, who's saying goodbye to a group of staff on their way out.

"I can stay."

He looks relieved. "Thanks, I owe you one. It's just you, I'm afraid; you're the only person to say yes."

She's alarmed. It could take forever on her own. "You're kidding, right?"

"No, sorry. But just think of the money. It'll only take you an hour or two. Concentrate on picking up all the empty fireworks, would you? I don't want them sparking back into life and burning the place down overnight. Let Ricky clean up the vomit in the morning." He winks at her. "He loves it."

She rolls her eyes. Ricky's never going to let her forget it if she does.

"I'll be over in the office for another ten minutes, but then I've got to shoot. I'll leave the keys in the wheel's ticket booth. Just promise me you'll lock the front gates when you're done."

"But I didn't realize I'd be alone." She's never been here alone in the dark before.

"What's the matter? You're not afraid of ghosts, are you?" he teases.

She suddenly feels stupid. She used to be afraid of ghosts when she was younger, but her mom always says it's the living we need to be afraid of, not the dead. She never understood that properly until a couple of days ago.

"Honestly, you'll be fine. Grab a flashlight if you're worried, but turn off all the lights as you go. Thanks, doll. I owe you one!"

He turns to leave for the office. Nikki rubs her neck, wishing she'd had the confidence to back out. But she's already asked her dad to pick her up, which means he'll be mad if she turns down the opportunity to make some extra cash. She thinks about asking Mason to stay with her but she doesn't want to sound needy.

She finds Mason over by the hot-dog stand with a couple of other staff, and he asks if she's ready to leave.

"I don't need a ride home now. I'm staying to clean up."

He looks surprised. "But you've been here all day."

"I know, but Trevor offered me double pay. I can't turn that down." She doesn't tell him she'll be working alone, as she doesn't want him to feel like he has to stay with her. "And my dad's going to give me a ride home."

He hesitates, and she's touched by his concern.

"Okay. I wish I could stay, but I've got to get up early tomorrow to work for my dad. Sorry." He touches her hand. "Is it still your day off tomorrow?"

She nods.

"Let's catch a movie at the drive-in later on, okay? I'll pick you up at two."

She smiles. She loves going to the drive-in with him, as he treats them to snacks and they get some rare alone time. "Sure. Don't drive all the way to my house, though, remember?" She doesn't want her dad to know she has a boyfriend, and if Mrs. Hicks sees her getting into Mason's car, she'll tell her mom straight away. That woman's such a gossip.

He nods. "Of course. I'll be down the street, undercover." He smiles and kisses her again, with his arms around her.

She doesn't want him to let go. She wants to tell him she loves him, but she can't find the words, not in front of the others.

She waves as he walks away and joins a group of people. Is that Taylor with him? Taylor leans in to say something to him as they head toward the parking lot. He looks at her and laughs. He's going to give her a ride somewhere.

Nikki watches them disappear, consumed with jealousy and fear. How does he know Taylor? She thought they'd never met before.

She fights the overwhelming urge to ditch the cleaning and run after him, to drag him away from that bitch. To run away to New York with him tonight.

Instead, filled with self-doubt, she holds back tears as she grabs some garbage bags.

She can't compete with girls like that.

CHAPTER FORTY-ONE

As Madison passes under the big *Welcome to Fantasy World* arch, lit up in bright neon lights, she feels anonymous in the dark. Normal, even. She's not felt that in a long time. The park isn't packed tonight, not with just over an hour left until closing time, but there are enough people to create a good atmosphere. She only wishes she was here to enjoy herself.

Brody happily follows her and Nate around, and people either stare at him in awe—he's a gorgeous dog, after all—or move out of his way, scared of his size.

They're surrounded by the happy screams of teenagers and the terrified screams of those who thought they could take the ride they picked but now know better. They pass a fortune-telling booth where a severe-looking woman wearing an excess of costume jewelry is glaring at them. *Madame Astrid*, the sign says.

Madison leans in to Nate. "She needs to smile at people if she wants any customers tonight."

Madame Astrid beckons them over. "Want to know if you'll find him?" she says.

Madison stops in her tracks. Has she been recognized already? She could ask the woman what she knows about Mason, but the mean look in her eyes stops her. "Find who?"

The fortune-teller smirks. "The one you seek. I have all the answers."

Madison looks at Nate who shrugs. "Can't hurt."

She walks closer to the woman's booth, which is draped in lace and twinkly lights. She's surprised there's no crystal ball. "Tell me his name and I'll pay for a session."

Madame Astrid laughs. "My vision is made clearer by coins crossing my palm." She pushes her cash tin closer to them.

Madison shakes her head in disgust and walks away, with Nate close behind her.

"You don't believe in psychics?" he asks.

"You do?"

"I'm probably less skeptical than you."

They stop at a shooting gallery, where a young man of about nineteen is scrolling on his phone, only glancing up randomly to look for some new suckers to relieve of their money. When he spots Madison and Nate, he smiles broadly.

"Step right up, folks." He hands Nate a plastic gun. "Here you go, six bullets for five bucks. Shoot the moving target, win the lady a prize." He points to the soft toys behind him: a choice of flamingo or unicorn.

"We actually just wanted to ask you some questions," says Madison.

He looks wary. "I'll answer anything you want as long as you play."

Nate looks at her. "Why not?"

Madison is frustrated that everyone here is more concerned with making money than talking about what's happening in this town. The guy grins at her as Nate takes his first shot, and she wonders how he can be so happy working here. The music is too loud and the bright lights are relentless. She could handle it for one night, but every night of the week? There's no way.

"What's your name?" she asks.

"Luke."

"Luke, am I right in thinking you know Mason McCoy pretty well, seeing as you both work here?"

His smile falters. "I know him, but I wouldn't say I know him well. He's not the most talkative guy. Why do you want to know; you a cop?"

"No." She almost tells him Mason is her son but thinks better of it. She doesn't need that kind of attention right now, because that would be outing him as Owen Harper, son of the famous Lost Creek cop-killer.

"We're private investigators," says Nate, having failed to hit any targets. "We're looking into Nikki Jackson's death and we don't think Mason had anything to do with it. We actually want to find him before the police arrest him."

Luke licks his lips and glances around nervously. "He was working here earlier today, but he left a while ago, I think."

"Could you call him for me?" asks Madison. She feels excited, like she might be just minutes away from speaking to her son for the first time in seven years.

He shakes his head. "I don't have his number. Like I said, he keeps to himself. He's pleasant enough to work with, but I don't know anything about him. He doesn't exactly socialize with any of us, even though he's worked here a couple of months. He's the complete opposite of his parents."

Madison bristles. "What do you mean?"

"You not from here or something?"

"No," says Nate. "We're new in town."

"Well, the McCoys are friendly, social folks; always putting on fundraisers and that kind of thing. My dad used to say they'd give you their last dime if you needed it." He pauses. "But that was before the falling-out."

"Your dad had an argument with the McCoys?" asks Nate.

Luke nods. "Over money, funnily enough. Wyatt McCoy gave my dad a loan a few months back, when we needed a new roof. I don't know what happened, but there's a lot of cursing now when he hears the McCoy name."

Madison can guess what happened: Wyatt's acting as the local loan shark and charging extortionate interest rates to the poorest people, knowing full well they won't be able to repay the money. "Did he ask your dad for any assurances on that loan?"

The look on Luke's face suggests he did, but he clams up. Madison would bet Luke's dad owes Wyatt the family home if he can't pay the loan back. "Goddam asshole," she mutters.

"Did Mason and Nikki ever argue that you know of?" asks Nate.

"Nah, they stuck together like glue and didn't have much time for anyone else. That's why I thought there might be something in that suicide pact theory. They seemed like two tortured souls, so it didn't surprise me when that was brought up as a possibility in the news. Plus, I heard she was seeing a therapist since she was like five years old or something."

Nate says, "But that doesn't mean she wanted to take her own life."

"More likely, though, if you ask me."

"So Mason doesn't have any friends here who might be helping him keep a low profile?" asks Madison.

Luke doesn't even have to think about it. "I highly doubt that."

She has to hide her disappointment as they thank him and walk away. The thought of her son being described as a tortured soul is upsetting so she tries not to dwell on it. "If he isn't at a friend's place, I have no idea where he could be. Angie wouldn't be stupid enough to conceal him on her land someplace."

As they reach the ticket booth for the Wonder Wheel, they see a sign indicating that it's closed. The lights are on but the huge structure is eerily still.

"This is where the girl was found," Madison says. The yellow crime-scene tape means no one can get too close. But there are teenage boys taking selfies in front of it, obviously for social media. She shakes her head at them and they walk away grinning. She spots two girls crying as they light a candle on the ground near the ticket booth, next to some flowers, but as she moves toward them, they scurry away, embarrassed.

Brody, who has been trailing behind Nate and stopping to lick up any spilt food or discarded hot dogs, walks past them and under the barrier for the Haunted House. He vanishes into the darkness.

Madison looks at Nate. "Is he allowed in there?"

He smiles. "Guess he wants to find a ghost. Come on, let's make sure he doesn't scare any kids."

They approach the ticket booth. A girl takes Nate's money and lets them into the house. She doesn't mention Brody, so it looks like he went unnoticed.

Inside the house, it's pitch black and the floor is purposely uneven to make them feel disorientated. Madison can't see Brody because she can't even see her hand in front of her face. Pre-recorded screams erupt all around them, along with random banging on the walls and flashing light displays, trying to scare them into believing the mannequins dressed like monsters are real. It's only when someone runs past her in the darkness that Madison actually screams and turns to Nate, trying not to grab him.

He's laughing. "I didn't think this kind of thing would scare you."

She holds her hands to her chest as she continues through the maze, cursing Brody under her breath. There's only one direction to go in. They climb four steps into a hospital operating room, where an actor has a girl tied to the table. She's screaming for help and it's so convincing that Madison gets as close as she can to check she's not a real victim about to be murdered.

"Hey, lady. Step back would you?" says the doctor. "You're ruining our act."

They continue forward into a room lit by battery-operated candles. She can see Brody ahead of her.

"What's up with him?" asks Nate.

The dog is sitting next to a coffin with his back to them. He looks over his shoulder and barks. Chills run down Madison's spine. He did that when he found Stephanie's blood in the house.

Just then the coffin lid swings open and a mannequin dressed as a vampire springs toward them. It makes her jump, and Nate laughs.

"Brody?" The dog jumps into the open coffin and sniffs the interior. Then he jumps out and barks again. Madison leans forward to see what he's found, mindful that the mannequin is probably about to fall back and the coffin close any minute. She spots a pocket knife. It has something on its blade but she can't tell what, as the lighting in here is too poor. She turns to Nate, who's peering over her shoulder. "It's part of the act, right?"

Brody barks again, louder this time.

Nate pulls out his cell phone and uses the flashlight to examine the knife. "That's a real knife. And Brody can smell blood."

"Shit." Her first thought is: what if it's the knife used to kill Nikki and it has Owen's prints on it? But she can't believe her son had anything to do with his girlfriend's death. The way Luke described their relationship, they were practically joined at the hip. Which means the prints on this knife could actually clear her son as a suspect. She needs to give it to Mike. She doesn't know if she can trust him anymore, but she knows for a fact she can't trust Douglas.

She has no choice. She pulls out her phone.

CHAPTER FORTY-TWO

As Mike walks into the fully lit Haunted House, he sees the cheap facade behind the clever light displays and shadows. The rooms are dingy and dirty and the mannequins all look like they've seen better days. A dog he recognizes from Madison's house approaches him with a ball in its mouth. It doesn't wait for a pat on the head. Instead it turns, leading Mike toward the voices.

When he enters the room, he spots Trevor kneeling on the floor next to a coffin, fiddling with some mechanical device. Madison's talking to a tall guy with brown hair and broad shoulders.

"You must be Nate," he says.

"The one and only." There's no move to shake hands.

"Thanks for coming, Mike," says Madison.

She doesn't smile, and he senses an underlying tension after what happened out at the McCoys' place.

"We've found a knife with remnants of dried blood on it, and because of the Nikki Jackson case I thought you'd want to have it tested for DNA and prints before anyone else stumbles across it." She points to the coffin, where a vampire mannequin is standing glaring at him.

"If I lean in, is this thing going to fall on me?" he asks.

Trevor stands up, screwdriver in hand. "No, I've switched him off."

Mike's a little annoyed that Madison found something his team have been searching for. The officers obviously didn't look everywhere. Maybe the coffin was closed when they came in here, but still, they should have opened it. That's the problem with a small team: not enough staff for a thorough job. He looks at the dog. "Did he find it?"

"Yeah, he's a cadaver dog," says Nate. "He could smell the blood."

Mike raises his eyebrows. "So you're a cop?"

Nate looks disgusted at the suggestion. "No. Brody's previous owner was a cop. I'm an investigator."

A private investigator? Mike suddenly realizes why Madison's been travelling with this guy. She's hired him to look into her case. That pisses him off. Most PIs he's met who weren't cops themselves at some point tend to have a thing against law enforcement, assuming they can do a better job. In Mike's experience, they're more like paid vigilantes. He wonders why Nate and Madison came here tonight; it clearly wasn't to enjoy themselves.

"Let me take a look."

Trevor steps to one side as Mike pulls out a pair of latex gloves and crouches down next to the dog, who makes no attempt to move out of the way. Instead he bites into his ball, which makes a high-pitched squeal right next to Mike's ear. He winces. "None of you have touched the knife, I assume?"

"Of course not," says Madison. "Do you think it's the same knife used on Nikki?"

"Well, if not, it could mean there was another crime committed here at some point. There could be a second victim somewhere."

"Shit, I hope not," says Trevor. "I could really do without more bad press right now."

Madison is peering over Mike's shoulder, and he can tell she's excited to be at a potential crime scene for the first time in a while, but she has no right to any information. "I'll bag it up and give it to forensics."

"Would that be Alex?"

He's surprised. How does she know that? "Yeah. I find him irritating, but you'd probably get on with him."

Madison almost smiles and Mike can tell that Nate's suddenly uncomfortable. He wonders why. Are the two of them screwing each other? Maybe that's how she's paying him.

He uses his cell phone to snap some photos of the knife and its location before turning an evidence bag inside out to pick it up. Then he stands. "Thanks for calling this in. I'll get Alex in to do a sweep of the place."

"No problem," Madison says.

Trevor excuses himself. "I've got to go put out the next fire." At the door, he turns back. "Just do me a favor, Detective: let me know when I can reopen this building to customers, would you? I'm already losing money while the wheel's closed. That was my biggest earner."

Mike nods. "Sure."

When he's gone, Madison steps closer. "Has there been any progress on the guy Douglas was questioning for Steph's murder?"

He sighs. "I really can't tell you that, Madison. You know the drill."

"I'm not asking for his name, but you could at least tell me if he's confessed. I mean, Stephanie was my friend, and let's not forget *I* was considered a suspect at one point. I'd like to know if that ridiculous assumption is off the table now so I can tell my attorney I won't be needing him again."

He knows she's right. "He hasn't confessed, but you're no longer considered a suspect. So if you want to leave town, you're free to do so."

Clearly annoyed, she shakes her head at him. "If you want me to leave town then help me find my son and I'll happily leave tomorrow. *With* Owen."

He tries to hide his irritation. He doesn't like her talking to him this way, especially in front of the PI. "I'm not going to argue with you, Madison; it's getting late and I've had a really long day. I'm glad you called me about this," he waves the knife, "but I've got to go. Nice meeting you." He nods to Nate.

As he walks out of the Haunted House, he finds himself wishing Madison would just leave town already. She's causing more trouble than she knows.

CHAPTER FORTY-THREE

Angie's sitting on the porch with her morning coffee, watching the horses frolic in the paddock as the sun rises above them. There's a chill in the air and she's struggling to wake up after a bad night's sleep. Trying to relax, she focuses on the birdsong and the horses gently neighing, but it's spoiled by the tinny echo of the radio in the repair shop, along with the staff's crude laughter and the sound of the car crusher sporadically grinding steel and shattering glass.

She sighs in frustration. She never gets any peace around here. What she'd give for another woman in the family, someone to empathize with her. Someone to complain to. Not for the first time, she resents not being able to get pregnant. She would have loved a daughter.

Wyatt approaches and takes a seat in the wicker rocking chair next to hers. He places his coffee on the small table and removes his dirty baseball cap to wipe the sweat from his brow. He's been working since the crack of dawn. If she were him, she'd leave the real work to the staff and enjoy the fruits of their other business. But she's glad he doesn't. It's bad enough having him close by every day, but actually *in* the house? They would have killed each other by now.

He was impressed that she'd got Mason out of the way before the cops—or Madison—could track him down. But he pointed out that it wasn't an adequate long-term solution to the mess the boy had got himself into. She had to agree.

Before they can discuss it again, she hears footsteps on the graveled driveway. She looks up and is shocked to see Mason walking toward them.

She stands up. "What do you think you're doing here? You're supposed to stay in hiding." She looks around to see if they're being watched. No one can see them on this side of the house, unless one of the guys from the scrapyard comes looking for Wyatt, but she knows they'd keep their mouths shut.

Mason climbs the steps to the faded wooden porch and leans against the railing. Wyatt says nothing, but he's watching his son with a hard stare. She doesn't think Mason realizes how bad this could be.

"I don't want to live in hiding," he says. "I haven't done anything wrong."

She rolls her eyes. "That's not the point, for God's sake! The cops are going to try to pin that girl's death on you. What part of that don't you understand?"

He looks like he didn't sleep a wink last night either, and she feels for him, but she's trying to protect him.

"She's not 'that girl'; she was my girlfriend. I want to explain myself to the cops, to stop the media making me out to be a murderer." He nervously looks at his dad.

Wyatt laughs, but it's not jovial. "Are all teenagers this goddam stupid, or is it just you?"

Mason looks away. "I'm not being stupid. It's called doing the right thing. I'm going to speak to the police. I've seen what that reporter's been telling people about me on the news."

"You mean you would seriously have us risk all this?" Wyatt motions to the property. "I'm telling you now, Mason McCoy, you need to do what we say and lie low until they close the case. That girl killed herself, it's obvious, so the fact that they want to speak to you about it tells me they're up to no good. They want to use her death as a motive to get a search warrant for my property and my businesses. You know what can of worms that would open?"

Mason's face is red with pent-up anger. "If you had nothing to hide, they wouldn't be after you. That's on you, not me."

Angie shakes her head. Challenging his father like this is going to end—at best—in tears. But she can't help feeling this conversation is long overdue. She steps between them, as it's undoubtedly going to get ugly.

Wyatt stands up. He's four inches shorter than Mason but about ten times meaner. "It's time to pick a lane. We've been too lenient until now. You need to quit that shitty job of yours at the park, stop dreaming that you're going to be a goddam lawyer of all things and help me run this place full-time instead. Maybe if you prove your loyalty I'll let you help with the other side of things too."

Angie knows this is Wyatt's last-ditch attempt at keeping Mason with them. He wants his son to stay forever; he wants someone to leave all this to when he retires. He wants the McCoy name to continue long into the future. But if Mason chooses wrong now, Wyatt won't give him another chance. Despite everything, Wyatt loves his son, but he can't understand how the two of them are so different. Angie knows it's because Mason spent longer with his mother. Madison has clearly rubbed off on him, despite their attempts at making him a McCoy.

Mason's shaking his head and his eyes are wild, but he doesn't speak. Angie can tell he's considering his options. He takes a step toward his father, making her catch her breath. He's not the kind of kid to stand up to a bully. Wyatt would have him on the ground in seconds.

She pulls on his arm. "Help me in the kitchen for a second, would you?"

"That's right. Go help your momma clean dishes like a good little girl."

"Screw you!" shouts Mason. "You don't even care what I'm going through! My girlfriend *died*. She was…" He stops as if realizing there's no point trying to explain her qualities to his dad. He's right, Wyatt doesn't care. "Nikki was worth ten of you, you asshole. We were going to leave this dump. We were going to escape both of you!" He looks at her. "And now it's ruined."

Wyatt glares at him and Angie can tell he's as surprised by the outburst as she is. Then he lunges forward and her heart jumps into her mouth.

"Wyatt, he's just a kid. Leave him alone."

Wyatt's eyes are mean. "You thought some tramp was going to save you from your family? Let me be real clear, boy: your choices in life are limited. You either work for me or you're on your own. I won't pay a red cent toward you from this day onwards. You won't be able to afford to finish high school, never mind go to college, and I'll make sure no employer in Colorado will hire you. Not even Taco fucking Bell. You'll be blacklisted, just like your bitch of a mother."

Mason gasps.

"So go make out with your little high-school girls and find out if love pays the bills." Wyatt picks up his coffee cup. "Now you better get out of my sight before I whip your ass."

Mason's eyes are red but he's never looked more like his father. He looks like he could kill right now. "Don't you dare talk about my mother like that." Tears are threatening to spill from Mason's eyes. He pushes past Angie and heads into the house.

CHAPTER FORTY-FOUR

Angie hears Wyatt laughing as she follows Mason inside, up to his bedroom. She's worried that if he leaves now, she'll never see him again. He pulls out a large sports bag and starts stuffing it with clothes. Then he fills his backpack with his laptop and more expensive items.

"Mason, please don't go. You can't leave me with him. Not like this."

He spins around and she stops dead in her tracks, worried he's going to hit her, completing the transformation into his father.

"I want out of here, for good!" he yells.

"Please, just calm down."

He's breathing hard and returns to pulling things out of drawers, but more slowly now. She thinks he's listening. There could still be hope.

"Don't do anything rash. You have to believe him when he says he'll cut you off. You can't do anything in this country without money, Mason. You know that. Why do you think I stay with him?"

He turns to face her, calmer now. "Because you're as bad as each other."

She takes a step back, his words like a slap to the face.

Mason appears instantly regretful. "Why is he like this? If he didn't want me living with him, I could have lived with Stephanie!"

Anger bubbles in her chest at the thought of Mason going to live with that woman. He was devastated when he read about her recent death. He disappeared all day and wouldn't talk to her about it when he returned. It was only the next day that she was able to explain to him that Stephanie Garcia was more than likely murdered by someone who worked for his mother; someone Madison had paid to kill her. He couldn't argue with the fact that if his mother could kill a police officer, she was capable of killing anyone.

She thinks about Madison being back in town. If Mason finds out, he'll undoubtedly want to see her. When he first came to live with them, his mom was all he ever talked about. Her and Stephanie. He couldn't understand why he couldn't see them anymore, so Wyatt explained what Madison had done, even though the social worker had told him not to. She had said it would have serious consequences for his mental health to know at that age that his mother was a killer. But they had to get him to stop asking after her and to move on with his new life with them.

He didn't believe them for the longest time. He said his mother would never have hurt Officer Levy because they were friends. After Madison was convicted, and child services had approved him living with them, he stopped asking after her. He finally accepted he had to live with his dad, and things slowly got better. They settled into their new routine and it was like he'd always lived with them.

She has put so much into raising Mason that it feels like he's her own son. The home-schooling, which she's in charge of, has given them what she always thought was a special bond. Having him live with them has distracted her from her own inability to have children. He's given her life purpose and she's been able to overlook the underlying reality that he's her sister's son. But as she looks at him now, a teenager on the cusp of adulthood, she wonders whether he ever really gave up on his mom.

Anger swells in her chest as she realizes he'd welcome Madison back with open arms, which means that everything she's done for him over the last seven years has been unappreciated. This is exactly why they changed his name from Owen Harper to Mason McCoy. It's why they took him out of the school system and never told anyone who his mother was. So Madison wouldn't find him.

As far as she can tell, Mason doesn't know she was released from prison early. He hasn't asked about her for years and she never told him which prison Madison was in. He thinks she still has just over three years left to serve. She can't help wondering how he would react if he knew she was back in Lost Creek. A bitter taste rises in her throat.

"Your father does want you here, Mason. He's just bitterly disappointed that you're thinking of moving on and not staying with us. You're his *son*. He really wants you to take over the business one day."

He's shaking his head. "No way. I want nothing to do with him. And I still find it hard to believe my mother ever slept with that asshole."

He's confirming her worst fears. He's not showing one ounce of gratitude for the life they've given him. Her heart hardens against him. He's turning his back on them and for that she can't forgive him. "Then you need to leave. You're not welcome here anymore."

He looks at her, first surprised and then resolute. He zips his bag closed, shoulders his backpack, and makes for the door. She clutches his arm as he passes.

"Let me give you some final advice before you go back to being a Harper. If you speak to the police about anything—your girlfriend, our businesses, us—you'll be considered an enemy."

He looks afraid, and rightly so.

She drops his arm. "I'll give you a head start before I tell Wyatt what you've just said, but you do not want to be in Colorado when he finds out."

Mason stands up straight. "He's my dad. He wouldn't hurt me." He searches her face for reassurance. When he doesn't find it, he turns and walks out.

Angie watches from the window as he throws his bags into his car and drives away. She feels defeated. She loved him like her own, believing he would repay her kindness. She should have known he would always pick his mother. The only consolation is that he's leaving town before Madison can find him.

CHAPTER FORTY-FIVE

Madison's showered and dressed before Nate. She heads to the living room with a bowl of cereal and watches the TV as she eats. It's another bright start to the day. Her mind wanders to what Mike's probably doing right now with the knife. She'd love to be a fly on the wall when he finds out whether it was Nikki's blood on it, and who the prints belong to. She just has to hope he'll tell her, seeing as she gave it to him. At least it should settle whether or not Nikki was murdered. How else would the knife make it all the way into the Haunted House after she supposedly slit her own wrists on the Wonder Wheel?

Brody is panting on the floor at her feet. He's already been out this morning to check the property for potential threats. She smiles. He's missing police work too. She glances at her cell phone: no messages.

Nate walks in with a coffee. "Hey." He rubs Brody's head and sits on the couch.

"Hey." She puts her bowl on the side table and glances at him. "Did you manage to get any sleep?" He looks a little tired and is still in his sweats.

"I did. That bed's surprisingly comfortable. It's just a shame I have to share it with a dog."

Madison smiles. "I wondered where he was sleeping."

Nate looks at the TV. "Turn it up."

The local news is showing an aerial shot of the park, taken by either a drone or a helicopter. Madison turns the volume up and

Kate appears on the screen. It looks like she's not been allowed in, as she's in the parking lot with the rides standing empty and motionless behind her.

"Good morning, folks. There have been some significant developments in two ongoing police investigations overnight. Firstly, Detective Don Douglas has confirmed that a forty-year-old man from Prospect Springs has been arrested and charged with the recent rape and brutal murder of local woman Stephanie Garcia. The suspect's name is being withheld at this time, but his lawyer has said his client denies any involvement."

Madison looks at Nate. "Mike didn't tell me they'd charged the guy. They must have something on him. Some evidence that he killed Stephanie." She grabs her phone. "I need to know his name so I can see why he was looking for me and whether I know him."

She shoots Shelley a text.

"Who are you asking?" says Nate.

"Officer Shelley Vickers, a friend in LCPD. She passed me some inside information on Steph's crime scene that day you went AWOL. Hopefully she'll give me a name."

They turn back to the TV, where Kate's still talking. "And secondly, unconfirmed sources have suggested that a bloodstained knife was found here at Fantasy World last night, but not near the Ferris wheel. It has been taken away for forensic analysis and it might be linked to Nikki Jackson's death. If this is the knife that was used, it would of course be extremely worrying for the community, as it would confirm once and for all that she was murdered. And with it happening so close to the slaying of Stephanie Garcia, it could suggest we have a serial killer in our midst. So the question now is: do the police have the right person in custody?"

Madison's surprised. "I can't believe Kate's made the leap to serial killer. There's nothing to suggest that."

"No, but it's good for ratings, I guess. Keeps people tuned in."

She shakes her head. "You know, if I hadn't have gone to prison, I'd be there right now looking into it." She sips her coffee. "I'd give anything to be working that case properly."

She keeps going over things in her head, thinking about the fact that her son has been in town all along, with that despicable couple taking care of him. She tries to imagine what it would have been like for Owen as a scared and sensitive ten-year-old boy being brought up as a McCoy.

She shudders. Why did child services allow him to live with them? But, having worked alongside the department many times, she already knows the answer. When a child is removed from a parent, they will always try to place them with a family member before considering fostering or adoption. And unfortunately, Wyatt is his biological father. He has every right, legally, to take Owen in. But no right morally.

She could cry. There have been so many injustices that have led up to this.

Her attention shifts to Brody, who's sniffing around the rug on the floor. He gets his nose underneath it and whines.

"I can smell it again too," says Nate, looking at her. "Can you?"

She hadn't noticed it before, but now that Brody's shifted the rug, there is a faint aroma of dried blood in the room. She's overcome with a feeling of hopelessness. "I can't get over the fact that Stephanie never told me Owen was in town all along. If I'd known that, I would have come straight here after my release instead of heading to California to track you down. I've wasted so much time."

"Your sister's husband must have threatened her into keeping quiet. I'm getting the impression they're pretty influential around here, so they could have scared her."

Madison has considered that. "It would make sense, I guess.' She shakes her head, feeling guilty all over again. "God, I bet she wished she'd never met me."

Nate touches her hand. "Don't go down that road. Trust me, I'm still there with Stacey and we don't need any company."

She smiles sadly. "We're pretty screwed up, aren't we?"

He laughs. "It's a good job we have each other to complain to. No one else would believe the shit we've been through, never mind put up with us."

"Have you heard from Father Connor lately?" She remembers how badly Nate reacted to the priest's emails he received when they were working on their last case in California.

"Nothing. The trail's gone quiet. Rex doesn't know where he is at the moment."

"And Rex hasn't got back to you with background information on Ryan's dad or anyone at LCPD?"

He checks his phone. "Not yet. He's pretty thorough, so it might take a little while longer. The minute he knows anything, he'll call."

She's quiet for a minute, then she stands up. "I can't sit around here waiting for Mike to update me or for Douglas to drag Owen in and frame him for murder. We need to try and find him ourselves."

Nate looks unsure, but to his credit, he nods.

CHAPTER FORTY-SIX

Mike removes his jacket even though it's still early morning. He's got another throbbing headache threatening to ruin his day. Chief Sullivan has joined him at Fantasy World, as he wants the speculation and press coverage around Nikki's death to end as soon as possible. He's got the DA on his back pushing for an explanation. Five of their officers are searching the park. Detective Douglas is back at the station interviewing Paul Harris again about Stephanie Garcia's murder.

Sullivan approaches him. "The whole park's secure and the uniforms have been instructed to do a proper search this time. We may have the knife, but whoever put it there might have dropped something else—a shirt, a glove, I don't know. Just something to help us identify him." He lights a cigarette and takes a long drag. "I can't believe this place doesn't have security cameras. Apparently some of the staff have dash cams in their cars, so I've got Officer Vickers calling round and getting them to drop their footage at the station. You never know, we might get lucky and spot someone arriving as people were driving away that night."

Mike nods. "The nearby gas stations will have surveillance cameras. I'll get an officer to go check those out."

"You said Dr. Scott gave Nikki's time of death as between midnight and two a.m., so there shouldn't have been many people about at that time of night. If necessary, I want you to identify the owner of every vehicle picked up on CCTV."

Mike tries not to sigh at the thought of such a labor-intensive job. "Where's Alex?"

"He's back at the station analyzing the knife. Dr. Scott is performing a second autopsy on the girl's body this morning, this time with a view to it being a homicide."

"It could still be a suicide, you know."

Sullivan shakes his head. "How do you explain the knife being found in the Haunted House if it was a suicide?"

Mike thinks about it. "Maybe Ricky Gregor panicked after finding her and hid it in there. I don't know. I've not been able to track him down, even now I know his real name."

"Why haven't we brought Mason McCoy in yet?"

"I visited his place last night, but he wasn't there. Angie said he was camping. There's a BOLO out for him, so it shouldn't be long before he's spotted."

Chief Sullivan shakes his head. "My money's on him. I mean, she asked him to meet her here. We find him, we find out what happened that night. And we need his prints to see if they match the print on the girl's face." He pauses, as if deciding whether to start pushing further. "You know what? I'll get a search warrant for Angie and Wyatt's cell phones and their premises. They could be hiding him."

Mike remains silent.

After another drag of his cigarette, Sullivan stares at him. "You're not afraid of the McCoys, are you, Mike?"

Mike raises his eyebrows. He knows what kind of upset that will create in the community. The couple have a lot of friends in both Gold Rock and Lost Creek, though they're mostly paid friends, or people under their control.

"Because I don't need cops on my team who are afraid of criminals," continues Sullivan. "You understand me?"

There's a lot Mike could say, but he bites his tongue. "I'm not afraid of them. But you know as well as I do that they play dirty. If we search their premises it's going to start a shit show. Are you ready to see who they have in their pockets, Chief? Who really controls this town?"

Chief Sullivan looks away, and Mike thinks he's considering whether this is a battle he wants to start, especially so close to his retirement. "I'm ready. It's time Wyatt McCoy was taken down a peg or two."

Mike's impressed. Chief Sullivan is taking this seriously. But that also makes him nervous.

After Sullivan instructs Mike and Douglas to haul the McCoy boy in, Mike drives them to Gold Rock. They're followed by two cruisers, silent with no flashing lights. They're going to try to do this without drawing too much attention.

A red Ford Mustang speeds past him on the opposite side of the road, going way too fast toward Lost Creek. "Asshole." Brad Skelton. Someone else Mike can't stand. He has an attitude problem as well as six arrests for drug offenses. Plus he works for the McCoy family, although Mike has never been sure what exactly it is he does for them. He doesn't know what most of Wyatt's employees do other than stand around pretending to fix cars. It's probably better he remains ignorant.

He pulls up to the McCoys' ranch and looks around before getting out, but it's so bright the sun is bouncing off the windows, making him look away. He hears a horse whickering to the left, but that's not as loud as the male voices singing along to eighties rock music in the auto repair shop to the right of the house.

They both get out the car and Mike glances into the workshop as they pass. Two men are under separate vehicles, banging away, so he goes unnoticed. Douglas continues on to the scrapyard just beyond, presumably getting a feel for who's around, just in case things take a turn for the worse.

Mike's always amazed by the number of cars spread over the site. They're all in various states of disrepair, with parts missing or obvious signs of collision. There's a huge scrap-metal weighing scale in the middle of the yard, but no staff anywhere. A sudden loud crunching and smashing sound makes them look to their right as a car is compressed in the huge metal crusher at the rear of the yard.

By the time they reach the front of the house, they've been spotted. Wyatt opens the front door with Angie behind him.

Mike slowly climbs the porch steps, followed by Douglas. The uniforms behind them keep their distance.

"Morning," he says. They don't respond. "Is Mason here?"

"Nope," says Wyatt. "We told you he's gone camping. Haven't been able to get a hold of him. Reckon he could be gone for a week."

Mike leans against the porch, trying to keep it casual, but Angie's looking past him to the cruisers. "Mind if we come in and check his bedroom?" he asks.

"I do mind, actually," says Wyatt. "I think we'll wait for a warrant."

Douglas pulls out the arrest warrant for Mason. "We need to check if he's inside, then we'll be on our way."

Angie looks like she's biting her tongue.

Douglas brushes past her and the uniforms follow. Mike stays outside to keep an eye on the McCoys. Out of the corner of his eye he spots Brad Skelton arriving. He must have turned around when he spotted the cruisers. A few other guys who work for Wyatt have come out from the scrapyard to see what's going on, but they keep their distance. At the moment they're just smoking and shooting the shit. Everything appears relaxed, but there's always an underlying tension bubbling away at this place and Mike can't wait to get out of here.

"It will be worse for Mason if he's brought in by one of our officers," he says. "There's a BOLO out for him, so it's just a matter of time. In the meantime, we'll be contacting his friends and visiting the places he liked to hang out. If he wants to explain himself before anyone else has their say, he needs to get in touch asap."

Neither Angie nor Wyatt responds. They just stare at him until Douglas returns.

"Mr. and Mrs. McCoy, if Mason returns home, I suggest you ask him to turn himself in," says Douglas. "If he wasn't involved in his girlfriend's death, he won't be charged."

Angie laughs. "What on earth could you charge him with anyway? The girl killed herself. There's no crime there."

Mike speaks up. "We have reason to believe it wasn't suicide."

"So what was it then?"

"You'll find out when we charge your son," hisses Douglas.

Mike wishes the guy would keep his cool. He always goes in all guns blazing and it's not going to work here.

Angie steps forward. "You need to get off our property." She's clearly fuming. She looks at Mike. "Both of you."

Douglas turns to leave, but then looks back at them. "You could help us discount your son as a suspect, you know. You could start by telling us where Mason was between midnight and two a.m. on July fourth?"

Angie doesn't hesitate. "He worked until around eleven, arrived home at eleven twenty and then joined us for the end of our party. We were all here together celebrating. Even had a firework show."

"Is there anyone other than your husband who can corroborate that?"

She gives him a deathly stare and then calls Brad over. "Hey, Brad, do you remember seeing Mason at midnight on July fourth? We were all celebrating together here with a BBQ, weren't we?"

Brad smiles widely. "Sure we were. It was a good night. God bless America."

Angie and Wyatt laugh and Mike knows it's winding Douglas up.

"Madison Harper's back in town," says Angie. "Maybe it was her. Have you asked where *she* was that night? I mean, she's a convicted cop-killer and then her ex-girlfriend dies around the time she shows up. She might have got a taste for blood. Maybe she's the serial killer they're talking about on the news."

Feeling disgusted that she'd implicate her own sister, Mike says, "We've already arrested someone for Stephanie Garcia's murder. It wasn't Madison."

Both Angie and Wyatt look surprised.

Douglas turns and walks to the car.

When he's gone, Wyatt says, "You need to remember who pays your wages, Detective Bowers. You cops work for us, so you don't want to upset the locals. You should make your friend aware of that. He clearly doesn't understand how things work around here."

Mike feels his face flush with anger. He's grown to hate this couple. "If you really want to protect Mason, you'll bring him to me before we drag him in."

He walks away with a feeling of dread building in his chest. He just knows something bad is coming.

CHAPTER FORTY-SEVEN

Owen Harper is about to do something stupid. He knows it, but he has to do it anyway. He takes a shot of bourbon straight from the bottle and wipes his mouth on his sleeve, just like his father would. He winces as it burns his throat. He doesn't even like the taste, but he needs all the courage he can get. This last week has been the worst time in his life since his mother's arrest, and he can see no way out that doesn't involve some kind of pain.

He sits in his car near the railroad tracks, watching a train speed by. It's so fast you wouldn't even feel it if you happened to get in front of one. You'd be dead before your body hit the ground. It would be a shame for the train driver, but they probably have access to therapy through a company scheme. Not that therapy ever worked for Owen.

He takes another swig from the bottle and tries to weigh up his options. He truly feels like he has none. He's barely holding his shit together and he can't stop thinking about Nikki and the way her life ended so unexpectedly.

He pulls his cell phone out and looks at the photos he took of her sitting on the hood of his car just hours before she died. She was funny, complicated and beautiful. Which is why it's hard to understand why she was so unsure of herself, so self-conscious. It was her head playing tricks on her, but she wouldn't believe him. Nikki was the best thing that ever happened in his shitty life. She was way more beneficial than his therapy sessions. It's not just because he can't tell her now that she's dead, but he knows he was in love with her. They understood each other because they both came from screwed-up families.

Nikki tried to introduce him to her mom once, when they bumped into her in the grocery store. Not as his boyfriend, though, as she didn't want her parents knowing she was dating. Her mother cast a critical look over him with cold eyes, judging his appearance, then just walked off. Nikki was mortified. She kept apologizing to him, but he knows she's not responsible for her mom's actions. Parents can be the worst. That's why he never had any plans to introduce Nikki to his dad and Angie.

He's always resented them. They talked so poorly of his mother, never waiting until he was out of the room, preferring that he heard. He can't be the son his dad wants. Mainly because he hates him. Wyatt McCoy is a bully and a criminal and there's no way Owen would ever work for the real family business.

His feelings about Angie aren't so black-and-white. Even though she's not his mother, she does have a maternal side, more so when he was younger. She took him to see the Thanksgiving and Christmas parades in Prospect Springs every year without fail until he outgrew them. And whenever he was sick, she'd put him under a duvet on the couch while she fed him chicken soup and ice cream and checked his temperature every hour, which always reminded him of his real mom. Probably because he remembers being unwell the night she was arrested, which was the last night he ever lived with her.

But despite Angie's attempts at mothering him, he's also seen a darker side to her. She has a ruthlessness that's more concerning than anything his dad has ever done.

Together they're a dangerous combination, and the closer he gets to turning eighteen, the more he realizes that if he doesn't give up on his plan of going to college to study law, his dad and Angie will make his life hell.

Not for the first time, he wishes he could visit his mother in prison. He needs to hear from her what happened to Officer Levy. Angie is adamant she was guilty. She says his mom was ten times worse than her when it came to her temper—a family trait—but he doesn't remember that about her. He shakes his head. His memories of life before her arrest are so hazy. He wishes he could recall more.

He probably remembers Stephanie better. He would see her around Lost Creek sometimes, but she would never speak to him. If he was alone, she'd wave, but she wouldn't come over. He'd asked Angie why and she said the woman probably hated him because he reminded her of his mom and what she'd done. That left him devastated and was one of the reasons why he had to start therapy. He couldn't understand why he was being blamed for what his mom had done. It made him retreat into himself and avoid ever getting close to people.

He has few friends, even now. As soon as Nikki died, he deleted his Facebook account because he was getting trolled. People accused him of driving her crazy, of having a stupid suicide pact. He couldn't handle it.

When Angie pulled him out of school and changed his name so that people would stop connecting him with his mother, it confused him. Whether or not they were related to him by blood, Wyatt and Angie were strangers to him. The McCoy name meant nothing, so to suddenly be told it was his new identity messed him up. His social worker recommended he attend therapy, but his dad was dead set against it until threatened with a visit from the social worker's manager.

Owen shakes his head and sighs at how messed up his life has been.

The worst part is that his mom has never once tried contacting him over the years. Early on, he found out that inmates were allowed to make phone calls and send letters, so he waited patiently. Angie told him she'd given their address to the prison so his mom would know where he was, and he wrote her plenty of letters for Angie to post, but he never received one response. He has to assume she's not interested in how his life turned out. He lost his mom and now he's lost his girlfriend. There's nothing else left to lose.

Which makes his decision easier.

CHAPTER FORTY-EIGHT

Madison's feeling defeated. She's slumped in the passenger seat of Nate's car while he drives them around town looking for places that would attract a seventeen-year-old boy. The thought that Douglas is eager to charge her son with the murder of Nikki Jackson fills her with dread. What's more terrifying is the thought that living with Angie and Wyatt might have turned him into someone who is capable of that. Does he enjoy living with his father? Has he discovered that they're similar?

She shakes the thought from her head. She has to believe he's nothing like Wyatt. That's not how she's been picturing him all these years. If she finds out he is, she doesn't know how she'll cope. "I just need to see him for myself," she mutters.

Nate glances at her. "You need to be checking out everyone we pass," he says. "Stay alert."

She's trying, but it's hard to concentrate. "What's the point? I'm not going to recognize him after all this time. I have absolutely no idea what my son looks like now. Do you know how that feels?"

"Madison, focus," says Nate. "We need to find him before Douglas gets to him. There'll be plenty of time for emotion later."

She looks at him and can tell he's as worried as she is that Owen will end up serving time for something he didn't do. She's lucky to have met Nate, but he must be getting sick of her problems. "You're right, I know. But I have no idea where he could be."

Nate's phone rings. When he answers, she hears Rex's booming voice.

"We're a bit busy at the moment, Rex," says Nate. "Now's not a good time."

She touches his arm and whispers, "It's fine."

"Scrap that. What have you got?" Nate pulls over and puts him on speakerphone.

"I can't get any dirt on Davis Levy. No criminal record as far as I can tell. Nothing bad in the press other than his son's death and a few arguments with disgruntled customers at the shooting range he owns." He pauses. "About their son's murder… I read that Officer Levy was shot dead, which means I finally found out who your new friend is. Thanks for the heads-up."

Nate looks uncomfortable. "Sorry, I was going to tell you next time I visited. I was planning on bringing Madison with me so you could meet her for yourself."

She feels tears building, but not because Rex knows she was convicted of Ryan's murder. It's because Nate isn't planning to ditch her and her problems anytime soon.

"She was wrongfully convicted, like you and me," he clarifies. "That's why we're here: to find out who framed her."

Rex is quiet while he digests the information. "Okay. In that case, I need to step things up a gear. So: the Levys have no financial problems or bad debt. But I'm only going by their names and address. If you get me their dates of birth or social security numbers, I can delve deeper."

Nate looks at Madison again. She shakes her head. She doesn't really suspect Davis of hurting his own son. His reaction to her in the grocery store was that of a devastated father.

"Hold off on that for now," says Nate. "How about the cops?"

"I've tracked someone down who might've known Don Douglas when he worked in Prospect Springs—heard of it?"

Madison sits up and leans forward. "Hey, Rex. Prospect Springs is the nearest large town to Lost Creek. It's about a two-hour drive away."

"Right. Well, my contact seems to think he's heard of your guy. Is he black, mid forties, about six feet tall?"

Her heart starts racing. "That's him."

"Okay. Well leave it with me and I'll do some digging while I wait for my guy to get back to me."

Nate speaks up. "Thanks, Rex. As always, we owe you one."

Rex laughs. "You owe me more than one, my friend. And I'll want all the gory details about your wrongful conviction when we meet, Madison."

She smiles. "You got it."

Nate leans back as he ends the call.

"You know what's going to happen, don't you?" she says.

"What?"

"I bet Douglas left his previous job due to an internal affairs investigation. He probably did something shady and they told him to move on or risk being exposed by the press. I bet he's been hiding something all this time. If Rex finds out it involved another cop, it could mean he's the best suspect for Ryan's murder."

Nate appears to think about it. "Did he and Ryan get along?"

She shakes her head. "They had no relationship at all as far as I know. Bear in mind we only worked with Douglas for a few months before Ryan was killed."

Nate looks reinvigorated. She knows what he's thinking before he even says it, because his hatred of bent cops is still strong—and rightly so after he discovered the detective who arrested him for his fiancée's murder was working for Father Connor. The police in Texas effectively helped frame him for murder and she knows he'll never forgive them for it.

"If Douglas was responsible, we need to make sure he gets prison time, Madison. We can't let him get away with what he's done. And we can't let him get to Owen before us."

He starts the car and pulls away so fast Madison thinks her neck is going to snap.

CHAPTER FORTY-NINE

Mike and Douglas return to the station after lunch. Before Mike even makes it to his desk, he's accosted by Alex.

"Do you have a minute, Detective? It's urgent."

He nods and notices Douglas rushing straight back out the door. Turning to Stella from dispatch he says, "Where's he going?"

"We had a call to say Mason McCoy's been spotted. He's checking it out. Officer Greenburg's meeting him there as backup."

Mike rubs his face. He's still worried about the implications of blaming this on Mason. He follows Alex to his office. "Any tox results from Lena yet?"

"Yes, we just got them. There were no drugs in Nikki's system other than a daily dose of prescribed antidepressants. No alcohol either."

So she didn't try to overdose or to numb the pain of slitting her wrists.

Chief Sullivan is already in Alex's office when they arrive. Alex sits in his expensive-looking ergonomic chair and pulls out a couple of sheets of paper. He pushes his glasses up his nose. Mike can tell he's excited about something.

"Okay, so the blood on Nikki Jackson's face is definitely all hers. The thumbprint on her forehead—which was a partial, remember—is a match for a print found on the knife from the Haunted House."

Mike nods. "Good. We're getting somewhere. Did you run them through the database?"

"Of course. No match. And before you ask, they're not Nikki's either."

Not so good. "Are Nikki's prints on the knife at all?"

"No."

Chief Sullivan sits up straight and looks at him. "So we can rule out suicide."

Mike nods. "I take it they don't match the prints you lifted from Ricky Gregor's ID badge either?"

"That's right, they don't," says Alex.

So they can eliminate Ricky as a suspect. Mike looks at the chief. "We'll take Mason McCoy's prints as soon as we bring him in, but in the meantime, I want to check the prints against Mr. Jackson's."

Chief Sullivan raises his eyebrows. "You think our victim's father could have killed her?"

"It's a possibility. I mean, he was supposed to collect her from the park, but he says he blacked out on the couch. Mrs. Jackson was asleep, so there was an opportunity where he could have gone to the park, killed Nikki, and got home all before his wife noticed he was gone. And he wouldn't let me search his house for the knife."

Sullivan's thinking about it. "But the knife wasn't found there and I'm guessing no one's pointing the finger at him, so what's our reason for bringing him in?"

"You mean apart from the fact that the guy's an asshole who treated his daughter like shit?"

Alex chimes in. "Come on, Detective. We all know you could say that about half the parents out there."

Mike stares. "Is that a dig at me?"

Alex looks confused. "What? No, not at all. Sorry, it was just an observation based on the kind of people we arrest."

There's an awkward silence. Mike thinks of his daughter, and how she's counting on him not to let her down this weekend. Maybe he's being too sensitive.

"Anyway," Alex continues, "I also found the same prints on the controls of the Ferris wheel *and* on the safety bar of the car that Nikki was found in. Now, each car's safety bar snaps down automatically once the ride is in motion. But to get *off* the ride, you need to lift the bar up yourself. And if you look at the position of these prints…" He picks up an iPad and shows them an enlarged image of the fingerprints illuminated on the metal bar. "You'll see they're pointing inwards, not outwards. In other words, whoever left these prints lifted the bar whilst standing outside the car, and therefore they weren't sitting with Nikki. The safety bar was in the open position when we arrived. I assumed the maintenance guy lifted it when he found her, but we can rule that out now we know his prints don't match these."

Mike nods. "According to the owner, Ricky insisted he didn't touch a thing when he found her. Looks like he was telling the truth."

Alex continues. "That amusement park will get hundreds of visitors every day and you can bet a lot of those people would have a spin on the Ferris wheel, but with only one set of prints found, it looks as if someone wiped the whole car clean, then went back for some reason and forgot to wipe his prints the second time, including from the knife."

"Maybe because he was interrupted?" says Sullivan. "Or maybe he had an accomplice, and these are their prints."

Mike takes a second to think about it. Finally he says, "And there's no way of knowing what order the killer did things in?"

"Oh, there's a way of knowing," says Alex. "It's called CCTV. But obviously there were no surveillance cameras at the park."

Mike shakes his head. Damn, this guy's annoying.

"The other thing is that I've had the results back from the state lab about the fibers and hair samples I took from Nikki's sweater. The fibers are navy and aren't from Nikki's clothes. I took them from the left sleeve of her sweater, so they might belong to whoever was sitting next to her at some point that day, either on the Ferris wheel or at work, or it could belong to one of her parents if they sat together for breakfast. The hair turned out to be animal, maybe a dog, as it was thicker than human hair. Do you know if she had a dog?"

Mike thinks of her home. There were no signs of a dog there; no water bowl or chew toys. He shakes his head. "Don't think so."

"Well, it could've been picked up from any pet owner who rode the wheel that day, or maybe she petted a dog. I wouldn't call it significant evidence in this case. Not unless it turns out she was killed by an animal, anyway."

They ignore his attempt at humor.

Mike checks his phone out of habit. "Okay, let me know if you find anything else."

He heads out of the station for some air and feels raindrops on his face. He loosens his tie, but it's not just the heat making him sweat. He pops two headache pills and rubs his forehead. It's going to be another long day.

CHAPTER FIFTY

Owen checks his watch. He has about two minutes before the next train speeds by. He takes one more slug of bourbon, starts the car's engine and looks up the tracks, waiting. Rain suddenly splatters on his windshield, so he switches the wipers on and rolls down the passenger window, giving him a clear view of the tracks.

He hears the train's horn off in the distance. It's coming. He turns the radio up loud but doesn't recognize the rock song he's going to die to. He revs the engine, keeping his foot on the brake for now. His mom's face flashes before him, followed by Nikki's. When the train appears, his sweaty hands grip the steering wheel and his body is flooded with adrenaline. It's now or never.

Just before he can accelerate and end his shitty life, a police cruiser with its lights blazing skids in front of his car, blocking him from the tracks.

He looks up in a daze as the train goes speeding by. He should be dead right now.

He watches in the rear-view mirror as a black sedan grinds to a halt behind his car, blocking him in. The guy who arrested his mother all those years ago is approaching his open passenger window. He's holding a gun.

Anger builds up inside him. Detective Douglas is going to arrest him for Nikki's murder, he just knows it. He looks around to see if he can somehow get away, but he's trapped. Desperate, he opens the glove box and pulls out the hunting knife he keeps in there.

"Stay away from me!"

Douglas stops next to the window. He bends down to survey the inside of the car, and when he's satisfied there are no guns present, he slips his own back into its holster. Then he raises his hands in front of his chest. "Calm down, Mason. I'm not here to hurt you."

"The damage is already done. You ruined my life when you arrested my mom. You started all this!" He's surprised by his own tears. It must be the shock of still being alive. Should he feel grateful? Because he doesn't. He feels like it's yet another thing he can't do right.

The detective looks confused. "What are you talking about? I haven't arrested Angela McCoy."

Owen's confused himself until he remembers that most people don't know who he is. "My name isn't really Mason McCoy; it's Owen Harper. Surely you remember Madison Harper?" he spits.

A look of contempt replaces the confusion on the detective's face, and Owen knows then that he's screwed.

"I watched you drag her away when I was ten years old. You ruined my life!" He tries wiping the tears of frustration away with his free hand, but they keep coming.

Detective Douglas crouches down next to the passenger window and rests one hand on the door. "I'm sorry, I didn't know you were her son. I guess nobody tells me anything around here." He pauses. "Your mother killed a police officer, so I had to arrest her. She was convicted by a jury, not by me." He nods to the knife in Owen's hand. "Will you put that down? I'm not here to hurt you."

Owen doesn't trust this guy. He saw how aggressive he was with his mom that night, and he saw how frightened she was. Convinced that he's trying to trick him, he moves the knife to his own throat as the detective's eyes widen.

He notices Officer Jim Greenburg slowly approaching his car. Jim's been to their house many times, for card games with his dad. He knows who Owen is, so how come Douglas didn't?

"Don't come any closer!" he shouts to Officer Greenburg. "I'll kill myself, and it'll be on you. You'll have to explain it to my dad."

The cop hesitates and then backs off.

Douglas looks worried. "Listen to me. We just want to make sure you're safe right now, that's all. We won't ask you anything about Nikki Jackson's death. This is about getting you to safety and letting a doctor check you over."

"I didn't kill her!" He knows they won't believe him.

"Okay, well it's the first time you've told me that because it's the first time we've spoken." He's so calm. "Now that I know that, I know to look for someone else. And when you're ready, you can tell me what you do know about that night. But for now, drop the knife. You don't want to hurt yourself."

Owen's hands are so sweaty the knife is slipping from his grip. "Yes, I do." He nods to the railroad tracks. "What do you think I was about to do before you showed up?"

Douglas realizes what he means. "There's no need to do that, Owen. You hear me? If you've done nothing wrong, we can figure it out. You can tell us why Nikki might have wanted to kill herself, so we can stop investigating her death as a homicide."

Owen shakes his head. "Nikki did want to kill herself, but you'll never understand why. How can you? I bet you had parents who loved you and fed you properly and didn't constantly berate you. I bet you've never known anything bad in your life."

Douglas looks away. "I've had my fair share of shit too."

"Like what?" Owen lowers the knife.

Douglas turns back to him, and the look on his face makes Owen realize he's misjudged him. "No one's life is easy, kid. Now if Nikki was being emotionally abused at home, we can investigate her parents. But we don't know anything about her now she's no longer with us. You can be her voice. You can tell us what was going on in her life. Killing yourself isn't going to help her, because then

we'll only have her parents' version of events. Do you want them
to speak for her?"

Owen looks at his hands. This guy is making sense. But he doesn't
want to believe Nikki *did* kill herself. They had plans for the next
day. She was fine when he left to go home. He would have known
if he was never going to see her again.

"Would it help to speak to your mom right now?" asks Douglas.

Owen slowly turns to look at him. He frowns. "What?" Why
would speaking to Angie help him?

"Your real mom. I can take you to Madison."

Owen's mouth moves, but no words come out.

"Oh shit, you don't know. She's back in town."

He doesn't believe it. It must be a trick. "She's in prison."

Douglas shakes his head. "She was released early. She arrived
back a few days ago to deal with Stephanie Garcia's death. You
want me to take you to her?"

Owen starts trembling. Why didn't Angie tell him? He feels
like he might vomit. He gulps, drops the knife and starts the car.
He has to find his mom.

Before he can try to get away, Officer Greenburg tears the door
open and pulls him out onto the ground. Douglas rushes around
the car and looms over him. "You need to keep still while I arrest
you for the murder of Nikki Jackson."

All Owen can do is surrender as he's painfully handcuffed and
dragged to the police cruiser.

CHAPTER FIFTY-ONE

Madison watches Nate and Brody as they walk back to the car. They've pulled over at a gas station to fill up, giving Brody a chance to empty his bladder and for Nate to grab some coffees. It's been a frustrating day so far, but she feels a spark of hope that something's going to happen.

Nate lets Brody into the back of the car, then passes a coffee through her window. "No one behind the counter has seen Owen. But they're not especially friendly to outsiders, so maybe they're lying."

She shakes her head as he walks around to the driver's side. "I need to call Shelley. She's not yet given me the name of the guy Douglas arrested." She sips her coffee and wonders if Shelley's decided that passing inside information to her isn't worth the risk to her job. She wouldn't blame her, but it's frustrating all the same. She pulls out her cell phone. Before she can touch the screen, it lights up. She looks at Nate hopefully. "It's Mike."

When she answers, Mike sounds out of breath. "We've got him, Madison." He pauses. "Douglas has brought Owen in."

Her heart sinks and she's suddenly covered in goosebumps. She looks at Nate. "We're too late."

Nate takes the phone off her. "Where is he now?"

She hears Mike say, "At the station." Then, before Nate hangs up, he adds, "But you can't see him so don't bother—"

Nate drops the phone in her lap and speeds away.

*

Madison pushes open the door to the police station so hard she thinks it's going to shatter. It holds up, but the look she gets from the officer behind the desk could kill. He stands up straight and crosses his arms.

"Can I help you?"

"I'm here to see my son."

She can't believe she's said those words. This is it. This is the moment she finally gets to see Owen and explain she's not a killer. That she didn't leave him voluntarily and she wants to rebuild their relationship. He can move into Steph's house with her. They can live as a family again. She'd rather not be saying all that here and in front of an audience, but she'll take it over the alternative, which is never getting the chance to say it at all.

Her breathing speeds up and she feels Nate's hand on her back.

"Take a deep breath," he says. "Just breathe."

The cop behind the desk watches them, unimpressed. Finally he looks at Nate. "You want to fill me in on what's going on?"

His tone is patronizing and Madison doesn't recognize him. She wonders how many staff have come and gone in seven years.

"We're here to see Owen Harper," says Nate. "He might have been booked in as Mason McCoy. Either way, Madison is his mother."

The cop raises his eyebrows. "Let me get the arresting detective to come see you. Take a seat right there."

"We're fine here," she says.

"Ma'am, he could be a while. I suggest you take a step back from my desk."

Nate motions her over to the seats. "Let's not aggravate anyone. We need this to go smoothly." He looks out the window and she knows he's checking on Brody, who they left happily wandering around the parking lot.

Her cell phone buzzes in her pocket. It's Kate. "I'm busy right now, Kate. Can I call you later?"

"Wait, I just need to ask you something."

Madison shuts her eyes; she can't take much more bad news. "What is it?"

"Is it true? Is Mason McCoy your son?"

Madison finally sits down. "Shit. How did you find out?"

"We just got a tip that he's been arrested, and the caller said his real name is Owen Harper."

"Who the hell is leaking this stuff?"

Kate hesitates. "I can't reveal my sources, you know that, but to be honest, I don't actually know who it is. They're doing it anonymously by text, but so far they've been one hundred percent accurate."

Which means it must be Douglas. Madison rubs her temple. "Look, it's true, but please keep it out of the news. I have enough to deal with right now."

"Where are you?"

"At the police station. I'm waiting to see him. This will be the first time in seven years." She swallows. "I never expected to be reunited with him like this."

"I really hope it goes well for you." Kate sounds sympathetic. "I can't even imagine what you've been through. But Madison, I can't keep it out of the news. It's my job, and Nikki Jackson's murder is all anyone's talking about. The community needs to know their children aren't at risk of being next. You must understand that."

Madison's stunned. She feels betrayed all over again. "Please don't repeat anything I just said. We can't be friends if you cover this."

"You're asking me to risk my job."

"No, I'm asking you to be my friend."

Kate hesitates. "I'm so pleased you'll be reunited with Owen. Good luck." She ends the call.

Madison has no idea what Kate's going to do.

CHAPTER FIFTY-TWO

Mike isn't looking forward to this, but Douglas is charging ahead of him, ready to rub Owen's arrest in Madison's face.

"Don't forget who you work for, Bowers. It's time you had my back instead of hers."

Mike could punch him for that, but Douglas doesn't give him the chance. He walks through the secure door that separates the front desk from the offices behind, and into the waiting area.

Madison jumps out of her seat and stands to confront him. Nate joins her, which pisses Mike off because he has no business here.

"I want to see my son," she says.

"He's about to be interviewed," says Douglas, folding his arms.

"I don't care. Let me see him."

Douglas shakes his head. "You're not his legal guardian or his lawyer, so you're not permitted to speak to him while he's here."

Mike can see she's trying to contain her anger. "I'm his *mother*."

Douglas doesn't flinch. "When was the last time you mothered him?"

Even Mike gasps at that comment. He watches the fire in Madison's eyes, but one touch on the arm from Nate and she appears to calm down. He frowns. This guy is meant to be her PI, so why are they so close?

"When are you releasing him?" she asks through gritted teeth.

"That depends on what he tells us in the interview. But it's not looking good for him."

"What do you mean?"

Mike knows Madison's about to get a reality check.

"I'm only telling you this so you know you're wasting your time by hanging around here," says Douglas. "We've taken his prints and they match those found on the victim and the knife. I've arrested him for Nikki Jackson's murder."

Madison's mouth opens, but she's lost for words.

It's hard to watch her reaction, and Mike doesn't know if Owen killed the girl; he can't see it himself. He's more inclined to believe they had some stupid suicide pact planned. All he knows is that either way, Owen's going to serve a long time for this.

Finally she asks, "Who's his lawyer?"

"He doesn't have one. His father's lawyer declined to represent him." Douglas smirks. "Looks like the McCoys have turned their back on him. He's asked to be referred to as Owen Harper from now on."

With tears in her eyes and a look of desperation, Madison turns to Nate.

"I'm on it." He pulls out his cell phone and walks away from them, presumably to call the same lawyer they used for Madison a couple of days ago.

The door to the station opens and Kate Flynn walks in. Mike glances out of the window. Bob, her camera guy, is getting his equipment ready. Great, that's all they need. "Not now, Kate," he says sternly.

Madison glances at her. "Really? Do you have no shame?"

Kate looks away, and Mike thinks she might actually leave, which would be a first for her. She hesitates by the door.

Madison turns to Douglas. "I'm staying here until you let me see him."

Douglas shakes his head in frustration. "You try talking some sense into her, Mike."

"Fuck you, Douglas!" She's shouting now. "This personal vendetta you've got against me is out of hand!"

Mike feels his headache intensifying. He rubs his temples. He'd rather be anywhere else but here.

"There's no personal vendetta, Harper."

She steps forward. "Then why did you kill Officer Ryan Levy and set me up as the fall guy?"

The hairs on Mike's neck stand up at the same time as Kate Flynn gasps. He looks at Douglas for his reaction.

"What did you just say?" Douglas takes a step forward. Mike pulls him back, but he gets shaken off. "That's a serious allegation, Harper."

"It's a serious crime. I should know; I served your sentence."

Mike steps between them. "Whoa! Madison, you're out of line. You need to leave before you get yourself locked up."

"Go ahead!" she says. "At least I'd see my son."

He pulls her arm, hard, forcing her to look at him. "Seriously, you need to go."

"You're going to take Douglas's side, then?" she says. "Just like you took Angie's side for hiding my son?"

"She didn't hide your son; and she gave him a home after you got yourself convicted. You should be thanking her, but once again Madison Harper acts the victim. If you ask me, Owen was better off without you."

Madison retreats as if he's slapped her. "What? How can you say that?"

He feels bad, but he's being pushed. "Just get out of here, would you? You're making things worse."

Nate ends his call and joins them. "Let's go, Madison." He looks at Mike. "Owen now has an attorney, Richie Hope. He'll be here in two hours. Someone needs to call us when Madison can visit her son. She has every right to see him."

Douglas is clearly still fuming. "You should be thanking me. I stopped your son from killing himself today."

Madison gasps. "What?"

"That's right. When I found him earlier, he was about to drive his car in front of a train because his life is so fucked up. That's on *you*, not me." He walks away, back toward the office.

Mike's anger wavers, because Madison looks like she's on the verge of losing it completely. "Listen," he says. "I'll make sure the lawyer sees him tonight. Now go home. I'll call you with an update in the morning." He turns to Kate. "You need to leave too."

He watches as Kate holds the door open for Nate and Madison. When they leave, he sighs and walks back to his desk. He grabs his mug, sensing he's going to be here for a lot longer than he'd like.

Douglas walks up to him. "I'll be interviewing the boy as soon as his lawyer turns up. Now that we have his prints and can confirm they match those on the murder weapon, it should be easy to get a search warrant for the McCoys' ranch."

Mike's head is pounding.

"I'm intending to strike early tomorrow morning; catch them off guard before they're awake and before their staff turn up for work. I'll be taking five officers with me. Are you in? Or do I need to find someone else to have my back?"

Mike doesn't trust himself to speak. He just nods.

CHAPTER FIFTY-THREE

Owen needs a change of clothes. He's just spent almost two hours being interrogated by Detective Douglas, and the stress of it has made him sweat so much he can smell it drying on his T-shirt. He's never been interviewed by the police before and didn't know what to expect. Turns out it was exactly like the movies. Although Detective Douglas was less bad-cop than he'd anticipated.

"Are you sure there's nothing else you want to tell me?" asks Douglas as the interview comes to a close.

Owen tries to get comfortable in the plastic seat. There's no air in this room and he's sure it's a tactic to make the suspect want to talk, just so they can get it over with and get out of here. "I've told you everything that happened that night." He looks the detective in the eye, but the guy stares back so intently that Owen is the first one to break contact.

"I think my client has already been incredibly open with you, Detective," says Richie Hope.

Owen looks at his lawyer. He underestimated him when the guy walked into his cell. He thought he was too old to be effective and he couldn't understand who'd hired him, as he knows Richie doesn't work for his dad. The McCoy lawyer is ruthless, and if he's honest, Owen would have preferred she showed up to battle the charges against him. He's guessing that the fact she's not here signals that his life with Angie and Wyatt really is over. He struggles to know whether that's a good thing or not. He could be completely alone in the world.

Richie's busy typing away on his laptop. They didn't get an opportunity for any alone time together before the interview, so the only thing the lawyer managed to advise him was to tell the truth. That was it. Owen took that advice against his better judgment.

Detective Douglas gathers his papers. "I appreciate your cooperation. If you think of anything else, ask for me. Can I get you a sandwich or a coffee?"

Owen relaxes slightly. This means the interview really is over at last. He feels like he's been in a boxing ring, but it was draining mentally as well as physically. He nods. "Both. I'm starving." He wants to eat and then sleep for ten hours. It's been a long day. The clock above the door tells him it's just turned seven.

Douglas leaves him and Richie together for a minute.

Immediately Owen asks, "Who hired you?"

Richie smiles at him. "Your mother and her friend Nate."

Owen's shocked. "My mother? You mean Madison Harper?"

"Yes. She's worried about you being treated unfairly because of her conviction. She did the right thing hiring me because I believe this detective may have it in for her. In which case he won't hesitate to take his feelings out on you."

Owen still doesn't know what's more shocking: that his mother really is back in town and looking out for him or that he may be convicted of murder because this cop has a beef with her. "Can I see her?"

Richie looks regretful. "Probably not anytime soon. It depends on what Detective Douglas decides to do next. We won't know until the morning, so you just hang tight and stay out of trouble. And by that I mean don't talk to anyone." He puts his hand on Owen's shoulder. "And by anyone I mean detectives, the other inmates or even a pretty female officer who might stop by with coffee. Everyone in here could have an ulterior motive for talking to you. Got it?"

Owen frowns, then nods.

"Good. Be smart. If I were you, I'd just go to sleep early like it's Christmas Eve. And then, who knows, Santa might bring you your freedom overnight." Richie smiles reassuringly and then gathers his things together.

Douglas comes back with a vending machine coffee and a pre-packed sandwich. "Officer Greenburg will escort you back to your cell. I'll be by to see you in the morning. Will you be coming back, Mr. Hope?"

"Of course. See you tomorrow, son." Richie winks at Owen before leaving.

Officer Greenburg enters the room. "Ready?"

Owen's not sure he is. Jim is a friend of his dad's. What if his dad wants him threatened so that he doesn't tell the police anything? He looks at Douglas but he can't speak up in front of Greenburg. He has no choice but to follow him down to the holding cell. There's a large white guy in one of the other cells who is staring at him like he wants to beat the shit out of him. Is he just being paranoid?

When he gets to his own cell, he sits on the bunk and sips the coffee. It's bitter.

"Here you go, kid." Greenburg stands in front of him with his cell phone. He turns the screen for Owen to read. It's a text. "A message from Angie. You need to read it unless you want trouble."

Owen's heart pounds out of his chest. He looks up at Greenburg. This isn't how it's supposed to be. Cops are supposed to be neutral. He realizes he's not safe in here, even if he's only in overnight. He looks back at the screen and reads the text.

Remember what I told you before you left? Your neighbor in there knows what to do should you ignore my advice.

Chills run down his arms. He reads the text three times, memorizing it. Officer Greenburg locks him in his cell without further comment.

On trembling legs, Owen stands up to look at the cell further down the corridor. The big guy is staring at him through the bars. Owen steps back. He's trapped. If he tells the police about his dad's businesses, this guy will kill him. He needs to ask Detective Douglas to get him away from here. But Richie said not to trust anyone. He collapses onto the uncomfortable bunk and tries to figure out what the hell he should do next.

CHAPTER FIFTY-FOUR

The rain clouds from earlier are still looming overhead and blocking the sun that's setting behind them. Nate knows that Madison's exhausted and frustrated, so they drop Brody home and he drives them to a nearby bar, where they can let off some steam. It's not like either of them can get Owen released tonight, no matter what they do.

At the dimly lit bar he orders them two shots of bourbon each and a couple of Buds, ignoring the sideways glances from the locals. It's like they've never seen a stranger in these parts before. He wonders what they'd do if he switched the jukebox from a country song to a death-metal one. The thought makes him smile.

He joins Madison at a booth under a Bud Light sign that's flashing in a way that suggests it's about to give up and die any minute. She downs both shots, one after the other, then sips her Bud. "I knew coming back here was going to be difficult, but I had no idea it would be this bad. In all the scenarios I ran through in my head whilst locked up, I never contemplated the thought that Owen would be arrested for murder. And all because Douglas has it in for me."

He sips his beer. "Well, technically, Owen's prints *are* on the knife. Which means he must know something about what happened to Nikki." He thinks that if anyone else dared to point this out to her she might hit them, but he feels like they're close enough now for him to be completely honest. "It doesn't look good for him."

She nods as she peels the damp sticker off the bottle. "I know. I just hope Richie can work his magic. Maybe Douglas planted Owen's prints on the knife?"

Nate doesn't think so. "He would've had to do it after they brought Owen into the station, so I don't see how he could have got away with that."

"He could if they're all in on it."

He's not so sure. "I agree that where there's one corrupt cop there are likely others covering their back, but a whole department? It's unlikely."

She sits back in frustration. "So what was my son doing with the knife?"

"Maybe the knife belonged to him and he gave it to Nikki to protect herself, or she took it from him without asking. I don't know much about forensics, but couldn't his prints have been on there before it was used on Nikki?"

She nods. "Probably. I don't know." She takes one of his shots and downs it. "I'm so sick of fighting everyone. It's been non-stop for years. I just want to hug my son." Her voice catches.

He reaches across and puts his hand on hers. "I know."

Nate can't help thinking that if Madison's right and Detective Douglas killed Ryan Levy and is now framing Owen for Nikki's murder, he's already got away with so much and nothing they do will expose him because he's protected by his badge. No one's going to believe their accusations, as Madison's not respected around here and Nate's a total stranger. They need concrete evidence, but the case is so cold it's difficult to catch a break.

"I can't believe Kate had the nerve to show up," she says.

"I don't think you need to worry about her contacting you again." Madison gave the reporter a mouthful, which he knows she'll regret once she calms down.

She sits up straight and looks at him. "I have a horrible feeling about something and I need to say it out loud to see whether I'm being ridiculous."

He's intrigued. "Shoot."

"Just before I left the McCoys' ranch yesterday, Mike turned up. He said he was there to talk to them about Owen. But he looked shifty, as if he didn't like the fact I was there. He almost looked like he'd been caught doing something wrong."

"That's odd. What's it to him whether you visit your sister?"

"Exactly. And in the police station earlier he told me I should be grateful to Angie for taking Owen in. It felt like he was sticking up for her. But she's nothing to him so why would he do that?"

Nate thinks about it. "You don't think he's having an affair with her, do you?"

"No way. Wyatt would kill him, and he was home so it's not like they were hiding anything from him."

"Could Mike be working an angle? Maybe he's getting close to them to investigate something. Do you know if they're into anything illegal?"

She scoffs. "I think everyone at LCPD has their suspicions that Wyatt's up to something but no one has ever been able to investigate properly. Chief Sullivan always thought Wyatt's preservation foundation was a front for money laundering and probably drug trafficking, but he was never able to secure permission from high up to look into it. We were a small PD, we had other fish to fry, and it was felt that as long as the McCoys were helping the community with their fundraising and not causing any obvious problems, it was best to leave them to it. Sullivan thought they'd shoot themselves in the foot one day and that would be when we would pounce. But it's hard to find anyone local who will say a bad word about them."

"What do you think Wyatt's up to?"

She sips her beer. "Bad loans, financial fraud with the charity work, possibly distributing drugs. He's always had more guys working for him than I've ever been able to put jobs to, and they all seem to do a lot of driving back and forth. Think about where we are: near America's Four Corners. It provides a perfect opportunity to traffic drugs through and from four states. That's why I can't bear the thought that Owen had to live with them. I mean, what must he have learned from them? What must he have witnessed?"

Nate understands how that could weigh heavy on her for years to come. "Then perhaps that's what Mike's been looking into."

She considers it. "You know, that could be the case. And maybe he's pissed at me for potentially ruining his set-up. But…" she takes a deep breath, "I have a horrible feeling he's working for them."

Nate downs the final shot. "Doing what?"

She leans back with a determined look in her eye. "That's what we need to figure out."

CHAPTER FIFTY-FIVE

Owen is lying on the cell's hard bunk, but he can't sleep. He keeps thinking of Angie's message and the finality of no longer being a McCoy. He's always considered himself to be Owen rather than Mason, but he feels even further removed from being a Harper after all this time. Is he supposed to change his name again now to something new? He wishes he could speak to his mom and find out what her intentions are. Will she take off and leave him languishing in prison?

"Hey, kid."

He daren't move. He and the big guy are the only people down here. "McCoy?"

Owen doesn't want to talk to him. He stays on his bed.

"I know you can hear me."

His whole body is tense and he daren't breathe for fear of this guy hearing him. Thankfully he can't see him unless he walks over to the bars.

"You better do what Angie says," the man continues. "Their lawyer told me that if you tell the cops anything about them, I have orders to silence you. So fess up. Did you tell them anything earlier? Are you a snitch?"

A door at the top of the stairway creaks open and Owen is thankful to hear footsteps descending the stairs.

"Hey, darling. You want to come join me in here?"

"Quiet, Harris," a woman says.

Owen sits up and waits for her to reach them. He remembers what Richie said to him about speaking to no one, not even a pretty female officer who wants to offer him a drink. But when he sees her face, he feels like he recognizes her from somewhere.

She approaches his cell. "Everything okay?" She must have been watching them through the security cameras and noticed that the other guy was trying to talk to him.

He stands up and walks to the bars. Trying to keep his voice as low as possible, he asks, "What's he in here for?"

She must see the fear on his face. "I can't tell you that. Is he threatening you?"

He swallows. "I really need to know what he's in for. *Please*."

She looks over her shoulder at the guy. He's smirking at them both like being in jail is a game to him. She turns back to Owen. "You might not remember me after all this time—you certainly look different from the last time I saw you—but I worked with your mom. My name's Shelley."

He looks at her kind eyes. "I think I do."

She smiles. "His name's Paul Harris. He's been arrested for the murder of your mom's friend Stephanie Garcia."

Owen feels dizzy. He takes a step away from the bars as his ears ring. Shelley unlocks his door and comes inside. She pushes his shoulders so he sits on the bunk.

When his head clears, he looks up at her. "Did he really kill Stephanie?"

"That's for a court to decide."

Owen starts hyperventilating. He's putting everything together in his head and the result is horrifying.

Shelley sits next to him, trying to get him to slow his breathing. "Do you need a doctor?"

He's shaking his head. "No. I need to speak to Detective Douglas."

"I wouldn't do that if I were you, kid," says Harris from the other cell. "Remember what I just told you."

"Shut up, Harris." She appears to understand the seriousness of Owen's request. "I'll see where he is, but it's late, he might be off duty."

Owen grabs her arm. "Please. He's going to want to hear what I've got to say."

She looks him in the eye, trying to figure out if he's just acting up. Finally she stands and walks to the door. As she locks him in, she says, "I'll see what I can do. Hang tight."

Owen lies back on the bunk, trying to regain control of his breathing.

"Oh, you're done for now, buddy."

He stares at the ceiling, trying to come to terms with what this means.

CHAPTER FIFTY-SIX

The next morning, Madison is up early despite the bourbon hangover. She was awake most of the night trying to figure out what Mike had to gain from helping Angie and Wyatt, and why he would even consider doing so. She talked herself into some pretty outlandish theories so she got up and showered, trying to clear her head.

After breakfast, she heads outside and stands leaning against the chest-high fence, watching the sun come up over the cornfields beyond Steph's—her—land. She can sense Stephanie here this morning. It's a strange feeling. It's tricking her mind into believing that if she turned her head to the right, Steph would be standing next to her.

A swarm of excitable flies catch her attention. They're buzzing around something in one of the corn tunnels ahead. From here it looks like the corpse of a raccoon. She's heard the raccoons at night, grunting and rummaging around the barns for food. She wonders what killed this one, but she can't tell from here; all she can see is open intestines and the flies. Her mind wanders to Nikki Jackson. She still can't believe Owen's prints are on the knife that killed her. She knows that if she were Douglas, she would come to the same initial conclusion; that it's more than likely Owen was present when she died.

Douglas told her he'd stopped Owen from driving in front of a train yesterday. She swallows. He was so close to dying. Has he been suicidal for a while? Is that why he was with Nikki when she died; because they *did* have a suicide pact? The thought of it makes her heart thump harder. If Douglas had found him minutes later, if he'd been held up at a red light, or stopped somewhere for a coffee, she'd be visiting her son in the morgue this morning.

She takes a sip of her coffee and watches the distant horizon.

Nate appears. "Morning." He's holding his cell phone in one hand and a coffee in the other. He stands next to her and leans against the fence. "What a great view."

He's right. The sun is peeking between the distant mountains and illuminating the cornfields and scattered scarecrows ahead of them. There's a cool breeze in the air that makes her pull her cardigan a little tighter. "Mike said he'd update me on Owen's situation this morning."

Nate raises an eyebrow. "Think he will?"

"Who knows?" She stands up straight. "I've managed to convince myself that he's been dealing drugs for Wyatt, which would be really fucking disappointing because I thought he was one of the few good guys around here. I don't want to believe he's as dirty as everyone else."

He frowns. "You really think he'd do that? And how would we even begin to prove it?"

She sighs. "I don't know. Locate someone who's running drugs for Wyatt? Offer them money in return for information?" She checks her phone. Still no word from Mike. She's heading to the station if he doesn't call soon. "You know, I heard all sorts of rumors about Wyatt when I was younger, which is why I warned Angie off him. After he attacked me, I had to stay away and keep quiet. If I'd wanted to investigate him for any of the drug rumors or the financial fraud once I made detective, I would have had to report the rape, which would have made me seem like I had a personal vendetta against the guy." She sighs at the unfairness of it all.

Nate's phone buzzes. He looks at it before answering. "Hey, Rex."

It's a video call this time. Rex looks exactly as Madison pictured him: a little overweight, with a thick brown beard and hair that's about two years' overdue a cut. He has a small dog curled up on his lap and a black kitten balancing on the back of his computer chair. Nate told her he runs some kind of animal shelter from his ranch in San Diego.

"Hi. You both managing to stay out of jail?" he laughs.

"So far so good," says Nate.

"Good for you. So, I found out more about Detective Don Douglas."

Madison leans in. Are they finally going to hear concrete evidence that he's corrupt?

"I don't think it's what you're expecting, though. In his previous police department, he was partnered with another detective, Joseph Ramirez. They were close buddies by all accounts; their families socialized together and even shared vacations."

Madison raises her eyebrows. She's surprised Douglas ever socialized with anyone.

"Anyway, one day they were having a birthday party for his six-year-old daughter."

"Wait," she says. "Whose daughter was this? Joseph's?"

"No, Don's."

"Douglas has a child?" She can't believe it. "I didn't even know he was married."

"Well, let me finish," says Rex. "They were enjoying her birthday party on the front lawn one summer's day when there was a drive-by shooting."

Madison gasps.

"Apparently someone wanted Joseph dead in retaliation for a conviction. And they took their opportunity while everyone was out front."

"Did the shooter get him?"

Rex sighs. "It sounds like Douglas and Joseph jumped in front of the kids the minute they heard gunshots. Douglas managed to save Joseph's son and daughter. Joseph tried to save Douglas's daughter. Unfortunately, she was fatally shot, as was Joseph. That day Douglas lost his daughter and his partner. His wife was clipped, but she survived."

Madison turns away with her hand to her mouth. For the first time ever, she feels sympathy for Douglas.

"Shit," says Nate.

"Within a year of that, his wife left him and they divorced. Just six months later, he started at LCPD, which is obviously when you would've first met him."

She realizes Douglas must still have been raw from what had happened. "This is why he has a massive chip on his shoulder about cop killers."

"I feel for the guy and all," says Nate, "but Madison didn't kill Officer Levy and he should have been able to see that if he'd investigated properly."

Rex doesn't look so sure. "From what I've read of Madison's conviction, her gun was the weapon used. It had her prints on. It's a pretty compelling case."

Nate glances at her, probably wondering if she'll react. She doesn't, because he's right: on the outside it looks obvious that she killed Ryan.

She's overcome with disappointment. With no alternative suspect, she's never going to clear her name.

CHAPTER FIFTY-SEVEN

Madison looks at her coffee, but she's feeling too nauseous to finish it. "After hearing that, I think we need to eliminate Douglas as a suspect. He had nothing to gain. All this time I've mistaken his determination to convict me for a personal vendetta instead of a need to see justice done for a fellow cop."

"I agree," says Nate. "Which leaves the Levys, or someone else from your department."

She tries to think. "But no one from my department had a motive either." She thinks of Mike's face when he saw her with Angie. He went pale. He was concerned. He must have thought she'd figured something out. "Wait a minute."

"What?"

"If Mike is working for the McCoys…" She tries to think. "What if it was *Wyatt* who shot Ryan and he got Mike to fix the crime scene to frame me?"

Nate's apprehensive. "Surely Mike wouldn't just let someone kill another cop? Was he friends with Ryan?"

She tries to think back. "Yeah, he was."

"So there was no reason for him to want Ryan dead?"

Her memory is patchy. It's been such a long time since they all worked together. "No. There was no beef between them that I knew of."

"So why would Mike let Wyatt get away with it?"

Eighteen years ago, Wyatt threatened to hurt her mom if she ever told anyone about the rape. She believed him, but as time went on, the threat diminished because she kept out of his way.

She was busy raising Owen and caring for her mom here in Lost Creek. Angie never visited. She and Wyatt weren't the pillars of the community they seem to be now; they were busy building up Wyatt's scrap business in Gold Rock and Madison had stopped thinking about them.

"I was five days into my new role as detective when Ryan was killed, and I can't shake the feeling that that's significant in some way." A thought occurs to her. "Was Wyatt scared I was about to arrest him for rape? Or for anything else he was up to? Did he live in fear that I was going to take him down because I finally had some power?"

Nate nods slowly. "Maybe he was working on the belief that you had spent all those years in law enforcement to become a detective for that very purpose. Though if he was that worried, wouldn't he have just killed you instead of Ryan?"

She considers it. "No, because who would they pin my death on? The unsolved murder of a female detective would've made the national news. It would be difficult to get away with. Whereas framing me for murder would discredit me in the eyes of the law and the community, so that no one would take me seriously if I accused him of anything. Plus, he gets the satisfaction of seeing me serve a prison sentence. He was probably banking on me getting life without parole for murder, not a lesser manslaughter conviction."

Nate is slowly nodding as he pieces it all together. "That's the most likely theory yet. And whether or not it's true, Wyatt has another motive you've not mentioned."

She looks at him. "What's that?"

"Owen."

She turns away and thinks about her son. Angie said Wyatt had suspected for a while that Owen was his. Angie couldn't have children, so he might have longed for a son to keep the McCoy name going. No wonder Angie was hostile toward her. For the last seven years she's been living with a constant reminder of her husband's betrayal. She must have believed him when he told her that Madison had seduced him. And Owen had been caught up in it all.

She takes a deep breath. "Mike must have been the one to frame me. He'd been to my house many times and knew where my gun safe was. He knew where I kept the key, and I'd told him Ryan was taking me for a birthday treat after work. He knew that day was the perfect time to make it look like Ryan and I were in a relationship." She realizes how badly he's betrayed her. But it does answer another puzzle. "He probably made a copy of my safe key."

"How would he get your keys away from you for long enough to make a copy?"

She shakes her head. "I don't know. I could have left them unattended at work, I guess. Although I don't remember ever doing that." Her heart sinks at the costly error. "But it was a police station, they should have been safe!"

Nate's looking doubtful now. "I get Wyatt's motive, but why would Mike agree to frame you for a murder Wyatt committed? What's his motive to hurt you that way?"

She's not a hundred percent certain yet. "He must have been desperate. Wyatt must have had something on him. Maybe Mike owed him money. I don't know. We need to find out." She faces him. "This is some serious shit, Nate. I need to take it to Douglas."

"I agree. This is way bigger than us."

As she reaches for her cell phone, it rings. "Hello?"

It's Douglas himself. "I need to see you at the station. It's urgent."

Even though she was about to contact him, she feels the same dread as always when she hears his voice. "On my way."

CHAPTER FIFTY-EIGHT

Detective Douglas is sitting in the interview room with Owen Harper across from him. The boy is shaking, spilling the coffee Don brought him, and he hasn't touched his breakfast. He's clearly afraid of the repercussions that come with his decision to disclose his father's secrets. The boy has a habit of regularly pushing his blond hair out of his eyes, and Douglas can see the resemblance to Madison. They share the same frown.

"So before I ask you to sign this," he nods to the statement in his hand, "I want to read out the main points to make sure you agree with what's been recorded, okay?"

Owen looks at his lawyer, who gives him a reassuring nod. "Okay."

"You've told me that you think Paul Harris—who is a suspect in the murder of Stephanie Garcia—works for your father, Wyatt McCoy. You suspect this because Harris threatened you last night by stating he has orders to harm you if you disclose anything to us about your father or his wife."

Owen nods.

"You also stated that Officer Jim Greenburg showed you a threatening text message from Angie McCoy. You said Officer Greenburg is a friend of your father. That correct?"

"Yes."

He'll have to deal with Greenburg next. He takes a deep breath and wishes Mike would arrive so he can help get this latest problem contained in half the time. "So why do you think your father would harm you? What's he up to that he doesn't want you to tell us about?"

As he battles his emotions, the boy looks younger than his seventeen years. He glances at his lawyer again.

"Go ahead," says Richie. "Everything you tell Detective Douglas will help solve Stephanie's murder and keep you safe."

He runs his hand through his hair, then tries to get comfortable. It's clearly hard for him to give his father up to the police. Don admires the boy's bravery. The McCoys are fierce opponents and not to be underestimated. He's going to have to protect Owen from any retaliation.

"You promise you're not going to put me back near Paul Harris?" Don nods.

Owen takes a deep breath and sits back in his chair. "My dad traffics coke, pot and meth across Utah, Colorado and New Mexico. He doesn't do it himself; he pays people to do it for him. His scrap business is just a front that barely makes any money. He earns way more from the drugs but he also offers loans to anyone in need. Except…" He hesitates. "I've heard rumors he's taking people's homes and cars when they can't pay his interest rates."

Don feels excitement building in his stomach. Owen's confirming everything he's suspected over the years but Chief Sullivan would never let him investigate. He always said the problem was too big for such a small department to bring down alone. In other words, he turned a blind eye, probably because he wanted an easy retirement.

"What about all the fundraising he and his wife do?"

Owen scoffs. "About seventy percent of that lines their own pockets. They give away just enough to avoid suspicion and to keep people digging deep for local causes." He takes a sip of his coffee, but he looks exhausted.

Douglas suspects that everything he's saying is true, but he doesn't have the luxury of probing into details and interviewing potential witnesses right now. If Wyatt McCoy hired Paul Harris to kill Stephanie Garcia, he needs to act fast. Because Wyatt has already put a hit out on his own son, and if he's capable of that, he's capable of anything.

He thinks about how all this ties in with Madison's conviction. If Wyatt did order the hit on Stephanie, and the hit man was hassling her about Madison's location, then it means Wyatt wanted to know where Madison was after her release. But why? He considers whether Wyatt could have killed Officer Ryan Levy to deliberately frame her. But he's her brother-in-law. Why the bad blood?

He looks at Owen.

It dawns on him then. Madison had something Wyatt wanted. *Fuck.* This is bad. If he was wrong about Madison, his career is at stake. But worse than that, he made a fellow detective serve time for something they didn't do.

"Are we done now, Detective?" asks Richie.

He takes a deep breath and looks at the documents in front of him. "Almost. For the record, you still maintain everything you told me during your initial interview: that you did not kill Nikki Jackson?"

Owen looks pained. "Of course I didn't. I loved her. We were going to move away together." He swallows hard.

Richie puts a hand on the boy's back. He looks at Douglas. "Why is Officer Greenburg passing messages to someone in custody? Is that normal practice in this police department, Detective? Is there anyone we can trust around here?"

Good question. Before he can reply, the door to the interview room opens. It's Officer Vickers. "Detective? Madison Harper's arrived."

Owen looks up incredulously. "My mom's here? " He stands up. "Can I see her?"

Don stands up and moves to the door. "Not yet. I need to speak to her first. Wait here."

He leaves the boy with his attorney and speaks to Officer Vickers. "Stay here and don't let anyone in this room. Not even his mother." He's not taking any risks.

Shelley glances over his shoulder at the boy, then she nods. "Understood."

CHAPTER FIFTY-NINE

Independence Day

Owen approaches the Ferris wheel, the only ride currently lit up. Everything else is in darkness because the park is completely empty. Well, almost. He checks his cell phone. Nikki messaged him almost half an hour ago, at 11.30, asking him to meet her here.

As he meanders through the park, he stops to take a photo of the wheel. It looks cool surrounded by darkness. Its red, yellow and blue lights are flashing away merrily, but without a park full of people and music it feels a little ghostly. Having worked here almost every day this summer, he never thought he'd miss the sound of kids squealing in delight as they're terrified to the point of vomiting. He can still smell the mixture of sugar and meat in the air from earlier.

After he takes the photo, he uses his cell phone to zoom in on the top of the wheel. He smiles. It looks like Nikki is up there waiting for him. She must have got bored. He pockets his phone and walks toward the ride, wondering what was so urgent it couldn't wait until they see each other tomorrow afternoon. Perhaps her dad bailed on her and she needs a ride home after all.

When he reaches the ticket booth, he jumps the barrier and waits as the Ferris wheel spins achingly slowly. When he first started here, Trevor told him it turned that slow so that people felt like they were getting their money's worth. He pulls his phone out and snaps a few more photos to pass the time. Then he waves at her. She doesn't wave back. He hears something behind him and turns, his eyes searching the darkness. There's no one there. But it would be hard to tell unless they were a couple of feet in front of him. The hairs on his bare arms spring up. Something's wrong here.

He looks up at Nikki's car on its slow descent. He checks the text she sent him.

Meet me at the Wonder Wheel.

There are no kisses. And she didn't reply to his text asking whether everything was okay. He swallows hard. It must be this place freaking him out. The park is always creepy when it's empty.

He has his hand ready on the wheel's control as he watches Nikki's car approach the unloading point. She still hasn't acknowledged him.

When her feet are level with the ground, he switches the ride off. The brakes squeal as the huge wheel bumps to a stop. "Hey." He approaches her and realizes her head is slumped. Has she fallen asleep? "Nikki?"

Panic washes over him as he notices the blood accumulating around her pale wrists. "Shit! Nikki!" He pulls the safety bar open and crouches at her feet. The knife she used is on her lap. He picks it up and drops it to the ground at their feet, thinking about trying to stem the flow by grabbing her wrists. But one tentative touch of the blood tells him it's starting to clot. The damage has been done. "No!"

He cups her head in his hands, pushing her hair to one side and looking for any reaction in her eyes. There is none. She's looking through him. The awful feel of her cold face and rigid neck makes him pull his hands away in fear.

"Nikki, what have you done?" Tears build in his eyes as he realizes his girlfriend has killed herself. Was she hoping he'd arrive in time to save her? Shock works through his body. His teeth start chattering and his heartbeat throbs in his head. Then he realizes he's touched the knife. His prints will be on it. Could the cops make it look like he killed her? Probably. They were quick enough to arrest his mom for murder.

He doesn't know what to do, but he knows he doesn't trust the local police. He picks up the knife. He has to ditch it somewhere. If he leaves here with it, he could be pulled over on the way home. He looks at the Haunted House. There are plenty of places to hide it in there.

He takes one more look at Nikki before he goes, but the girl he's in love with is no longer there in the body in front of him. She's lost to him forever.

CHAPTER SIXTY

Nate watches as Madison paces the waiting area in the police station for the second time. It's not even seven o'clock yet, but the station feels warm with the sun shining brightly through the glass-paneled front. Madison's nervous energy is rubbing off on him; he's jittery, wondering if she's finally going to be reunited with her son.

"Remember," he says, "don't aggravate Douglas. He's the only person who can grant you access to Owen. Let's focus on what we came here for."

She rolls her eyes at him. "I don't need a pep talk, Nate. I know how to behave myself."

The main door opens and Mike walks in with his sunglasses on, presumably arriving for a new shift. He stops when he notices them, then removes his shades. "I told you I'd update you this morning. You didn't have to come in."

Nate doesn't like the look on his face. What's he got to be unhappy about?

Madison appears lost for words. She's probably worried that Mike will realize they're onto him.

"We're waiting to see if Douglas will let her talk to her son," Nate says. "She's desperate to see him again. I'm sure you can understand that?"

Mike looks from him to Madison. "Of course. Let me see what's going on." He walks through to the back office, leaving them in the waiting area.

Madison turns to Nate. "Shit! What if he does something to Owen?"

"Keep your voice down." He glances up. The male officer behind the desk is watching them. "Just stay calm. We don't know who's bent and who can be trusted at this point. All we can do is hope Douglas will listen to you and then take it from there."

She takes a deep breath. "I can't believe Douglas is my best bet at this stage." She laughs bitterly. "It just shows how desperate I am."

Detective Douglas appears. He holds the internal door open, indicating they should follow him.

Madison shakes her head. "Can I have a quiet word here first?"

Douglas sighs but joins them in the waiting area. "What is it?"

"I have reason to believe we can't trust Mike Bowers."

He raises his eyebrows but says nothing.

"You're just going to have to go with me on this one. I don't want him present while we talk. Once you've heard what I have to say, you can make up your own mind."

Douglas looks at Nate. "I suppose you want to join us?"

Nate smiles. "You suppose right."

The detective turns and leads them through the door and on to an interview room. Once inside, he closes the door behind him and tells them to sit down.

Nate's nerves kick in and his hands feel clammy. He has bad memories of police interview rooms, and this one smells like all the rest: of desperation. He looks at the camera high up on the wall in the corner. It's pointing at them but he can't tell if it's recording. He has to resist the urge to flee the room, even though he's not here to be questioned.

"Is Owen still here?" asks Madison.

"He is." Douglas takes a seat opposite them. "Now, I called you earlier because I need to update you on some things."

Madison stretches her hands across the table like she can't contain herself. "Before you start, can I please tell you what I suspect about Mike?"

Nate thinks she's pushing her luck. Douglas seems like the kind of guy who doesn't appreciate being interrupted. But he leans back in his seat, throwing his hands in the air.

"Sure. Why not? Let's do this your way."

Madison ignores his frustration. She takes a deep breath and keeps her voice low, as if she's afraid that Mike's standing outside listening in. "I believe Wyatt McCoy killed Officer Ryan Levy and paid Mike to frame me for it." She stops, waiting for his reaction.

Nate stops breathing. He's fascinated to see how Douglas reacts.

Douglas raises his eyebrows. Taking a deep breath, he locks his hands behind his head. "Go on."

Madison seems surprised that he wants to listen. "I was at the McCoys' place the night before last and Mike turned up looking sheepish, like he wasn't happy I caught him there."

Douglas is difficult to read. "What were you doing at the McCoys' place?"

Madison explains patiently. "Angie's my sister. Wyatt is Owen's biological father. They took Owen in when I was convicted and changed his name. I was never told that. I had no idea where child services placed him. I only found out this week. I went to see Angie to ask about my son and whether she knew where he was. But that's not important. Mike turned up and he seems to have some kind of relationship with them. I think he's been working for Wyatt all along."

Douglas pulls a notepad and pen toward him. "What time did he show up?"

"About seven thirty."

Douglas frowns. "He better not have been tipping them off that I'm trying to secure a search warrant for their premises."

"You're searching their premises?" says Madison. "That's great! You might find evidence that Wyatt killed Ryan."

"So you're not blaming me for that anymore?"

He's so calm that Nate can't tell whether he's holding onto any animosity for that outburst.

Madison looks exasperated. "Look, I'm sorry. I was wrong to say that and I don't believe it now. I really think we need to focus on Mike and Wyatt for Ryan's murder."

To his credit, Douglas lets it go. He must realize the gravity of what Madison's alleging. "The fact that I'm going to search the McCoys' ranch is not information I want out in the public domain, so keep it to yourself."

Madison leans back in her chair. Nate can tell she's relieved he's taking them seriously.

They hear a cough through the wall and Madison looks at Nate, then at Douglas.

"Who was that?"

Douglas says, "Someone I've been interviewing."

Madison stands up. "Is it Owen? Is he on the other side of this wall?"

Nate watches as Douglas slowly nods. "Yes."

CHAPTER SIXTY-ONE

"You have to let me see him." Madison reaches for the door.

Douglas stands up, blocking her from getting out. "I need to update you on some things first." He points to her seat. "Let's finish this, then you can have five minutes with him. And then I can head to Gold Rock and search the McCoys' place. I need to act quickly if they've been tipped off."

She turns to Nate, who's giving her a sympathetic look. How is she supposed to wait, knowing her boy is just inches away from her? She sits down and rubs her sweaty hands on her jeans. Her stomach flutters with nerves and she worries she might throw up.

Douglas clears his throat. "Owen tells me that he suspects Wyatt might have had Stephanie Garcia killed."

Madison gasps. She always suspected Stephanie died because of her, but she was clinging on to the hope that it might have been a random home invasion because she doesn't know if she can live with the guilt. "Why does he think that?"

"Because according to your son, the guy we've arrested for the murder works for Wyatt. And he's under orders to kill Owen if he snitches on them." He stops. "You okay to continue?"

She nods and wipes away the tears that are falling down her cheeks. How could Wyatt order a hit on his own son? She feels Nate's hand on her back. "I'm okay."

Douglas looks unsure, but he continues. "He thinks his dad was already mad at him for not wanting to stick around and work for the family business. Owen had plans to leave town as soon as he graduated, if not before. He wanted to study law at college. He wanted to take his girlfriend and get out of Lost Creek. In essence, he wanted to get away from the McCoys."

The tears don't stop. Learning this about her son from the man who split them up is mind-boggling. Owen should be able to tell her these things himself, but she's grateful for any nugget of information about him. And the thought that Nikki Jackson was there to comfort him when she wasn't makes her feel sad that she'll never meet her. She'll never be able to thank Nikki for being a light in his life, however temporary.

"Is there anything linking Wyatt to Nikki's murder?" she asks.

"Not that I've seen."

"Did you know Nikki was working for Stephanie?" She feels a need to solve Nikki's murder even more now she knows Owen loved her.

Douglas frowns. "I didn't know that."

"I think Nikki witnessed some part of what happened to Stephanie. She must have been there, and perhaps she fled when she heard screaming. Perhaps the hit man threatened her or she got away before he saw her. She must have been terrified that he'd come for her next, and maybe she was right."

"So if Wyatt ordered the hit on Stephanie," says Nate, "it stands to reason that he wanted Nikki silenced."

Madison shakes her head. "That poor girl. What evidence do you have that you can check for Wyatt's fingerprints or DNA? Was she raped?"

Douglas frowns. "No, she wasn't raped. Why do you ask that?" He pauses, eventually putting two and two together. He leans forward. "Madison? Are you telling me Wyatt McCoy is a rapist?"

She slowly nods and swallows back her fear. "I couldn't report him. I was young. It was—"

He stops her. "You don't need to explain your reasons for not telling the police."

She looks him in the eye. She doesn't know what to say, but she's never seen this side of him before.

"I think I know enough now to nail that son of a bitch for something. It sounds to me like the McCoys have a lot to answer for." He closes his notepad. "I need to run this by Chief Sullivan and get his take on how to link all three deaths to Wyatt."

She feels her stomach flip and turns to Nate. "Oh my God. Is this real? Is Wyatt responsible for all three?" But that would mean all three deaths are also linked to her. Ryan was killed so she could be framed for murder, Stephanie was killed because she wouldn't give up Madison's location, and Nikki was killed because she worked for Stephanie and was in the wrong place at the wrong time. Madison doesn't want to believe it.

Nate's shaking his head. "He needs taking down."

"I agree," says Douglas. "Not a word about this to anyone or we risk them destroying evidence. Understood?"

Madison stands. "Can I see Owen now?"

"Yes. Follow me."

CHAPTER SIXTY-TWO

When Madison opens the door to leave the interview room, she notices Richie Hope walking away. She considers calling after him to thank him for representing her son, but she doesn't want anything to delay their reunion any longer. Shelley is standing outside the other interview room, and she gives Madison a reassuring nod. Then a look comes over her face to suggest she forgot to do something. She must be remembering Madison's request for the name of the hit man. But it doesn't matter now. They all suspect Wyatt was behind that.

As Douglas dismisses Shelley from Owen's door and leans in to open it, Madison feels like she's on the verge of a heart attack. She's never been so overwhelmed with so many different emotions at one time: fear, hope, anxiety, love. And it's taking a toll on her.

Nate has opted to stay behind in the other interview room in order to give her some privacy, and she's grateful to him. She's going to be a blubbering mess and could do without an audience.

Before Douglas can open the door, a man walks up to them.

"Detective?" He's got a British accent, so this must be Alex. "I can't find Detective Bowers so I thought you'd want to know: I've been scanning through the CCTV from the local gas stations and I've spotted something you're going to want to see. It's from the station after the turning for Fantasy World, as if you're heading out of town to Gold Rock. It shows a white pickup truck driving away from the park after midnight with what appears to be one person in it."

Douglas looks at Madison. "You okay to go in alone?"

She can't even speak she's so tense. She nods.

"I'll be back as soon as I can. Don't leave the station before I return. And no running away with your son, okay?" A joke. He actually smiles at her.

As Douglas and Shelley follow the British guy down the hall, listening to the latest developments in Nikki's case, Madison touches the door handle, trying to build up the courage to open it. How is Owen going to react to seeing her? Does he even *want* to see her? She realizes she didn't ask Douglas. She didn't even ask if her son was well. Before her anxiety can get the better of her, she swings the door open and steps inside.

She looks at the teenager sitting at the table. He glances up at her with weary eyes and she recognizes her ten-year-old son in this young adult's face. She covers her own face with both hands as she's overcome with tears.

"Mom?"

He rushes to her and wraps his arms around her, pulling her close. The first thing she notices is how tall he is; he's taller than her now! And he's strong. Eventually he lets go of her to grab some tissues from the table.

She laughs through her tears when he gives them to her. "Thanks." Once she's wiped her face, she looks at him properly. He's dressed in faded jeans and a navy T-shirt. His blond hair is in need of cutting and he's tanned, probably from working outdoors at the park all summer. She suddenly finds herself mourning ten-year-old Owen. She'll never get that little boy back, and although she knew that, being with the teenage version of Owen makes it hit home hard. "I can't believe it's you," she whispers.

"Me neither."

She grabs his hand and can feel it shaking, so she leads him to the table and chairs and they sit next to each other. She has to let go of young Owen and remember that this is still him. "How have you been?"

He shrugs like a teenager. "Okay, I guess."

She laughs. "Really? You're in a police station charged with murder!"

He grins. "Yeah, but I've got my mom back."

She hugs him again, trying desperately to stop crying so she can form a coherent sentence. She has to accept that those last seven years are lost to her. But it's hard, because it's so unfair. She tries to focus on the here and now. There's so much to tell him. So much to ask him.

"I didn't kill my girlfriend," he says when she pulls away. "My prints are on the knife because I found her after she died and I panicked."

"I never suspected you did. And I need you to know that I didn't kill Ryan."

"I never believed you did." He laughs. "Why does trouble follow us, Mom?"

She gets serious. "Because of who your father is."

He looks away and his face clouds over. "I can't believe he's my dad. What did you ever see in him?"

She feels deeply ashamed that she inflicted Wyatt on him, even though it wasn't her fault. "I didn't see anything in him, Owen." She struggles to find the words to tell him what really happened, and eventually changes the subject. They can discuss that another day. "Did they at least take care of you?"

He nods. "They weren't as bad as you're probably imagining. Not until they realized I had no intention of living with them any longer than necessary."

She's relieved. "You didn't go without anything?"

"Only you."

The tears start again, but she laughs through them. "Oh my God, you're *killing* me!"

"Poor choice of words," he grins.

He has her dark sense of humor. She smiles, thinking she could get used to this version of her boy. "Who chose the name Mason?"

"I did. It's only two letters away from your name. I liked how it sounded similar and I guess I thought it would be a clue for you if you ever came looking for me. It was stupid, I know. I was just a kid." He reddens.

She hadn't made the connection, but she loves the way he thinks.

"What was prison like?" he asks.

"Worse than I expected. But don't worry, you're not going to end up there. Detective Douglas is going to search Wyatt's place this morning. We think he's responsible for the deaths of Ryan, Stephanie *and* Nikki."

He looks shocked. "Nikki too?"

"We think she must have been at Steph's the night she was killed. We think she saw what happened and who did it." She can tell from his reaction that Nikki never confided in him. She must have been scared for her life.

Owen shakes his head in disgust. "Is it because of me?"

Madison takes his hand. "No, Owen. Only Wyatt is responsible for his actions. And I'll make sure he pays for everything he's done. I know things about him that will see him put away for a long time, whether or not they find evidence he killed anyone. He's not going to be able to hurt anyone else."

He doesn't look at her. "Why didn't Stephanie let me live with her? When I saw her around town, she would turn away. Angie said it was because I reminded her of you and of what you'd done."

Madison feels like her heart could break into a million pieces. Owen has had so much to deal with, and all without her. "Your father would have made sure she kept her distance. She never once told me you were living with them, and eventually she stopped visiting me in prison. I didn't hear from her for years. You can't blame Steph for anything. She was affected by all this too and she paid the ultimate price for knowing me."

He looks at her. "Hey. If I can't think like that, neither can you. Deal?"

She smiles. "Deal."

The door opens and they both look up. Douglas walks in with Nate behind him. Chief Sullivan follows, and all of a sudden Madison feels closed in.

CHAPTER SIXTY-THREE

Madison watches as Douglas holds up a bunch of papers. "I've got the search warrant and now an arrest warrant for both Angie and Wyatt. I'm heading there next."

She glances at Owen and can see fear in his eyes. Looking back at Douglas she asks, "What are you going to do about Mike?"

"He's left the station and he's not answering his phone. Maybe he's gone ahead of me to the McCoys' place. Or maybe he figured out we're onto him and he's on the run. If he approaches you anywhere, call 911 and get away from him."

Chief Sullivan looks at her. "Do you really think Mike was working for Wyatt?"

She hesitates. "If he's got nothing to hide, why isn't he here right now?"

Sullivan nods. "If it's true, this department owes you a massive apology."

Although being vindicated and having her conviction overturned is what's driven her this far, she can't even think about the implications yet. Not until Wyatt and Mike have been arrested and are sitting downstairs in cuffs.

"Officer Greenburg has vanished too," says Douglas to Owen.

Owen gives her a quick explanation. "He's a friend of Dad's who works here."

Sullivan says, "I've asked the state police for backup, because this is more than we can handle on our own. They were reluctant to get involved but said they'd send some uniforms over to the

McCoys' place mid morning to help with the search. Where are you going to be?"

She stands up. "I'm coming with you."

Both Sullivan and Douglas are shaking their heads.

Chief Sullivan says, "No way, and it's not negotiable. You're not a cop anymore, Madison. If I let Douglas take you out there with him, the McCoys can accuse you of planting evidence. It would be foolish."

She wants to argue her case but he gives her that look she remembers from when she worked here. His "don't bother, my decision is final" look. He always meant it, so she doesn't waste her breath.

"I think you should all stay here," says Douglas. "It's probably the safest place for now." He follows Chief Sullivan out, closing the door behind them.

Madison looks at Nate, then at Owen. She realizes she hasn't introduced them. "This is Nate, by the way. He's a private investigator who came all the way here from California to help me find you."

Nate leans in and shakes Owen's hand. "Your mom actually didn't give me much choice. But I guess it was worth the journey." He takes a seat opposite Owen. "They could've at least offered us a drink."

As the two of them make small talk, Madison paces back and forth, every now and then stopping to listen to her son's voice, to watch him laugh. It's like watching the ghost of her ten-year-old. She glances at her cell phone to check the time and sees a new message from Shelley.

Sorry for the delay. I got sidetracked then forgot to reply. His name is Paul Harris.

She almost drops her phone. Paul Harris was Angie's boyfriend in high school. He was a bully and would go around lifting girls' skirts or pinging their bra straps. When he started seeing Angie, he was like her lap dog, doing whatever she wanted. Then Angie switched her attention to Wyatt, and he and Harris would go at it, fighting over her. Harris hated Wyatt with a passion.

Goosebumps cover her arms as she tries to think about the implications. It doesn't surprise her that Harris is capable of rape. Then it hits her.

She tries to steady her breathing as she realizes Harris wouldn't have killed someone for Wyatt. There was no friendship there, no loyalty. No. His loyalty was to Angie. What if they've been blaming the wrong McCoy?

"Oh my God."

"You okay, Mom?" asks Owen.

She swallows. She doesn't want to believe it. "Do you think enough time has passed?"

"For what?" says Nate.

"I'm going out there. I'll stay out of sight, but this has been about me from the beginning so I want to be there at the end. Plus, I want to make sure it's handled properly. If Officer Greenburg is in Wyatt's pocket, who's to say Chief Sullivan isn't?"

Nate looks wary—he can probably tell she's figured something out—but then he nods. "You're probably right. We still don't know for sure who is and isn't working for the McCoys. Just make sure neither of them sees you there. Do you have your gun?"

"Yes." She taps her ribs where the Glock is sitting in its holster. "I'll take the back road. It leads to the rear of the scrapyard." She turns to Owen. "You need to stay here, okay? It's the safest place at the moment."

He looks unsure.

Nate stands up and hands her his keys. "Take my car. And take Brody with you for protection. I'll stay here. You know I'm no good with guns." He smiles at her.

Madison could kiss him. What he's really doing is offering to protect her son, and he's probably the only person in the world she'd trust Owen with right now. "Thank you."

Owen gets up and hugs her. "Please be careful." She can tell he's nervous of something happening to her so soon after their brief reunion.

"I promise I will."

CHAPTER SIXTY-FOUR

Angie's panicking. She's in Owen's bedroom, frantically searching his things before the cops turn up. She and Wyatt are checking the whole place for anything incriminating. She's had a tip-off from Mike that Douglas and his team are on their way, and is grateful to have had time to destroy anything she doesn't want them to find. She just hopes she hasn't forgotten anything.

Wyatt walks in. He's holding a small metal safe covered in dirt.

"How did you do?" she asks.

He smiles. "They won't find anything in the house or the repair shop, and I managed to locate this."

She knows what's in there: evidence from Officer Ryan Levy's crime scene. It's been buried in the scrapyard for seven years, but Wyatt couldn't remember the exact location, so finding it took longer than her nerves would have liked.

"I need to get rid of it before the cops get here."

"How?"

"I have a car ready in the crusher. I'll slip it in there. The contents won't be recognizable once they've been through that machine, and let's face it, the cops don't even know any of it exists. Is there anything else that needs to go in?"

"No. Everything I found has gone in the fire pit." Her hands are shaking. "I feel violated, Wyatt." It's a horrible feeling. They've never had their property searched before and she's worried they've overlooked something. She takes a deep breath to try to relax. "You know, it would have been less trouble to kill Madison all those years ago. She's the reason all this is happening."

He raises his eyebrows. "We would never have got away with it."

She knows he's right. "Have you spoken to Brad yet?"

He nods. "Told him to spread the word that no one is to come into work today. The last thing we need is any of them getting arrested or making deals with the cops."

She agrees.

"Message Jim Greenburg on the burner phone," says Wyatt. "Tell him to notify Harris that he's to go ahead with killing the boy."

Angie's eyes widen. She can see he's deadly serious. She never thought he'd kill his own son, but the impending search of their property is the final straw for him. Because it means Owen has done the unforgivable: he's sold them out to the cops. "You sure?"

"Yeah. Jim can unlock their cell doors and let Harris deal with him. Then we'll put a hit out on Harris once he's transferred to prison so he can't point the finger at us. The stupid asshole should never have killed the Garcia woman, and I'm not going to let him tell the cops it was us who hired him to scare her."

Angie nods. "Goddam rapist couldn't keep it in his pants."

Wyatt never told Harris to kill Stephanie Garcia. Angie wanted to keep track of Madison once she heard about her early release from prison. But months passed and there was no sign of her. Sick of waiting for her to show up out of the blue, she talked Wyatt into hiring Harris and his brother to scare Stephanie into telling them where she was. She wanted to know if Madison would come back to claim Owen and start trouble. When it was clear Stephanie wouldn't talk no matter how much pressure they put on her, Wyatt called Harris off. But he doesn't know that Angie overruled him. He thinks Harris took it upon himself to go back one final time, but the truth is, Angie wanted the woman dead.

She uses the burner phone to text Jim.

Let Harris out. It's time to get rid of the boy.

But she hesitates before pressing send. She does have feelings for Owen; he was the son she should have had. They shared many good times. Does she really want him dead? What if he's had time to reconsider where his loyalties lie?

She hears something. Cars. More than one. She stands and looks out of the window. A black sedan followed by three police cruisers block the road outside their house. That enrages her.

He's picked Madison over her.

She sends the text. Then, collecting herself, she passes the phone to Wyatt. "Put this in the crusher too. Now go. You need to get out of here."

Wyatt runs down the stairs and she follows him slowly, but as he heads for the back door, she hovers on the bottom step. When the knock on the door comes, hard and heavy, she stalls, giving Wyatt time to get all the way to the rear of the scrapyard, where the car crusher is. It's only when Douglas knocks for a third time and shouts, "Police! Open up!" that she opens it wide and stares at him with her hands on her hips.

She sees Douglas and five officers. But no Mike. Could he have been arrested? Maybe he's fled.

Detective Douglas leans in to spin her around, grabbing her wrists painfully and cuffing them. "Angela McCoy, I'm arresting you for conspiracy to distribute cocaine and methamphetamine. Other charges may follow once we've searched your property."

She shakes her head in disgust as he reads her her rights. When he's done, she turns to face him, her hands tightly clasped behind her back. "I want to see the warrant."

"You can read it at the station. Where's your husband?"

"How should I know? I'm not his keeper. And I'm not responsible for anything he's done either. I want to call my lawyer. When she's done with you, you're going to wish you never became a cop."

Douglas ignores her. "Officer Vickers will escort you to a squad car. You'll be driven to the station once we have your husband."

He pushes past her with four officers following him into her home.

Officer Vickers takes her arm. As she leads her across the road, Angie looks back over her shoulder, watching the cops crawling around her property like parasites.

CHAPTER SIXTY-FIVE

Madison took the back road to the McCoys' place and is waiting in the driver's seat of Nate's car, parked behind the boundary of their scrapyard. If Angie or Wyatt do anything unexpected, like trying to run from the cops and use this way as an escape route, she can surprise them. Brody is alert in the passenger seat, panting. He knows something's going down. She's tempted to let him out, but she doesn't trust Wyatt not to shoot him. Nate would never forgive her. She opens the car's windows so she can hear any gunshots or shouting.

This morning has been insane. She can't even think about her reunion with Owen yet, as she's desperate to see if the cops find anything that proves who killed Ryan. She'd give anything to be in there with them.

As she looks toward the scrapyard, all she can make out over the chain-link fence and overgrown shrubs and trees is a pile of burnt-out cars and the metal walkway that sits on top of the car crusher.

A shadow covers the driver's window, blocking out the sun. It's Mike. He's looking down at her with a strange expression on his face, and she wants to grab for her gun, but a quick look at his hands reassures her they're empty. His weapon sits in its holster. Perhaps he hasn't figured out she's onto him yet. She decides to play it cool by smiling and casually getting out of the car, making sure he can see her hands are also empty.

"Hey," she says, slamming the door shut. Brody is watching them from inside and she leaves her hand on the handle in case she needs to let him out quickly. He sticks his head out of the window.

Mike looks exhausted. Something's clearly eating away at him. His sleeves are rolled up and he's not wearing the tie he had on when he arrived at the station earlier. Instead, his top button is undone and she can see his white T-shirt underneath. He already has large sweat patches under his arms, despite the cool start to the day.

"I take it Douglas is in there?" He nods in the direction of the house.

"Yeah. Shouldn't you be in there with him?" She wonders why he's come the back way if he doesn't know she and Douglas are onto him.

He rubs his temples, then grimaces with pain.

"Everything okay?" she asks.

"It's my head. Feels like I've got a tumor growing in there with the number of headaches I'm getting lately."

She doesn't comment that they're probably caused by guilt and the pressure of working for Wyatt.

He looks at her. "You seen Owen yet?"

She nods. "Briefly."

"I'm pleased for you, Madison. He should never have been taken away from you." He runs a hand through his hair, his eyes devoid of emotion. His strange behavior is making her nervous.

"You okay, Mike?" she asks.

He shakes his head. "Not really. I haven't been okay for a long time." Taking a few steps away from her, he looks up at the sky.

"Why not?"

He turns to face her. "Have you ever been addicted to anything?"

She thinks of cigarettes; she would love one right now. "Nothing serious."

"I was addicted to coke and pot before I joined the force. I managed to clean up my act for work. But when Viv left me and got custody of Sally, I felt the old cravings coming back. That last year you and I worked together, I started using again. I'm surprised no one noticed."

"Addicts are good at hiding things," she says. "I saw a lot of that in prison." It dawns on her that he wasn't selling drugs for Wyatt. He was *buying* them.

He nods. "I still can't believe you ended up inside."

She senses he has a need to confess. It angers her, because she doesn't want to give him any relief. "Even though it was your actions that put me in there?"

A flash of surprise crosses his eyes. "How long have you known?"

"I've had my suspicions for a while, and seeing you here the other night confirmed it for me. What happened? You owed Wyatt so much money for coke that he offered you a deal to wipe out your debt?"

He looks pained as he nods. "Addiction is a disease. It destroys your life. Back then I didn't know why they wanted to frame you—it was none of my business—but I knew I could never pay off my debt. They offered me a way out. But once I killed Ryan, my life became unbearable."

"Wait, what?" She steps forward, shocked at his words. "*You* killed Ryan?"

"I thought you'd figured it out." His voice is robotic, his face expressionless.

"I thought it was Wyatt. I assumed you somehow gave him my gun to make it look like I did it. I had no idea *you* shot him!" She doesn't want to believe it. How could he kill a friend? Ryan lost his life for such a stupid reason. Her hand moves to her waist, ready to pull out her weapon.

Mike looks away and she finally sees a flicker of emotion. Remorse, perhaps.

"So how did you get my gun out of the safe? Did you steal my keys and make a copy?"

"You left your purse on your desk when you went into a morning training session," he says. "I took your back door key and safe key and had copies made. Then I replaced them. Didn't take longer than thirty minutes."

She silently curses herself. They had lockers for personal items at work. She doesn't remember leaving her purse out.

"When you told me you were going out with Ryan after work to celebrate your birthday, I knew it could look like you were on a date. I followed you home after and waited for you to go feed your neighbor's cat with Owen."

She shakes her head. If she hadn't told him in conversation that she had offered to feed that damn cat for a week, he wouldn't have had the opportunity to get in her house that night.

"I took your gun from the safe and locked it behind me so you wouldn't notice it was missing. Then I got into Ryan's house through a basement window." He looks at her with anguish written all over his face. "He didn't hear me walk up behind him." His eyes are red-rimmed now. "I shot him in the back of the head. He died instantly. The noise he made when he hit the ground... It still keeps me up at night, all these years later. Except I see my daughter dropping to the ground."

She has no sympathy for him. "And then you staged the scene?"

He nods. "The candles and pizzas... I made it look like you and Ryan were continuing your date." He wipes his eyes. "Wyatt never set foot in the house, but he was waiting for me afterwards. He took the copied keys, the clothes I was wearing and the latex gloves I used to ensure only your prints would be found on the gun. He said he'd hide them for me, but I knew he was keeping them as collateral, in case I ever told anyone who ordered the hit. Because they implicate me, not him. They're here on his land somewhere. No doubt Douglas is about to find them." He takes a deep breath. "You know, I found out later that it was Angie's idea. She wanted you in prison."

"What?" And there it is. Confirmation that her sister was behind it all. That her sister started this terrible chain reaction that has resulted in three people losing their lives.

"She hates you, Madison. I've never seen someone so bitter over another person. She told me that when you made detective, Wyatt confessed to sleeping with you all those years ago, and that he suspected Owen was his. She was livid, and as payback she convinced him that you were about to investigate his drug business and needed to be stopped."

He's watching for her reaction, but she can't take it all in. It's despicable. If she had known sooner the timing of Wyatt's confession, she could have put it all together. She shakes her head in disgust. But it means she must be right about who told Paul Harris to kill Stephanie. They've all been assuming Wyatt was behind everything, and although he might have been an accomplice, Angie was the ringleader. Angie was the real killer.

"Ryan's parents invited me to give a eulogy at his funeral. Did you know that?" Mike's look of remorse has turned into despair. "That was the worst day of my life. I knew he was lying dead in the casket and you were rotting in a cell all because of me."

Madison is trembling. She's disgusted with him. "I don't know how you live with yourself."

"Neither do I." He pulls out his gun. "Tell my daughter I'm sorry." He puts it to his temple before she can react.

"No!" She instinctively runs forward, but there's no point. He's dead before he hits the ground.

CHAPTER SIXTY-SIX

Angie ducks her head as Officer Vickers guides her into the back of the squad car. When she hears a loud thud followed by something hitting the ground behind her, she turns to see Brad Skelton smiling. Relief washes over her.

Officer Vickers lies motionless on the ground, blood seeping from a cut on her forehead. Brad must have slammed her head against the side of the car, because he doesn't have a weapon in his hands. She leans down to check the woman is still breathing and is relieved to find a pulse. She doesn't want a cop's death pinned on her.

"She didn't see me coming and you were in front of her, so she can't implicate either of us when she comes to," he says.

"Get the keys to these." She holds her hands up.

Brad finds the keys on Vickers and unlocks the cuffs.

Angie rubs her wrists. It's become obvious that this situation is out of their control and Douglas means to take them all down, whether or not he finds anything. Anger washes over her. She won't spend time in prison like her bitch of a sister. She hears the faint rumbling of the car crusher starting up in the distance and smirks. At least Wyatt got there before the cops noticed.

"What do you need me to do?" asks Brad.

"Just keep them distracted while I find Wyatt."

Without her husband, she can't afford to get away. All their bank accounts and assets are in his name. If she had access to any serious money, she'd take a car and drive away without him, but she can't.

She watches Brad silently jog over to the house, where he pulls out his gun and waits outside the front door. The cops haven't split up yet, so the scrapyard is clear. She'll be able to grab a gun from the repair shop and then get the spare keys to one of the pickup trucks. She'll let Brad take the fall for injuring Officer Vickers and she doesn't care if he starts shooting the place up.

As long as he waits until she and Wyatt get away.

CHAPTER SIXTY-SEVEN

Nate's getting to know Owen, and feels a little guilty that he's spending more time with the boy than Madison is. It's stuffy in the interview room now and he'd give anything for a glass of water, but he can't go anywhere as it could be dangerous to leave the boy alone.

He's telling Owen about Brody and how he's a trained cadaver dog who helped them find a missing girl in California a few weeks ago.

"That's so cool," says Owen, leaning forward. "So let's say I cut my hand open and I'm upstairs in a house. If he's downstairs, would he hunt down the smell of blood even if no one told him to?"

Nate laughs. "Er, I'm not sure. We might need to experiment when you get home."

Owen frowns. "Where's home?"

"Stephanie left her house to your mom in her will, so we've been staying there."

He looks surprised. "I loved that place. There was a railroad track going all the way around my room. I used to count the trains before I went to sleep. I still remember how many there were."

Nate smiles. "It's still there. I know, because I've been sleeping in your room."

Owen's face lights up at the thought of seeing the trains again. Then he becomes serious. "Are you and my mom dating?"

Nate shakes his head. "No. We're friends. Plus, technically, she works for me as an investigator."

He hears a shuffling noise outside the door and stands up, suddenly wishing he was armed. Owen looks afraid as Nate approaches the door. The noise has stopped. He takes a step backwards just as it swings open, obscuring his view, but he sees the look of terror on Owen's face as he discovers who's standing there. The boy ducks just as a shot is fired. The bullet hits the wall behind him.

Nate pushes the door closed on the gunman's arm, making him drop his weapon. He hears a loud yell and a crunch followed by "Son of a bitch." Then he opens it wide to see who's shooting at them.

"He works for my dad!" shouts Owen.

The shooter is a uniformed officer, and he's crouched on the floor, picking his gun up. Nate kicks him hard in the chest, but this guy is big. He takes it with barely a flinch. Nate kicks the gun away from him and it lands at Owen's feet. He sees the look of temptation in the kid's eyes.

"Don't touch it!" he yells.

As the officer stands up, Nate punches him across the jaw and his fist screams with pain. That's the first time he's ever punched someone, and he wonders if he's broken his hand.

The officer punches him back, and through the stars dancing in front of his eyes, Nate sees Owen pick up the gun. "Owen, no!"

His fear of seeing Madison's son land himself on death row invigorates him. He goes for the officer's nose this time, upwards with the palm of his hand, making the man fall backwards as his bones crunch.

Owen aims the gun and Nate's convinced he's going to fire, so he reaches out to take it off him, but he's too late.

The gunshot is so loud in this small room that his ears ring and he can't tell who's been hit.

CHAPTER SIXTY-EIGHT

Madison lets Brody out of the car because he's destroying the interior in his bid for freedom. He runs to Mike's lifeless body and sniffs it all over. A machine has rumbled into life behind her, so she looks toward the scrapyard. She can see Wyatt standing on the walkway over the car crusher. He's facing the controls. Why would he be working during the police search? She thought Douglas intended to arrest them both.

"Shit." She realizes he must be destroying evidence.

She runs toward the chain-link fence and looks for a way in. It's so old that it's broken in several places, so she squeezes painfully through and, staying low, approaches the crusher, trying not to be seen. Metal and glass screech with the impact of the compression.

Wyatt doesn't hear her as she slowly creeps up the metal steps. She can't see any cops in the scrapyard, so she needs to be careful. She pulls her gun out just as Wyatt turns.

His face breaks into a smirk. He has an arrogant look in his eyes that she doesn't like. It's the same look he wore when he was driving her to the woods eighteen years ago. She glances at his hands. They're empty. At least he's unarmed.

"What's in the car?" she asks over the rumble of the machine as it vibrates beneath her.

"Doesn't matter now. There'll be nothing left of it by the time the cops realize it's evidence."

He must have got out before Douglas and his team entered the house. She's fuming at the thought. He always gets away with his crimes. She glances at the control panel next to him. She needs to turn the machine off before it destroys whatever's being crushed underneath them.

"Heard a gunshot," he says. "You been shooting people again, Madison?"

That smile on his arrogant face infuriates her. "Mike's dead. He killed himself because of you."

Wyatt has the audacity to laugh. He doesn't give a shit about Mike. "Well, I guess he can't testify against me and Angie now. And you'll never get your conviction overturned."

She's furious. Mike was a good cop once. At least she wants to believe that. This piece of scum preyed on his addiction and drove him to desperation. "He told me Angie was responsible for Ryan's murder. And you orchestrated the whole thing, you son of a bitch."

Wyatt takes a step closer. "You've been nothing but trouble since the day I met your sister. I told her we should just kill you instead of the cop, but she wanted you to suffer. She wanted you to rot in prison for the rest of your life."

Even though Madison has no relationship with Angie, it still stings that her sister hates her so much. Her loathing has clearly been gnawing away at her over the years. She raises the gun and points it at his chest.

"You wouldn't dare shoot me." He doesn't look so sure of himself.

"Why wouldn't I, after everything you've done to me?" She thinks back to herself as the young woman he took advantage of. Many times, alone in the dark, she's imagined how different she would be now had that never happened to her. She might not have become a cop. Joining law enforcement was her way of stopping other people from getting away with violent crimes. And she made an impact, she knows she did. Until she took the promotion to detective. That was one step too far for her sister and Wyatt. They knew then that she had more power than them for the first time. They panicked. She swallows back her emotions. "Are you ever going to admit you raped me?"

He scoffs. "It's not rape when you're clearly begging for it. You wanted me from the day you met me. I saw it in your eyes."

She shakes her head in disgust. "Is that why you had to hold a gun to my head while you did it?"

Doubt crosses his face, giving her hope that some tiny part of him feels guilty. But it's gone before he can accept it.

"You have a choice," she says. "If you don't want to die here, you can agree to tell the cops about Angie being responsible for killing Officer Levy, Stephanie Garcia and Nikki Jackson. You'd only be charged with being an accomplice. You could make a plea deal before Angie and get a lesser sentence."

He appears to consider it. "We had nothing to do with that girl's death." He smiles meanly. "Guess you're not as good a detective as you think."

"You expect me to believe that?"

"She must've been murdered by our boy." He stares at her. "You should be proud of him, Madison. He turned out just like us."

She ignores the dig and steals a glance over Wyatt's shoulder to where two expensive-looking pickup trucks, one black, one white, are parked side by side. Her stomach flips with dread. The forensics guy at the station told Douglas they had CCTV footage of a white pickup truck leaving the amusement park at the time of Nikki Jackson's murder. It was heading out of town to Gold Rock.

She looks at Wyatt. "If you didn't kill the girl, then you won't mind telling me who that white truck belongs to."

He must realize why she's asking, because he smiles. "Shit. Angie killed her?" He laughs. "She has bigger balls than I gave her credit for. She didn't even tell me."

Madison shakes her head and tightens her grip on the gun. She can't believe he would find that funny. "She was only sixteen, Wyatt. She'd done nothing to Angie."

His eyes burn. "She would have had her reasons. You know, you always assumed I was a bad influence on your sister. Made her do stuff a woman shouldn't be capable of. You never once stopped to think that it could be the other way around. I've done things for Angie that would give you nightmares."

She's starting to believe that could be true. "Actually, I think you're a fatal combination. Capable of things together that you wouldn't do alone."

"Like Bonnie and Clyde." He laughs again.

She doesn't like how close he's getting, and glances down nervously. From up here she can see how lethal the crusher is. It's ravaging the car and whatever he slipped inside. As a cloud disperses overhead, the sun reflects off the metal, temporarily dazzling her.

Wyatt lunges forward, spinning her around and knocking the gun from her hand. She hits the walkway and he looms over her as the crusher grinds below. A hard kick to her stomach sends pain shooting up her torso.

"Best make sure you don't have any more illegitimate kids," he shouts in her ear.

In her lungs, she can feel every cigarette she's ever smoked and she's struggling to control her breathing. She gulps back the pain and curls into a ball, protecting her head, as Wyatt prepares to kick her again. Before he can make contact, Brody bounds up the steps toward them and dives at him, His weight pushing him toward the edge of the walkway.

Madison holds her breath as Wyatt loses his balance. Brody hovers dangerously close to the edge too, until he manages to take a few steps back. Then he starts barking non-stop.

Madison knows she'll never forget the look on Wyatt's face as he falls backwards into the crusher. He sees his death coming and he knows it will be excruciating. Her instinct makes her reach out to him, but it's no good.

The sound of his screams as he's pulled under the compacter is harrowing. It stops abruptly just before a horrendous popping sound. The blood sprays upwards like a firework. Some lands on her and Brody.

She looks away, but it's too late: she saw it. She expects to see it again many times in her nightmares. She has to stop the machine. She forces herself up and hits the blood-spattered off switch.

There's barely enough time to catch her breath before she hears Angie's voice behind her.

CHAPTER SIXTY-NINE

"No!" Angie's advancing on her and she has a gun in her hand. She's just watched her husband die. "You bitch!"

"It was you who killed Owen's girlfriend, wasn't it?" says Madison as she carefully descends the steps. There's no way she's getting trapped up there.

Angie looks feral. "You killed my husband!"

Madison spots Douglas running toward them from the direction of the house. He's about to pull his weapon out, but he suddenly hits the ground hard, screaming loudly and clutching his shoulder, then he's out cold. Someone's shot him from behind. She notices Brad Skelton, long-time employee of Wyatt's.

"Get the others too!" Angie yells to him. "I'll take care of her." She nods to Madison.

Brad turns back to the house and disappears; Brody shoots past Madison, following him. Why didn't the dog go for Angie instead? She's the immediate danger here. Madison has to buy herself some time.

"Wyatt explained it all to me."

Angie looks surprised. "Did he now?"

"Yes. He said you wanted Officer Levy killed so I'd be put away for a long time. You were angry about what Wyatt had confessed: that I'd had his baby instead of you. It made you want revenge. I can force myself to understand your reasoning but I can't forgive what you did."

"Good job I'm not looking for your forgiveness."

Madison ignores her. "But Stephanie wasn't supposed to die, was she? You were meant to just be using Harris to squeeze her for information. At what point did you flip and order him to kill her?"

Angie smiles. "When I knew she wouldn't tell us anything about you. She was loyal to the end. I couldn't have her helping you; giving you a place to stay while you tried to figure out who framed you. She needed to go."

Madison shakes her head. "You were there, weren't you?"

"I was. Not in the house—I'm not stupid enough to risk leaving DNA behind. I was outside in a rental car parked down the street. Harris called me to say she wouldn't tell him anything, so I told him to do whatever he wanted with her as long as she didn't live to see another day." She pauses. "I hope it gives you some relief to know she fought for her life. I heard her squealing like a pig all the way from where I was parked." She's grinning now.

Madison has to swallow her hatred and grief. She needs answers for Owen first. "And Nikki Jackson? Did she see Harris go into the house?"

Shock crosses Angie's face before she replies. "I saw a girl with bright red hair wearing a Fantasy World T-shirt cycle past the car like a bat out of hell. I didn't see where she came from, but it wasn't hard to figure it out. I don't know how much she saw but she was a potential witness."

"Did you know then that she was Owen's girlfriend?"

For the first time, Angie looks away. It tells Madison she had no idea.

"I tracked her down on Facebook through the Fantasy World page. She was listed as staff and tagged in some photographs. I friended her pretending to be a teenage girl and tried to arrange a meet-up, but she was wary. Instead she wanted me to be her goddam best friend online. All she ever talked about was how her parents didn't love her and how she thought her boyfriend might leave her for one of the girls who bullied her for being poor—Taylor her name was. She told me all kinds of things but she never named her boyfriend, so how was I supposed to know? She was so goddam insecure, it was pathetic. Still, it worked in my favor. When I finally caught her by herself at the park, I was able to use what she'd revealed online to silence her. She didn't even put up a fight, she was that unhappy. If you ask me, I did her a favor by putting her out of her misery."

Madison can't believe how her sister can relay all this with no remorse whatsoever.

"There. Now you know. And now I can't let you go."

Her heart is beating out of her chest. Her sister is going to get away with everything. Douglas is lying completely still and she's starting to worry he's dead. She looks around and is about to run when Angie raises her gun.

"I should have done this years ago."

The sound of Brody's frantic barking comes to them, followed by a gunshot. The barking stops and Madison goes cold all over.

Angie smiles. "There goes your dog."

Madison's trembling. She sees someone approaching behind her sister and is careful not to let her eyes flicker over Angie's shoulder. Instead, she turns to run. As she does so, she hears a gunshot ring out behind her and braces for impact. Seconds pass and nothing happens. She slowly turns around.

Angie is sprawled on the ground, face down. There's blood coming from her thigh, but she's alive and swearing in pain. Officer Vickers has blood dribbling from her forehead and is aiming her gun at Angie's back as she approaches her.

"You hurt?" she asks Madison.

Madison shakes her head and sits on the ground, badly shaken.

Brody runs out from around the side of the house. He's unharmed. She's so relieved, she cries as she fusses him. His thick fur is covered in a fine dusting of Wyatt's blood. "Oh my God, Brody. I thought you were dead. Nate would never have forgiven me."

He lies down next to her, panting but happy.

The sound of sirens comes thick and fast, and Madison is relieved to hear backup finally arriving. Two state police take over. She stands up, trying to catch her breath, as they flip Angie onto her back and cuff her. The male officer asks Madison if she's okay and then goes to looks at the blood spray from the crusher. He slowly climbs the slippery steps. When he peers inside the machine, he immediately turns away and dry-heaves at the sight of Wyatt's remains.

Angie looks at Madison with hatred burning in her eyes. "I don't care if I end up inside, because you will too for killing Wyatt."

Madison shakes her head. "You're a monster, Angie, and our mother was always ashamed of you."

Angie looks shocked. Is that hurt in her eyes? "You don't get to judge me. You slept with my husband! You deserve everything you got."

"My God, you still think I *chose* to have sex with that man? You're delusional. You need a fucking psych evaluation, Angie."

A menacing smile appears on Angie's face. "Have you checked on Owen lately? Because he should be dead by now."

Madison stumbles backwards. "What?"

"That's right. You think Mike's the only cop we have in our pockets? You better get to the station, Madison. You might just get to hear Owen's last words."

The state police both tell Angie to shut up as Madison uses her last ounce of energy to run over to Douglas and the two uniforms who are trying to help him. He's losing blood from his shoulder but his eyes are open and he's holding it together through gritted teeth. His skin has turned pale and sweaty. She prays it's not a critical injury.

"You're going to be okay, Douglas."

He looks at her. "Are you a doctor now, Harper?" he pants.

"I need to borrow your radio," she says urgently. "Angie said someone at the station is going to kill Owen."

He nods and she takes the radio from him, explaining to the female dispatcher that her son is at risk. The dispatcher assures her she'll send someone to check on Owen and Nate immediately.

As she gives Douglas back the radio, she says, "Mike's on the back road over there. He's dead."

Douglas looks alarmed.

"I didn't kill him. He did it himself. He admitted he was the one who shot Officer Levy. Angie was behind it." She needs to tell him everything.

Douglas raises a hand. "I believe you. Just shut up, would you? I'm kind of going through something right now."

She's relieved that she's not going to be arrested. Ambulance sirens roar toward them in the distance. Satisfied that she can leave, she calls Brody over and heads toward Nate's car. She needs to get back to her son.

CHAPTER SEVENTY

Independence Day

Nikki's back is aching from all the bending down to pick up spent fireworks. She's been working non-stop and hasn't had time to feel scared at being in the park alone at night. But as she approaches the Wonder Wheel, she hears footsteps. She stops and the hairs on her arms stand up.

Someone's slowly approaching from behind the carousel. It can't be Mason yet, she's only just texted him. Seeing him with Taylor earlier filled her with dread. She needs him to come back so she can ask him whether he's only been pretending to be her boyfriend all summer.

"Who's there?"

When they step into the light from the Ferris wheel, Nikki can see a woman with long hair coming toward her. She's smiling and Nikki recognizes her.

"I'm sorry. I was here earlier and stupidly lost my purse so I came back to have a look for it. I hope you don't mind?"

Nikki relaxes. "I've been cleaning up and I didn't find anything."

"Oh well, that's okay. Maybe someone will hand it in tomorrow. I'll get my boy to check for me. He works here."

"I know. You're Mason's mom, right?"

"I am. Do you know him well?"

Nikki smiles proudly. "He's my boyfriend."

The woman takes her hand, looking delighted. "Nice to meet you. But I thought his girlfriend had blonde hair with pink streaks? Never mind, I can't keep up with who he's dating."

All of a sudden, Nikki feels sick. Her worst fears are confirmed. Mason's been seeing Taylor behind her back. So he didn't mean anything he said to her about moving away together. It must have been some cruel joke Taylor got him to play on her.

"Are you okay?" asks Angie. "You look like you might pass out. Here, come and sit down."

She leads Nikki to the Ferris wheel and they take a seat in the lowest car. "I'm sorry, have I said the wrong thing?"

Nikki starts crying; she can't help it. "I'm not Taylor, I'm Nikki. "

"Oh, my goodness. Sorry. That's so typical of Mason. He's always got more than one girl on the go. Takes after his father in that respect."

Nikki feels her world crumbling around her. She has an overwhelming impulse to cut herself, something she hasn't done since she was younger. "I thought he loved me."

Angie puts an arm around her and squeezes her shoulders. "Men are assholes, sweetie. The sooner you learn that the better."

Nikki looks at her and wipes her tears away with her hands. "Have you ever wanted to kill yourself?"

Angie leans in. "Of course. Who hasn't?"

The temptation to cut is building, and Nikki knows she's going to do it. "Did Mason ever mention me to you?"

Angie shakes her head. "Sorry. Recently he's only talked about Taylor. He's obviously been cheating on you, honey." She pats Nikki's hand. "You know, drinking too much vodka helps me relieve the pressure inside when I'm upset. What do you do in order to forget?" She looks at her. "Do you cut yourself? Would that help you right now?"

Feeling like she's no longer in control of her emotions, Nikki nods.

Angie pulls a pocket knife out of her cardigan. "I'll stay with you if you like. Make sure you're safe."

Nikki takes the knife from her and opens it up. But she can't bring herself to do it. It's been so long, and she can hear her various therapists from over the years telling her it won't solve anything. That it's a temporary release that will make things worse in the long run. She feels more tears spilling down her cheeks.

Then what is she supposed to do because she can't cope with this pain.

"Want me to help you?" asks Angie.

Feeling hopeless, and before she can think twice, Nikki nods.

Mason's mom puts the knife to the middle of her forearm and slices down to her wrist. The pain takes a few seconds to start, but it isn't as bad as the pain in her heart. It gives her something different to focus on.

She leans back and focuses on the stars that are shining brightly through the Ferris wheel. She doesn't feel any better yet. She can feel the warm blood oozing out of her. It's not taking enough of her pain with it. Her therapists were right: it doesn't work. But she doesn't know how else to deal with the rejection and humiliation. Everyone at school must be in on the joke and laughing at her behind her back. Her whole summer with Mason was a lie. A sick joke designed to ridicule her. She should have known someone like him was too good for her. Why would he go for trailer trash over someone like Taylor?

"Let me help you," the woman whispers into her ear.

Nikki doesn't watch but she feels the stinging in her other arm, deeper this time. She winces and tries to pull away, but Angie holds her hand tight.

"Teach him a lesson," she says into Nikki's ear. "Teach them all a lesson: your mom, your dad, Mason, Taylor. Everyone who's ever hurt you." Her words are comforting as Nikki starts to feel dizzy. "This will show them how much they hurt you."

She thinks about her mom; about how she never once put Nikki before her husband. That's something she doesn't think she will ever get over. Mothers are supposed to put their children first. Mothers and daughters are supposed to have a special bond. But her mom is a ghost to her.

She thinks about Mason; about how he was able to fool her so easily. All because she's needy and desperate to be loved. He probably told Taylor everything she ever confided in him.

She closes her eyes against the tears and feels her pain draining away.

CHAPTER SEVENTY-ONE

Chief Sullivan is waiting for Madison when she arrives at the station. The stress on his face makes her want to turn around and not listen to what he's about to tell her. Nate didn't answer his phone when she got back to the car, and because of what's happening at the McCoys' place, she wasn't able to get through to speak to anyone in dispatch.

She takes a deep breath. "What is it?"

He smells strongly of tobacco. "There was a struggle and someone got shot, but don't worry, your son is fine. Follow me." He glances at the blood spatter on her face and clothes before he leads her away.

She can't think straight. If Owen's okay, does that mean it was Nate who got shot? Brody runs ahead excitedly as she follows the chief to his office. When she steps inside, both Owen and Nate stand up, and she feels light-headed with relief. "Oh, thank God."

Owen approaches her and she hugs him tight. Over his shoulder she notices that Nate's holding an ice pack to his jaw. He must have protected her son. She walks over to him, removes the ice pack and kisses the corner of his mouth. It's cold but soft.

"Eww, Mom," says Owen. He's crouched down petting Brody, who looks exhausted but proud of himself. He should be. He saved her life today. He shook off most of Wyatt's blood onto the upholstery in Nate's car, then rolled around on the back seat to make sure he got rid of the rest. Nate won't be happy but she'll arrange for the car to be professionally cleaned. It's the least she can do.

She hugs Nate to her. "I don't know what you did, but thank you!"

When he pulls away, he checks her over for injuries. "Are you okay?"

She nods. "It's not my blood." She glances at Sullivan. "Mike's dead; he killed himself."

"What?" Sullivan turns pale and sits on his desk.

"And Douglas is wounded."

"So I've been told," says Sullivan. "He's on his way to the hospital but the paramedics are hopeful his injury isn't life-threatening. He's going straight into surgery. Officer Vickers told me over the phone that Brad Skelton shot him, but I understand Skelton is now deceased thanks to her."

"Did Angie get away?" asks Owen. "And what about my dad?"

Madison doesn't know how he'll react to the news. "I'm so sorry, Owen, but Wyatt's dead."

He looks down at Brody and rubs the dog's head.

"And Angie's got a gunshot wound to the leg, so she's on her way to hospital too. She tried to kill me. They both did."

Eventually Owen looks up at her. "My dad deserved it. And Angie deserves to go to prison. Do you know who killed Nikki?"

Madison has to swallow her heartache. "It was Angie. She was behind all of it. Nikki witnessed Stephanie's murder. Angie didn't know exactly what she saw but she tracked her down through Facebook and waited for her at the park that night. I'm sorry, Owen."

He nods. "I knew she wouldn't have killed herself. We had plans."

The look on his face tells her he's going to need therapy after everything that's happened. Wyatt's expression as he fell backward flashes before her eyes and she has to shake it away. They all have a long road to recovery ahead of them.

Owen stands up and notices his hands are pink. He wipes them on his jeans. She doesn't want to explain that it's the remnants of his father's blood.

"The feds are on their way," says Sullivan. "What with the drugs being trafficked across state lines, they'll be in charge of that investigation. A thorough search of the McCoys' ranch could take weeks, but I'm hopeful we'll find enough to get Angie sent down."

Madison's relieved. Then she remembers something else. "Before he killed himself, Mike told me he was the one who shot Ryan, not Wyatt. He was acting on orders from Angie. She wanted me put away."

Sullivan looks horrified before shaking his head. "I should have let Douglas investigate the McCoys years ago."

Madison stares at him. "Yes, you should have." She takes a deep breath. "Mike told me that the clothes he was wearing when he shot Ryan, along with his gloves and a copy of my keys, were kept on their property. Wyatt tried to destroy it all in the car crusher earlier. You might be lucky and find some fragments." She doesn't say how they'll need to get Wyatt's remains out first. Not in front of Owen.

Sullivan massages his temples. "Jesus Christ, this is going to create a shit storm in the media."

Madison thinks of Kate. She wonders if her old friend will help her undo years of damage to her reputation now they know who really killed Ryan. Then she thinks of the Levys. She doesn't expect an apology from them, but she's hoping Davis will leave her alone the next time their paths cross.

The forensics guy knocks on the door and Sullivan waves him in. "Everyone, this is Alex."

Alex smiles self-consciously. "Sorry to interrupt, but I just wanted to ask you something, Ms. Harper."

"Sure."

"I understand our primary suspects for Nikki Jackson's murder are the McCoys. To tie up loose ends forensics-wise, could you tell me whether they have a dog?"

She looks at Owen, who says, "No. But Angie has two horses."

"Ah," says Alex. He's nodding. "That would account for the animal hair we found on Nikki's sleeve. I won't be a hundred percent certain until I have a sample from the horses, though. I'm also waiting for any navy-colored clothes they own to be brought in so I can try to match the stray fibers found on Nikki's sweater."

Madison shakes her head. Her sister deserves life in prison for all the pain she's caused. She notices Owen is looking at the floor.

Before Alex leaves them, he stops at the door and looks back at Sullivan. "I can't remember if I've already told you this, Chief, but Paul Harris's DNA matches that found in the semen sample taken from Stephanie Garcia's crime scene. It doesn't prove he killed her, but he *is* the person who raped her."

"Thanks, Alex. Good work." Sullivan looks at Madison. "How are you holding up?"

She tries to raise a smile, but she's thinking of Stephanie now. "I've had better days." She frowns. "Wait. I thought you said someone got shot here?"

He nods. "Officer Jim Greenburg. Your son shot him."

She turns to Owen, shocked. "He's not dead, is he?"

"No," says Owen. "I only got his leg. But it was totally self-defense."

She's flooded with relief and can't stop herself from laughing. She doesn't think she could handle Owen being arrested for killing a cop. That would be the final straw.

"When we searched Officer Greenburg before arresting him we found a second cell phone which shows a text message instructing him to release Harris from his cell to kill Owen," explains Sullivan. "But I've spoken to Harris. Apparently, he refused to do it, sensing he was being set up by the McCoys. So Greenburg tried to do it instead."

She doesn't know how to feel. Today has been one despicable revelation after another, and she's exhausted by it all.

"Looks like he was our leak too," says Sullivan. "We found messages on his burner phone that show he's been passing inside information to Kate Flynn, including about your recent brief arrest. Someone obviously wanted it in the press so the locals would be outraged by your return and maybe drive you out of town. It's unclear whether Kate knew who was sending it to her."

"She told me she didn't," says Madison.

Sullivan nods. "Okay." He looks at his watch. "Well, I won't make you give your official witness statements this morning. You must be in need of some food and caffeine, no doubt."

Madison nods. A feeling of relief overwhelms her and she takes a deep breath.

Before any of them can leave, though, someone enters Sullivan's office without knocking.

CHAPTER SEVENTY-TWO

A tall woman Madison doesn't recognize moves to stand next to Chief Sullivan. She's striking in her sharp pant suit and with her immaculate dark brown hair.

"Carmen," says Sullivan. He gets up to shake her hand. "Thanks for coming in. I know I explained some things over the phone, but this is a fast-moving situation so I wanted to update you in person."

He looks at Madison. "This is Carmen Mendes. She's my replacement and will be taking over in the fall, once she's ended her role at the Colorado Bureau of Investigation."

Madison feels butterflies in her stomach. The woman is gorgeous but she has an intimidating stare. "Pleasure to meet you."

Carmen is looking at them all, even Brody, but she doesn't smile. "I gather you've had an eventful morning?"

Sullivan nods. "You could say that. And it means we now have a major staffing issue."

She raises a perfectly plucked eyebrow. "Oh?"

"After this morning's fiasco, we're down two detectives and an officer."

Madison's mind starts buzzing. Should she put herself forward while she's got the chance? No, they'd laugh her out of here after everything that's happened. But then she never did anything wrong, and LCPD owe her big time.

Her hands are shaking as she tries to build up the courage to speak. But what about Nate? She's supposed to be working for him. Would he mind? And does she even want to stay in Lost Creek?

She looks at her son. He's here. She'll stay for him. The McCoys can't hurt them now.

"Perhaps we should discuss this in private," says Carmen to Sullivan.

Owen takes the hint and heads for the door, followed by Nate and Brody. Madison is frozen in place. Both Carmen and Sullivan stare at her.

Does she even want to work here? And with Douglas? She realizes that now she's got Owen back and can begin the process of overturning her manslaughter conviction, she wants nothing more than to get her old job back. She deserves it after everything she's been through. And she'd be working for a woman this time. Carmen might be intimidating, but she's worked for the FBI. Madison could learn a lot from her and maybe even eventually become a federal agent herself. She thinks of her father, who worked for the bureau in Alaska. Perhaps he could help her if she can track him down after all these years.

"I'm available." She blurts it out, instantly reddening. "I mean, when you eventually advertise the detective role, I'd like to apply. You won't know this, Carmen, but I used to work here before."

Carmen nods, her face not giving anything away. "Yes, I know. Chief Sullivan has told me about you."

Madison's heart is beating out of her chest. "I'd love to come back. To prove myself."

Carmen almost smiles. Almost. "Things are a little uncertain at the moment, Ms. Harper. But why don't you and I talk again in the near future? I'm sure there are issues we need to resolve about how your case was handled."

Madison nods and Carmen finally smiles at her. She holds out her hand. "It was nice to meet you."

Madison takes it, hoping the woman can't feel that she's trembling.

She turns to the door, where Nate is staring at his phone with a serious expression. Has Father Connor got in touch? A feeling of dread washes over her. He'll never be free of that man until they have their long-overdue showdown. She can help Nate with that. He's done so much for her, and now that she's found her son, they can focus on finding the priest. It's the only way he's ever going to get over what happened to him and his fiancée.

He pockets his phone and tries to give her a reassuring smile. She looks at Owen, who is grinning at her, and she can't help feeling how lucky she is to have him back.

She walks toward them and puts her arm around Owen. "Come on, you two," she says. "Let's go home."

A LETTER FROM WENDY

Dear Reader,

Thank you for picking up this book out of the thousands available out there and giving it a try. You can keep in touch with me and get updates about the series by signing up to my newsletter, and by following me on Twitter or Facebook or on my website. I'm very interactive, so don't be shy—get in touch!

www.bookouture.com/wendy-dranfield

I hope you enjoyed spending time with Madison and Nate and that you'll want to see how their stories and lives progress in future books. If you want to know more about Nate's time spent on death row, you can read for yourself just how awful his experience was in book one of the series, *Shadow Falls*. You'll also find out how Madison and Nate acquired Brody as a companion!

You might be pleased to know that books three and four are well under way, so you won't have to wait too long for those to follow.

If you enjoyed this book, please do leave a rating or review (no matter how brief) as this helps it to reach more readers.

Thank you, and see you next time!
Wendy x

🖥 wendydranfield.co.uk

🐦 WendyDranfield

📘 WendyDranfield1

ACKNOWLEDGMENTS

Firstly, thank you to my readers for sticking with me and encouraging me every day via your tweets, comments and messages. I write all my books with you in mind and you provide a welcome distraction on the days the words won't come.

Thank you to Jessie Botterill, my editor, for working with me on this series, and to the team at Bookouture. It really does take a whole team to publish a book, and they've done another great job.

I must thank all the fabulous bloggers online who help spread the word about my books. I really appreciate your enthusiasm and support and I love reading and sharing your reviews.

Finally, I always thank my husband in case he reads this! He makes a great beta reader, even if I do usually want to divorce him after I've read his detailed and critical feedback!